YOURS FOREVER... MAYBE

Things in Life That Are Too Hard to Get Are Worth Fighting For

A NOVEL

KATHERINE [MK] MITCHELL

CHAPTER ONE

"Actors can't keep their pants on," Kathi said while gently zipping up Marla's wedding dress.

"A slight exaggeration, I'd say, Mother."

"Your dad couldn't keep his on."

"That's too much information, if you don't mind," Marla said.

The twenty-seven year old bride stood before the mirror in an understated white gown accented with gold embroidery patches that shimmered in the light with her every move. Gold threads ran through her shoulder length curly black hair as well as the edges of the veil. Although taller, more slender than her mother, Marla knew the older woman had been a beauty in her day. Her friends still called her Kathi, a girlish name, Marla thought, for someone nearing sixty. Kathi was slightly plump, her face somewhat weary, but she retained a strong presence. Besides Kathi's expressive dark eyes, Marla also inherited her mother's command of space which Marla innately used to camouflage her feelings. Both women appeared self-sufficient and strong on the surface which generated people's trust and confidence. Both women presented the façade of knowledge but their real power was in the ability to readily know where to find answers and solutions. It was a blessing and a curse. Kathi used to say "if you say nothing, everyone will think you know a lot but if you speak, everyone will know that you know very little." Because neither of them appeared needy, no one ever thought that they needed any support emotionally or other ways. They often were sounding boards for others. Marla wanted to distance herself from her mother who was more and more of a loner. She wanted to be unlike her mother and found it hard to talk with her mother. But, problem solved. Marla was saved by her love for Warren.

And now the day was here, the most wonderful day of her life. She and her mother had called a truce, a kind of a *wedding truce*. They spent the night in one of the mansion's two-bedroom guest suites. In the back of her mind Marla registered the tasteful and expensively furnished surrounds and while she appreciated the touch of class reflected in the stylishness, she was generally unimpressed with just money. Besides, as her heart was racing, her gown was the only thing that interested her. She halfheartedly listened to her mother's soft-spoken words without letting down the wall that had kept her safely screened from the woman who, as Marla knew, lived her life for her daughter. Kathi would not give up. She kept trying to make her point.

"It's not too late," she said. "Please. Hear what I am saying. Actors, without a script, are needy children." The older woman stood by the bay window that framed the vast flower garden but her thoughts clouded the view.

"Mother, in fifteen minutes I'm going to walk down the aisle and marry Warren. I'm sorry you're not happy for me."

"And his mother? She's controlling."

"I don't really know. I've only spent a few hours with her and yes, she seems to be full of ideas, but that can be a good thing." Marla was blind to notice the worry in her mother's eyes.

She slipped into high heel shoes, put on gold lace gloves and took another look in the full-length cheval glass. She grinned with satisfaction.

Kathi would not give in. "The woman bought the two of you a condominium without even knowing you." She stood a few feet from her daughter, her hands clenched together, torn by the distance between them.

"Listen, she approved her son marrying me instead of some society debutante. That's a first step. I can work around the rest." Marla concentrated on her mirror image.

Kathi attempted to reason some more. "Do you really mean that, Marla? I know it's hard for you to stand your own ground. You can be overpowered sometimes."

"Yes. It's hard. But now I count on Warren." The older woman moved to refresh her own make-up, turned around and looked Marla in the eye.

"I'm happy for you, honey," she said. "I'm also scared."

"So am I," Marla said. "Happy and scared."

There was knocking on the door followed by a polite voice, "We're ready for you."

Marla looked at her mother, took her hands and said, "Put on a smiley face, mom. OK?"

"OK."

They opened the door to a spacious antechamber where the flower girls of all ages and sizes, the bride's maids, maid of honor, were ready to go. The Wedding Planner signaled the twelve-piece orchestra and the sounds of the Grand March from Aida by Verdi, chosen by Warren's mother, marked the start of the procession moving to the garden overlooking the Pacific Ocean. The small crowd of a hundred invited guests was the best of the best that Southern California's Laguna Nigel had to offer.

The Traynor family was a leader of local society. Old money, well managed, secured the lives and dreams of each member. Their sprawling mansion in the hillside crowned several acres of manicured lawn, flower beds, guest cottage, pool, tennis court and all that makes for a luxurious lifestyle. The Traynor ancestry went back to the days of the 1820-s following Mexico's independence from Spain. Those who served in the government or who had friends in authority were routinely given vast lands for cattle grazing. A Traynor was at the right place at the right time. Warren did not care much about the Traynor family history and accepted the family motto of not abusing their privileges. Although he was spoiled and often bratty, he respected the recognition the family was enjoying and frequently experienced the resulting favorable fallout.

Marla walked in a dream, her Mother on one side and Warren's elegant father, in place of her own, on the other. They were delivering Marla to her husband to be, the love of her life.

Marla saw no one, only Warren, at the end of the white-carpeted walkway. Looking at him, some would say he was the next superstar, the next George Clooney, or Matthew McConaughey, oozing with sex appeal. His charisma and self-confidence made him irresistible to her and she melted under the gaze of his hazel eyes. As he took her hand, she trembled. Oh, yes. Marla knew this was a match made in Heaven. Their kiss would last forever.

Following the brief ceremony, Warren's mother took Marla by the arm and started introducing her around. Mrs. Traynor's attitude of owning the world reminded Marla of Joan Rivers. In passing, Marla wondered how long it took for Mrs. Traynor to develop her style or was it possible that she was born with it. Banish the thought! Marla knew from Warren that no one argued or disagreed with his mother. Everyone obeyed. His father stood by her unconditionally—at least publicly. Regardless of the overbearing mother, Marla was on cloud nine and didn't intend to leave that place. The tears misting her mother's eyes when she performed the obligatory dance with the host, Warren's father, went unnoticed by Marla. She was so in love, she did not see her own mother walk toward the flower garden, away from the party. This was the happiest day of Marla's life. No one else mattered.

Warren kept the top of his late model Cadillac convertible on for the hour-drive to the Hotel del Coronado, a beachfront luxury hotel in the city of Coronado, just across the San Diego Bay from San Diego. He excitedly told her about the unique hotel, the wooden Victorian structure that was a designated National Historic Landmark. She looked delightful in a pastel peach color loosely fitting pantsuit, hiding her trim body while emphasizing her luxurious hair. She was sincerely curious about what he was saying, eager to learn everything that interested him. The closer they got, the more impressed she was. On arrival, the Valet took Warren's name, entered it on his curbside computer and a porter appeared. Their luggage was placed on his cart and they were whisked away toward the Beach Village where their private cottage awaited. As soon as the door closed behind the bellman, they kissed. As if they had never touched before, the fervent kiss, like electricity, ran all the way through their bodies until their weakened knees buckled. Falling on the bed, they surrendered to their passion, giving and taking all. They took no notice of the complimentary champagne awaiting them. Their sexual fervor overpowered all senses and left them without energy to even move. A nap, followed by a titillating bath in the Jacuzzi tub this time with champagne, fruit and delicious finger-foods of pâté and caviar hors d'oeuvres stirred renewed erotic play, more climactic moments and finally, in the late night hours, they called for a light meal from room service. Next afternoon they slowly pulled themselves together, wearing casual beach wardrobe they embarked on a survey of the great outdoors, anything outside of their cottage suite. They were oblivious of other guests staring at the beautiful couple walking with arms around each other. The onlookers were probably wondering what kind of famous people they might be?

Warren's cell phone jarred them out of their dreamy beach walk. It was Warren's agent. They had to cut the honeymoon short. Warren had to report for an acting job.

"This is the most incredible thing, Marla. You brought me luck!" He was jumping with joy. "Four weeks of work, maybe more. Feature billing, I can really make my mark this time and get some good film footage."

Marla started to carefully pack the beautiful clothes she brought for this special two weeks, her honeymoon. In a way, she was sorry to have to leave, but glad for Warren's acting opportunity.

"I think that inviting the casting director and his wife to our wedding was a stroke of genius," Marla said. "That's what clinched the job. I had nothing to do with it."

"My mother's the genius. She always knows what to do." After a while, he turned to her again, "She wants us to give regular dinner parties. Be sort of a *networking center,* that's what she calls it."

Marla's attitude was simple and lighthearted. "It will work out as it's supposed to, Warren. We don't have to be pushy." She saw his face tighten. This was a different side of Warren.

"We'll have regular dinner parties. We'll be a networking center. People will come to our place to meet other important people." His voice was firm.

"Are we important?" she asked.

"The Traynor family is."

"Well," she said, but Warren interrupted her. "It's the family, Marla, that's all. People will come."

The rest of the drive had no heart. She was at a loss and decided to stay in her own thoughts.

Marla had never seen the condominium in the Beverly Glen Canyon somewhat upward from the foot of the hills. The pricey residential canyon connecting the Beverly Hills and The San Fernando Valley was a fashionable location. The beautiful hillside living was convenient to several of the film and television studios, just short of being in-your-face obnoxious, yet far from modest. The three-story building was unassuming on the outside with underground parking. Warren placed a barcode sticker on the window which let them access entry. They passed by the guest parking spots on one side until they reached one of the nine attractive garage doors assigned to their unit. Warren smiled ceremoniously, took the garage door opener from the glove compartment and *Voila!* their private two-car-garage-cum-storage space opened up. She helped unload the luggage. Her enthusiasm grew every step of the way to the glossy elevator lobby, into the designer decorated elevator. Marla became aware of many understated luxuries. Yes, Warren's mother had great taste, no one could deny that. Marla was almost giddy watching Warren's full-face grin, as he, like a magician, produced a key card and slid it into a slot to start upward and eagerly anticipated what would come next.

"This card programs the elevator to go directly to our floor. The top," he said and winked. "If we want to go anywhere else, we can just press the button."

"Oh, no magic? Just the usual?"

"There's more magic inside. Just you wait," he said.

She followed him with great expectations, rolling her suitcase down the wide carpeted hallway to one of three elegant double doors.

"There are three condos on each floor," he said and unlocked the door.

Before she could step inside, he dropped his bags, kissed her, picked her up in his arms and carried her over the threshold.

"I wanted to do this," he said and kissed her again.

"I love you so much," she said, tears clouding her eyes.

They walked through the marble-tiled foyer leading to a wide open living room with a full wall of sliding door windows to a wrap-around balcony and a marvelous view toward the City of Angeles sprawling below the elevation.

Marla ran out on the balcony and around the corner while Warren went through the master suite and opened the balcony door for Marla. She rushed in, happy with everything. She was almost dancing as she checked out the master bathroom spa, the guest wing, study and she totally fell in love with the kitchen. It had a cooking island, a wine closet with a few bottles of wine, breakfast nook and a long pass-through to the dining room. At the press of a button, a sliding door displaying a decorative tapestry design artistically closed the pass-through and unobtrusively melded into the wall.

"I can't believe this," she whispered. "Oh, m'G_d, she said over and over.

"Mother rented the furniture and some basic furnishings for a few months until we get the decorating and new furniture in."

"Oh, I want to do it! I want to do it so much!"

"It's a little larger than my Westwood place, isn't it?" Warren said. "It's 2900 square feet."

"Yes, it's pretty big. I will have a ball furnishing it, making it ours. A home." She was misting up again. "I love the open flow, Warren," she said dragging him around. "The wood flooring. Is it pinewood?" She got down on her knees for a closer examination. "Oh, and the corner location, the view. It's screened, no bugs, so we can eat out here, *al fresco*!"

Finally, Warren opened a bottle of wine and they settled down on the balcony. She continued to babble on but Warren's attention switched courses. He called his agent and asked him to have the script sent over. Marla started to unpack, prepare a bubble bath and luxuriate. She was so happy; she could not find words to express her feelings. She was thinking about calling her mother, telling her that everything will be all right. She made a mental note to call.

Two days later, before they even had a chance to settle in, the building's downstairs doorbell rang. Warren pressed the buzzer.

"Susanne," came a woman's voice.

Warren opened the front door while waiting for the guest to come up in the elevator.

"Honey," he proceeded to brief Marla. "This is Mother's decorator. She's been with our family forever. A dear friend. Practically helped me grow up," he said with a mischievous sparkle in his eyes.

"What does that mean?"

"She worked for Mother all the time. I was a young boy. She was there. All the time. She knew things… you know."

"What should I know?" Marla asked.

At that point a pretty woman in her youthful forties appeared. She had lush red hair, wore a soft North Beach of San Francisco leather suit and carried a folio case.

"Susanne Currie," Warren said. "Susanne, this is my wife, Marla."

"I saw you at my wedding, didn't I?" Marla said, extending her hand.

They shook and Susanne laughed. "Yes. I danced with your husband when you weren't looking."

"Susanne's here to decorate this place," Warren said.

"Says who?"

"Honey, you must've forgotten. I told you she'd come by before I leave for location. Turned out to be today. She has sketches and fabric samples and all that." Susanne walked to the dining room table and without a word pulled several drawings from her folio. Warren followed.

"Your mother really liked these," Susanne said to Warren. "She wants me to get your approval, of course."

"Well, I'll definitely approve mother's selections," Warren said.

"Hello," Marla said. "May I look?"

"Of course, of course," said Warren and Susanne almost at the same time.

Marla paged through the sketches and separated those she didn't like. She handed the three others to Susanne.

"This would be my first choice, second and last." Marla gestured to Warren. "What do you think?"

Warren nodded and mumbled. "Whatever."

Marla turned back to Susanne. "What about the time frame?" she asked Susanne. "When do you want to start? How much time will you take? Approximately, of course."

Susanne looked at Warren. Warren grunted. "Um. Hm."

Marla saw that her taking charge was not anticipated.

"How much time would each one take?"

"I'll work it up," Susanne said.

"You didn't bring it?"

Susanne faltered. "I wasn't sure." She looked to Warren again but no support came.

Marla wanted answers. "I thought you and Warren's mother had it all worked out already. If not, I'd appreciate a schedule so that we can arrange our lives around you."

"We're in no rush," Warren said. "Whatever's convenient for Susanne."

Marla looked at him. "Of course. Why not," she said. "Whatever's convenient." She turned to Susanne. "Would you like a drink?"

Susanne glanced toward Warren and smiled. "Is there any champagne in the house?"

"Always," Warren said, heading for the temperature-controlled wine closet in the kitchen.

The rest of the visit kept Marla ill at ease and on her toes. She felt like an outsider looking in on her own life. After a while she got up and said, "I'm going to start dinner. Susanne, would you like to break bread with us?"

"Break bread? What I quaint term," Susanne said.

"Great idea, honey," Warren said. "How about it, Susanne?"

And she stayed. She adored the angel-hair marinara, the jumbo shrimp scampi, even the salad was *mahvelous* because of the light dressing. "You must give me the exact measurements you used," she said to Marla with too much enthusiasm.

Susanne did not object to an after dinner liquor before she announced that, "I must go. Tomorrow is an early, early day. I have a million things to do."

———— ✦ ————

Three days later Warren left for location. He had a choice of taking company transport or driving his Cadillac to each California location. Marla kept busy. Played tennis, dealt with workers sent by Susanne, and hoped for the completion of the decorating. Susanne would call to check in with Marla but she did not stop by. She suggested that if there was anything Marla didn't like, she should give Susanne a call. That was OK with Marla. She didn't particularly want to bond with a woman who knew her husband so well.

One day Marla received a letter from her mother.

"You have caused me a lot of pain. I caused my mother a lot of pain. It was too late when I learned that what comes around goes around, that you make your own bed and lie in it. I saw all that happen. It happened to me. We create our own karma.

I didn't want you to make the same mistake I did and marry an actor. They have too many temptations and forget right from wrong. You married an actor anyway because you were so in love. Well, I was so in love also and married your father against the better judgment of my mother.

My next man, a film studio executive, wanted to send you to boarding school. In Europe. Wanted to separate us. I didn't marry him.

I did my best, still somehow I didn't raise you right and am paying the price. I wish we could have been friends, as adults. I don't know anything about you anymore. I don't know whether I should be sorry for you or for me? Who's to blame? Things happen the way they are supposed to happen.

To love and be loved is the ultimate human quest, but inner peace is the true reward. If your love and your career don't mesh, something has to give or give-up or give-in. You may not find a man's love in your life, but being honest to yourself reflects your love for yourself. You must be your own counsel. Respect for yourself, your marriage, pays off. Remember: love and respect.

Tears came to her eyes. Alarmed, Marla called her mother but she was not in. "Where did these thoughts come from? Why now?" Marla wondered. She decided she had to set things straight with her mother and make sure that she would not interfere in her marriage with more letters like this. She left a message, telling her mother that she was on her way to see her.

Marla's mind was traveling down memory lane as she got into her car for the half hour drive. The things her mother used to say, the moments that stuck in Marla's brain about growing up under her mother's roof.

Kathi worked all her life and often remarked about having "paid her way" and owing no one. She was proud, never went to a party without bringing food or wine. She never went to anyone's home as a guest for the first time without taking flowers or other mementos. She was first to take pictures at an event and made certain that those who were in the shot would receive a copy right away. She was ready to help and if she could not do it herself, she made sure that she found a way to get the help any friend needed. Kathi was a master of kind little acts, which, when recognized, made her feel as good as the recipient.

Raised in the *olden days*, one of Kathi's frequent expressions, she was an outspoken patriot. She stood whenever she heard the National Anthem whether in her living room, watching some event on television, or in public or private place. No matter. She stood and appreciated the goose bumps the masterful words produced in her. Young Marla was enthralled by this until her father made a joke of it and laughed at Kathi. Kathi's feelings were demeaned but she never changed her ways.

Frustrated by her failed marriage, Kathi frequently belittled her ex husband, the father of Marla. He lived close enough in the neighborhood and liked spending his kind of time with his daughter. Sometimes young Marla would overhear her mother on the telephone telling him that parenting is not a buddy-buddy relationship, that as a father he had to guide their child instead of showing her off at his favorite bars. Marla's father was an actor. She knew from her mother that he was extremely talented but she didn't like hearing her mother say that he was lazy. Her mother made derogatory remarks about him only after a few glasses of wine. Without any heart-to-heart talks that she actually registered, Marla sensed that her mother felt justified voicing the defeat of her youthful expectations. Kathi would tell her husband that "if you have to go drinking every night, go to the clubs where the directors and producers are drinking. Make friends with people who can help you in your career not with your car mechanic." But that went in and out of her father's ears. Estrangement with Kathi was his answer. When eighteen-year old Marla accompanied him on his outings some nights, she would notice that to the mechanic and his friends her father was a hero. They idolized him. Why would he go any place where he was the least famous or the least important? Although, he would agree with Kathi's theory when sober, it only lasted until he entered the Iron Horse, a watering hole in Studio City, near Universal and other studios and heard the accolades of the guys. He liked being their *TV star idol*.

Kathi, on the other hand, was intense about raising Marla, about pointing her toward a wide range of education, introducing her to art, music, sports other than football, and wanting her to have a well-rounded background. She discouraged Marla from romance with school-mates and younger men, implying that an older man with more experiences would have more knowledge and would fit her better. Although Marla did not do anything particularly for the purpose of pleasing her mother, she actually met no boy in high school who was worth her time. It was in community college where Marla discovered tennis. Yes, she could *see* the ball, *hit* it, *place* it and *score*— and get the attention of the local pro. Her mother was supportive of all her endeavors but she did not take well to hearing about Marla's sexual affair with the popular tennis champion, especially when they learned that he was spending only the summer season in California after which he was heading to an Ivy League university. Losing her virginity was not as bad as being left behind. Marla determined that she was not in love with him because love must feel better than he made her feel. Even though Marla knew that getting her sex thing out of the way was high time, she curled up in her own head, withdrew and built the highest wall between herself and the real world.

During her second year of community college Marla was growing more and more unsettled, unfocused until *the lights came on*. She realized that she could get away from it all and see the world as an interpreter. She concentrated all her future studies on languages, starting with French. She would become a linguist and specialize in international affairs. She could even be a simultaneous interpreter at the U.N., or a specialist in international law, maybe commerce. The possibilities were endless and she pursued her higher education with vehemence. All the practice, computers, voice labs and ear phones kept Marla in solitude.

After her father died of a sudden brain aneurism, Marla removed herself from the world and her mother's life even more. Although she lived in the home Kathi had bought in Newbury Park in the San Fernando Valley just north of Los Angeles, they talked less and less. Marla's passion for tennis became an added excuse to be away from her mother, still too deeply dedicated to parenting. Her tennis game was good enough for some inter-collegiate tournaments but not good enough to go pro. Still, she loved playing and loved picking up games at the tennis park with just about anyone who asked. She didn't have to get involved, she didn't have to communicate, just play. The break her brain got from studying was as good if not better than therapy.

That's where Warren happened into her life. Warren made her communicate, Warren made her get involved. Warren Traynor was in his late twenties, movie-star-handsome and, indeed, his goal was to become a movie star. Huge movie star! His rich head of blond hair sculpted in the latest style seemed to crown his perfectly proportioned six-foot plus body. He was studying acting and succeeding in small parts. He was full of *joie-de-vivre* attracting attention with his contagious laughter and wondrous energy. Dedicated to his craft, he would go anywhere and would accept any role to gain more acting experience. He invited her to his dress rehearsal in a production of the local theater company. She never imagined that Noel Coward's *Private Lives* could interest her in any form but there she was enjoying the play with Warren in it. Why Noel Coward? Why in The Valley? Just did not make sense, but there it was. After their dating became more exclusive, she invited him to dinner to introduce him to her mother. Well, Kathi felt a knife in her heart. "An actor?" That's all she had to say to Marla after Warren left.

Warren lived in a small studio apartment in Westwood that featured the electronic parking lift system in the back alley that could accommodate two cars suspended on top of each other. He had a membership in the local library and in the Westwood Tennis Club where he generously put her name on the list as his permanent guest. She could go any time but she only went when she was with Warren. It was with Warren that she understood for the first time the profound connection between sex and love. Everything made sense. Love was worth the wait. Her love for him lifted her spirit and being with him became foremost in her life. She stopped her studies to accompany him to every one of his career-related events, to take care of every one of his needs. They became inseparable and marriage was the inevitable next step. When he took Marla to the Laguna Nigel mansion of his parents, she actually understood that he came from a great deal of money. She was impressed with the informal charm of his parents but was annoyed by his mother's domineering attitude. Since Warren and Marla's plans did not include living near his parents, Marla didn't give it another thought. She graciously agreed with the mother-in-law-to be about grandchildren, about her duties to her son, Warren, and everything else. Confidently and with fearless clarity, Marla felt that in due course she will do what she needs and not the mother.

Her mind stopped wandering as she came to the last turn before pulling up at her mother's home. She was not there. Marla used her key to enter the small house in a nice tract community in Newbury Park in the northern San Fernando Valley. She had an eerie feeling walking through the house. She found everything neat and orderly. In the living room, serving as a coffee table, was a wooden trunk decorated with intricate carvings and inlays. It was a new piece, not in the house when Marla lived there. She did not stop to admire the artistry just headed toward the bedroom. Stuck to the mirror in the bathroom, however, were numerous telephone numbers of doctors. Frightened, she frantically dialed the first one.

"Oh, my gosh," the receptionist answered. "I was just calling your number. And here you are," she said. "Unreal. As if you knew."

"Knew what?" Marla asked.

"Your mother's in the hospital, very sick and she didn't want us to call you but now, right now, Dr. Marder told me to get a hold of you. And here you are. As if you knew. You must be really close to your mother to sense when something's wrong."

Marla turned snow white. "What's wrong?"

"You have to go to the hospital, she is… Well, you just have to go. How long will it take for you to get here from…"

"I am here."

"Here? Where?" the receptionist asked.

"I'm in Newbury Park," Marla said. "I just got to the house."

She wrote down directions, thanked the receptionist and headed over to the local medical center. She walked into her mother's room. The doctor was about to cover her mother's face with the sheet.

"Wait!" she called out.

The doctor stopped. Marla walked over to the bed, pushed the sheet aside to be able to see and touch her mother's face.

"Oh, my mother," she whispered.

————— ◆ —————

Sleepless, Marla needed comforting. She needed Warren's love. The only person who understood her. She searched for Warren's location itinerary on the computer and printed out the directions. Apparently, on that date, the company was only about a five-hour drive north. She packed a small suitcase and drove out before sunrise. Outside of Bakersfield, she spotted the road sign to the location lodging and drove through the entrance of the attractive two-story motel. Built in the 60-s style, there was a pool in the center of the courtyard only few feet away from the cars parked in front of the various rooms. She did not see Warren's car. The office wasn't open yet. She checked her notes for the room numbers. When she looked up, she recognized an actor walking across the courtyard and called out to him.

"Hello, Mr. North. You don't know me, but I am Warren Traynor's wife." She looked at him with a soft smile. "I am looking for his room, twelve-forty-two. Can you tell me which way?"

Jack North knew better. Jack North was not about to disclose any information to a wife.

"I'm afraid I can't help you," he said.

"You can't? One, two, four, two?"

"The numbers are very screwy in this place," he said avoiding her eyes. "We are moving around too much. I still get lost around here." She realized what was happening.

"Never mind."

She drove on, followed the signs and parked downstairs from the second-story room. She ran up the stairs and rapidly knocked.

"Just a sec. Hold your horses," came Warren's voice.

Sleepily and wearing only a towel, Warren opened the door. His smile disappeared.

"Who the hell is there so early?" a woman's voice asked from inside.

Warren was speechless. Marla saw the woman in his bed. Marla froze.

"Wait a second, Marla," Warren said. "I can explain."

Marla slowly turned around and Jack North watched as she went back to her car. Tears rushed to her eyes. She drove out of the courtyard with tires screeching, leaving a sharp imprint in the road.

The drive home seemed longer than on her way over. She breathed heavily, letting the flood of tears run off her face, down her clothes.

She was crushed. Unsettled, she tried to chase pangs of guilt out of her mind. She couldn't go back to her mother's house. She would not face her uncles and their know-it-all families. She would let them handle all that needed handling. All she wanted was a memento. She made some phone calls to have the beautiful trunk that belonged to her mother delivered to the condo.

Emotionally drained, completely alone, she curled up under the covers. Her thoughts were racing, disorganized, disconcerting. She knew nothing about her mother, her health, her interests, her lifestyle. Nothing.

"Oh, my mother," she whispered.

———— ◆ ————

A few days later, Friday night, Warren arrived home. He was genuinely upset.

"I'm finished. I'm home. I want to apologize."

He stood there like a five-year old. "Marla, I didn't mean to hurt you. I made a mistake. Can you forgive me?"

"I don't know if I can. I'd like to, but I don't know."

He put his arms around her. She did not resist. "I won't do it again, I promise." He kissed her hair, her cheeks, searching for her lips. She pulled away.

"I just don't know. Can I trust you again? I feel terrible," she said.

"I feel terrible, too."

"Why did you marry me if you can't keep your pants on?" She slapped her hand to her mouth in total shock at having said that.

"I love you. I can keep my pants on, Marla. I'll show you. I want children and family."

"And your mother? What does she want? A movie star?"

Warren's boyish grin was endearing. "I think so. I think she wants both, the grandchildren and the fame. Whatever it takes."

"I have to know that I didn't make a mistake, Warren. I have to know that you can respect our marriage." She was stunned at hearing herself repeat more of her mother's words.

"I'll turn a new leaf, just believe me, please." He held her tight, touching her gently, swaying with her. She could never resist him.

"I do. I believe you." They kissed with passion. As always, she was caught up in his sexual prowess, burning with desire, ready to make love.

It was a while before she could recover from the intense erotic moment they had shared. Her knees were weak as she got out of bed, walked to the bathroom and stepped into a steaming hot shower.

Warren came in. She could see his outline through the steam and knew that wearing his shorts, he was sitting on the settee, waiting for her to finish and get into a robe.

"Am I safe in hoping that you will come to the SAG dinner Thursday?" he tried unsuccessfully to appear insecure. There was no room for insecurity in a cocky person. "Do you need a new gown?" he continued. "Want to go shopping?"

"Maybe I'd wear a tuxedo and we would match. What do you think?"

"Not bad. If you wear it with a skirt we'd still match."

"How about the skirt and the jacket with just a dickey, like the girl in *Flashdance*. Remember?" she said playfully.

Unexpectedly, Warren became serious. "The 'girl' was Jennifer Beals. You're in the biz now, Marla, where we all have our real names."

"Excuuuse me," she laughed at her own imitation, then added, "Real name, Steve Martin."

"I got it," Warren said without appreciating the humor.

She turned to get a glass of water. Warren saw blood on the back of her legs.

"Oh, you have your period. Why didn't you tell me? Guess no more nookie tonight."

"I don't have my period. Besides, what's that word, 'nookie?' That's so not like you."

"I see blood," he said. "Anyway, that's a cute word."

"You think cute words fit you?" She went back to the bathroom to wipe off the blood. Warren heard the thump of her fall, rushed in. She fainted.

"What the hell?" he mumbled, trying to elevate her head while checking her pulse. He lifted her up, carried her to the *divan* under the bathroom window, and hurriedly soaked a washcloth in ice-cold water to put on her face and neck. She opened her eyes.

"I have to take you to the emergency room," he said. "Can you walk?"

She nodded, yes, but went under again. Warren dialed 911. The ambulance arrived in just moments and while riding, the paramedics logged the symptoms and contacted Dr. Blanche Shlagerman, the only doctor whose name Warren heard Marla mention. The gynecologist, Dr. Shlagerman, met them at the hospital.

"I'll eat my hat if this is not an *ectopic* pregnancy," the doctor said and immediately ordered an operating room. The tests proved her right and within an hour of their arrival to the hospital, Marla was in surgery.

Around midnight, Dr. Shlagerman found Warren sleeping in one of the waiting areas.

"Well, Mr. Traynor, I can assure you that she will be fine. You saved her life by bringing her right in. Her tube was about to burst. That would've been fatal. I'll see you in the morning," she added and left.

Once the nurses settled Marla in a private room, Warren was allowed to stay with her. It was almost the middle of the next day when the doctor returned. This time she looked old and tired as someone who was often awakened and who spent more time taking care of her patients than herself. Her eyes were alert, and there was a reliable, peaceful air about her.

"It is not unusual for women with one fallopian tube to bear children. Don't think it's the end of the world," she said to the two of them. "It may take a while. I wouldn't worry."

"My mother can hardly wait for her first grandchild," Warren said, earning a disapproving glance from the doctor.

"Is that your real incentive?" Marla couldn't help her frosty tone.

As the doctor was leaving, she winked at them from the door. "Just enjoy life. Have fun," she said. Marla smiled back. "Thank you."

She was ordered bed rest for a few days at home, after which she could resume her normal activities, but not tennis. Tennis would be out for a few months.

———◆———

Going to the Screen Actors' Guild awards dinner, however, was not too hard on her and she didn't mind. She dressed in the tuxedo-and-long-skirt creation over which they had their mini-argument a few days earlier. She decided to wear little more than a dickey and chose a halter-top chemise. The wide circular driveway to the banquet rooms at the Beverly Hilton Hotel was under the scrutiny of hundreds of fans cheering every arriving person from the narrow rows of spectator bleachers. Marla knew that they could have used self-parking but Warren wanted to be seen. He said he wanted to practice for the future. He walked slightly in front of her and waved to the fans as if he should be recognizable. She smiled as the flashing cameras snapped pictures of everyone, including her, without knowing who was who. Once inside, Warren mingled through the line of interviewers on the red carpet from television and news media, who were working hard at grabbing interviews with the big name actors. He reached back to take Marla's hand but his networking eyes were searching for people he knew, actors with whom he had worked and with whom he wanted to be noticed. Marla understood all his efforts.

Inside the huge banquet hall they found their table and she noticed there was water and soft drinks, nothing alcoholic available before the ceremony of the awards. She recognized Warren's agent and his wife who were at the wedding and was pleased to be sitting with them. Various major clients of the same talent agency joined them and Marla was introduced to some who had leading roles on television series. So many beautiful people, beautiful bodies, beautiful hair and jewelry were a feast for Marla's eyes. She graciously met all Warren's friends who stopped by. Pretty actresses gave her the once-over look which she ignored. She also met some people Warren considered important and some people who knew Warren's family. A publicist who was sitting at the next table stepped over and said he could *create Warren* and *jumpstart his leading man career*. The publicist gave him his card, asking that Warren meet with him. This was all too foreign to Marla who, throughout, remained charming, remained in the background, letting Warren shine. Marla was the perfect *actor's wife*. After all, she loved him.

Warren pointed out some of the famous faces to her, including science fiction writer-producer Eugene Romany and his actress wife, Sherrie. He also introduced her to a French director standing nearby and embarrassed her by asking her to speak French to him.

"I haven't spoken French since I met Warren," she told the director. "I'm afraid I'd better stay with English."

The director took a drink off the tray of a waiter passing by and looked away. He didn't care. However, Warren wanted to make points and be remembered.

"She, my wife, Marla, by the way, I'm Warren Traynor, my wife here, was studying to be an interpreter," he said in an effort to continue the conversation. Marla wanted to pull Warren away, but didn't. The director was looking around, looking through and past Warren. He really didn't care about Warren.

"Very interesting," he said. Suddenly, the director's eyes lit up as he noticed someone he knew. "Interesting." He walked away.

Marla chuckled. "I don't think he gives a damn, Warren."

"Nope."

"Is it a big deal?" she asked. "I didn't mean to let you down."

"He's preparing a movie. I want him to use me, that's all. This is how you make your mark."

"Honey, he'll remember my stupidity more than if I had been perfect in conversational French." She tried to settle him down.

"Maybe. Maybe you're right," he said, turning to talk with others.

On their way home, Warren evaluated the evening. "I made some good connections. There'll be work."

"Didn't you say footage from this movie will get you work?"

He looked at her with incongruity and spoke to her as if she were a child. "Marla, that's still in the can. No one will see it for ages."

"Ah, you're right." He was right. Just the same, acting jobs, although often meaningless roles, kept coming his way and his circle of business contacts grew.

Marla dutifully hostessed some very successful *networking center* dinner parties, invitations to which became highly sought after. Warren, following his mother's instructions, wanted theirs to be an *open house* and they began to attract higher power people in the industry.

"We're getting somewhere," Warren said one morning when he noticed his name mentioned in one of the entertainment news columns. "Look, Marla," he read:

> *"The famous industrialist Traynor Family is planting roots in Hollywood. Warren, a promising young actor, is a feast for the eyes. His wife's dinner parties, nicknamed* Table for Twenty, *are an irresistible invite but the B ticket for the after-dinner* soiree *is almost as big a treat."*

"His wife isn't named," Marla said. "Mustn't have impressed the reporter very much.”

“I’ll fix it next time.”

Marla saw some humor in that. “I like being nameless.” She laughed and kissed him. “As long as you know my name.” She kissed him again. They lingered. Their sexual heat was uncontrollable. Tearing off their clothes they devoured each other on the floor. The honeymoon magic was back on track full throttle. All was forgiven and forgotten.

CHAPTER TWO

Linda Reese, at twenty-five, had had more sex than ten people have in a lifetime. Buxom, dark in a sultry Italian way, wearing silk underwear and high-heeled slippers, she was swinging and swaying to a Harry Connick Jr. album. She packed several pieces of her prettiest clothes into the Floto Milano calfskin trolley luggage. Every once in a while she took a hit from a small cannabis pipe. On the coffee table was a screenplay, *Pioneer Trails*, written and produced by Michael Gaston.

She studied the precious pieces in her jewelry box. Touching the *Lapis lazuli* brooch gave her goose bumps. As Linda placed the beautiful pin in her travel case next to more sporty jewelry, memories rushed her mind and she heard her father's voice.

"Now, baby, baby, you've got it. Just right." He was breathing heavily in sexual ecstasy. She could still taste the chocolate-dipped condom around his erect penis. His one hand was squeezing the last drops of semen out, as his other hand released the rich deep blue stone to her.

"Good girls get everything they want," he whispered. "I'll show you the way. I'm your daddy."

He leaned back on the queen-size canopied four-poster bed with linen and pillows adorned in a colorful array of reds, oranges and bold greens. Except for the unusual combination of hard colors, this was the room of a typical teenager with everything young girls would keep in their own space, slightly messy, lived-in. A sly smile rolled off his face as he gestured toward the full length mirror on the back of the door.

"Go look in that mirror," he said to the twelve year old and watched as his naked daughter slowly walked over to look at herself.

"You'll blossom into a beauty and that little thing," he pointed at her lightly growing pubic hair. "That little thing will bring you everything you want, will take you places."

Linda covered up with a bath towel.

"Shy and modest girls don't get far in life. They might get a good job, like your mom, but there's no future in working. You know what I mean?"

"Yup," Linda said.

"Don't say 'yup,' Linda. Say 'yes.' You have to speak well. Not trashy. Gentlemen want their women to be trashy only behind closed doors. You know what I mean?"

"I'm not sure, Daddy."

"I'll explain it again later." He got up, zipped up his trousers and started for the door.

"You want some more?" she asked without expression, gesturing toward his male organ.

"Not now." He rubbed his nose against hers playfully, fatherly. "Now, shower and get ready for dinner." He left her room.

———◆———

Linda remained standing in front of the mirror. She dropped the bath towel to the floor. She could not imagine what was there to look at. She studied her budding breasts, her small butt and turned back again to look at the pubic hair. She picked up the *Lapis* from the bed and dropped it into a long sleek red jewelry box without giving it a second thought. The bewildered grimace on her face reflected exactly how she felt. Bewildered. A shrug of her shoulders shook off all question marks from her young mind. She headed to brush her teeth and shower.

Their small two-bedroom tract house was in a middle-class neighborhood in Fullerton, about an hour south of Los Angeles. Linda grew up in that house and did not know that it was only 1200 square feet and other people had bigger homes. It never mattered to her. Part of the garage was her father's carpentry workshop where he created pricey furniture for designer stores. He was paid well, especially for special orders, so he worked as many or as few hours as he liked. He never told anyone about his sexually abusive mother and how he had to escape from her. He sold his body to pay for carpentry school and was elated when his graduation piece earned the most money in his class. It brought him instant invitation into the commercial carpentry world. And Linda? She was not his mother. But she was his creation and like all the other creations, under his control.

An hour later he called her to dinner. Linda could smell the meatloaf her father made even in her room. The table was set for three. She poured her own water, got her father his chilled beer and sat down. He served the two of them, leaving the third place setting empty except for a glass of red wine. When he was ready to sit down to eat, he was the warm, loving father he should be.

The sound of the garage door opening and closing was followed by her mother's cheerful voice and then she appeared in the kitchen.

"Hello, everyone! I'm home!"

A classic Italian beauty, she threw her airline attendant uniform jacket on a chair, kissed both of them and patted Linda's silky hair as she talked.

"Oh, we almost got snowed in in Denver. I didn't want to lay over one more night," she said washing her hands, reaching for the glass of wine. Linda watched as her father kissed her mother on the lips. Her mother let her husband put salad on the plate and appreciated knowing that she had his undivided attention.

"I'll be home until Saturday. Linda, honey, we can go shopping and to the movies, whatever you want." She smiled at her daughter.

"Then Saturday I'm off on an overseas trip. I'm afraid I'll be gone at least eight days." She ate slowly, sipped on wine. "I hate the idea of lengthy separations."

She got up, walked over to kiss her daughter and gently rubbed the back of her husband's neck.

"Oh, I miss you always, Lindy. But," she lifted her index finger, "if all goes well, I'll be transferred to permanent domestic in about two months. I qualify and I put in for it. That means shorter trips. I'll be home a lot more."

"Oh, sweetheart, that'll be fantastic," her father said. "Now, Lindy, you go on, get ready for bed. I'll be there in five minutes to tuck you in for happy dreams."

"Yes, Daddy," Linda said, giving both her parents a hug.

"You're so good with her," her mother said to him. "I'm the luckiest woman in the world."

She put her arms around her husband. They didn't know they were being watched by their daughter. He held his wife tight, felt her heart beat faster and kissed her with passion.

"Will you tuck me in, too?" she teased him, eyes twinkling. "I could use some happy dreams."

"Have I ever let you down?"

His wife stopped to think for a moment. "No, dear. Never. You're perfect."

———◆———

As time passed, Linda's jewelry box was filling with various size emeralds, sporty costume gems and even precious diamonds. Her dad's endless love was never a subject for discussion and it made the sexual molestation seem like the natural course to adulthood. Linda believed when her father assured her that when the time was right there would be an upside awaiting her in life and choices.

In high school she quickly discovered that the prettiest kids, boys and girls, were in the drama club. She joined. She wanted to be seen and tongue-kissing her scene partners excited her. The boy would be either a handsome leading man type or a strange looking character actor with lots of personality. Either way, Linda liked the feeling and wanted more. Her popularity with the boys grew as word got around. One afternoon she went to rehearse at a senior's house who encouraged her to try marijuana. She liked the gentle fog that came over her and laid back on his bed. Without kissing, he immediately went for her panties. She let him pull it off then stopped him.

"There are rules. You can't afford to touch that," she said. Letting him look at her some more and watching as his pants bulged up.

"I have some more grass. You want it? It's worth a lot," he said, breathing slowly.

"What's a lot?

"Three-Hundred, maybe Five-Hundred an ounce," he said.

"What's the difference?"

"Quality," he said.

"Which one is this?" she asked and took another toke.

"Three," he said.

"And the Five is better?"

"Oh, yes," he said.

"Well, then, let me know when you have the Five and you can touch me," she said, pulling her panties up and getting ready to leave.

"Tomorrow? Same time?" he said.

"I'll be here. Don't lie," she said, and left. He knew he would do anything he had to do, meet all her rules to get those panties off again.

And he did. That and more. Linda was OK with that. She brought him a condom, watched him put it on and waited for something magnificent. She liked how the boy felt inside her and was inquisitive about others. She would have to experiment. Her English teacher tried to prove his superiority over the boys, but his fancy moves still left her curious about the *orgasmic excitement* she had read about. It had surely eluded her. However, she was impatient to report to her father about the high quality marijuana she lucked into.

"I don't understand why it's not legal," she said to her father.

"Well, people get hooked on it, so it's better not to start." He took it in stride. "Do you have any?" he asked.

"Yes. Are you going to get hooked, Daddy?" she chuckled.

"I won't get hooked from an occasional small toke. Usually no one does," he answered and watched her bring him a joint. "But it can be a dangerous addiction." They smoked, laughed, played erotic games, and said good night.

Linda was satisfied with her life and didn't think anything was wrong with it. Early in December she arrived home from school. There was a note from her parents letting her know that they were Christmas shopping at the mall. She was tired, went to bed and quickly dozed off. The quiet of the house was abruptly interrupted by the telephone.

"Miss Reese. There was a five-car pileup in the fog on the highway," the voice said.

"Your parents were killed instantly."

She stood still, her eyes staring into nothing.

"Thank you," she said without any emotion. "Where should I go?"

"The Coroner's office will call you as soon as they can."

"Thank you. I will wait for the call."

She had no feelings. She was sad, but not crushed. Linda didn't know whether or not she was supposed to hurt, scream, kick, cry, sit, stand, or what. She actually felt relief. She thought to herself that freedom will be interesting. Her father told her that there would be an upside awaiting her in life when the time was right. Was this the time?

———◆———

Linda's mother had a distant cousin in Superior, Nebraska. They came to the funeral, helped Linda pack mementoes important to her, including the red jewelry box, some pictures, music albums and her laptop. They took a few items they liked and agreed to accept a small portion of the life insurance money as a gift, since they were not named. Linda sold the modest tract home with most of its contents and headed to Hollywood. Why study drama and not do it? Although not yet nineteen, no one knew by looking at her, that she was under twenty-one. She learned the word *majority*, meaning that she had reached legal age. The insurance money was released to her. She found that the language of cash overrode potential problems in purchasing a townhouse, a new car and the rest went into an interest earning money market account. Her self-confidence was enormous.

She knew she wanted to act. She knew she wanted to move fast. She drove over to the Sunset Boulevard addresses of the show business trade news papers, the Daily Variety and the Hollywood Reporter, and subscribed to both. She read about Backstage, *The Actors Resource* newspaper and headed to the famous intersection of Hollywood Boulevard and Vine Street where she stopped at the huge newsstand to pick up a copy. She was educating herself about the business the best and quickest way she could find. She had to have an agent to represent her. She called one only to be told in a snide fashion that *they were not signing new clients who had no previous film experience to show.* She started to tell the receptionist that she was new in town but the person on the other end of the line didn't care and hung up the phone. She decided to call more agents and was told time-and-again the same thing. Most of the agencies were rude, almost crude. Linda had to devise a plan.

She picked a small agency from her list. Dressed to kill, she arrived at the David Sharper Talent Agency housed in the garden office building of the Sherman Oaks Galleria. She was not noticed when she opened the door and saw two middle aged women hurrying to finish up the day's work and get out of there. It was after five in the evening. Linda overheard one of them on the telephone, "Yeah. Big Boy will be back before six. I'll leave word." Linda quickly exited before she was seen and went around the corner of the hallway.

She peeked and saw the two women lock up and take the elevator. The office building was clearing out. After waiting for a few minutes, she returned to the agency entrance and sat on the floor, leaning against the door. She heard the elevator bell down the hall and started to breathe heavily as if hyperventilating.

The short, balding, middle-aged man was well dressed, loaded down with scripts and a heavy briefcase. He looked annoyed at the unexpected intrusion on his schedule.

"Can I help you, Miss?"

Linda's breasts were heaving through the slinky blouse, her sweet eyes pleadingly looked at him.

"Yes, please… I lost my balance… I'll be all right in a few minutes." She reached up for his hand and he automatically helped her up. He unlocked the door and she followed him into his office. He went for his messages and forgot about her. She sat down in the reception area and waited. She could hear him making calls in his office. Finally, there was silence. She went inside and handed him a sheet of paper. He looked at her and at the paper.

"What's this?"

"My *résumé.*"

He was tired and apparently without any fighting power.

"I'll be. The oldest trick and I fell for it," he said. He realized that he was had by an actor. He slumped back in his chair and reluctantly started to read. Linda watched him.

He studied the *résumé* she handed him and his polite smile turned to laughter. "There's nothing here, miss."

"Linda," she said. "Linda Reese."

She walked closer to him and sat on the edge of his desk. Her knee so close, his fingertips were burning.

"What can be done about it?" she asked.

"What can be done about what?" he looked at her.

"My *résumé*. You said there's nothing there. High school theater is nothing?"

He laughed out loud. "Not in this town."

He attempted to rise in conclusion of the meeting, but Linda let her knees down and stopped just an inch away from his legs. He slowly lowered himself back into his chair.

"What do you suggest?"

The agent did not expect Linda's wide, ear-to-ear, winner smile that lit up the office.

"Why don't I do what I do," she held her gaze on his fly, "and you think about the *résumé.*"

She was in his lap, moving just enough for him to…

"A dry hustle…. I've always wanted one," he said, trying to catch his breath.

The next evening, when Linda returned to see the agent, David Sharper, she had a smart *résumé* waiting for her. He handed it to her with pride. The list had *the film* she was lacking; small TV appearances that looked good enough and would never be checked. He also had a late-day appointment for her scheduled with a director at the CBS television studio in The Valley. Linda was tickled.

"Thank you. You're a good man. I'll make you money, David," she whispered in his ear and walked out of the office.

———◆———

The director was an old man. Once an actor, later a film director, he was now part of *the industry takes care of its own* concept by giving employment to its over-the-hill but once important talent. He still got work, directed television westerns by-the-numbers. When Linda entered his small, messy office, she instantly smelled freshly sprayed cologne in the air. He was leering at her with great expectations.

"So, you don't have a SAG card," the man said.

"Oh, I've just misplaced it," she answered.

"You don't misplace a SAG card, missy."

"Linda," she said. "Missy Linda Reese."

He laughed. "I like humor."

"I have plenty of humor," she quipped.

"Yeah, like misplace the SAG card. Don't you know, it only means you're not in the actors' union."

"Oh."

"You have to get into the union. That's the only way you can work. You need a first job that gets you in."

"I'm here for that first job." She spoke firmly and advanced toward him. "I want that first job." She was nose-to-nose with him. Beads of perspiration appeared on his forehead.

"I might just have such a job, missy."

He reached for a script and held it up to her.

"One line," he said. "The *Tootsie role*."

"What does that mean?"

"On every TV show there is someone's Tootsie in some small role," he grinned.

"Can I get the card?"

"We'll arrange it," he said and let himself be pushed gently into an easy chair. She didn't even move on his lap but as her ample bosoms brushed against his cheeks, his orgasmic rush made him limp. Linda crossed over to the chair opposite him. He was happily rubbing himself, his ugly face beaming.

And the work started. Her reputation preceded her. *Tit-for-tat.* Her *résumé* looked more and more like a real *résumé*. Directors, producers, writers, all had a piece of her and just like her jewelry box, her bookshelf containing the scripts of shows on which she had worked, was filling up.

———◆———

Linda sat in the reception area of a typical bungalow office at a major studio. The one-story office building held a series of independent office suites which were called bungalows same as some of the stand-alone smaller buildings that looked like private villas or cottages. The seat Linda took in the front room faced to the outside where she could see studio personnel coming and going. The short and overly made-up secretary told her that she had to rush, she couldn't wait for her boss to return. She apologized halfheartedly for not being able to introduce Linda to Buzz. Linda assured her that she will handle the introductions just fine. After the woman was gone, Linda stepped over to the reception desk and picked up Buzz Kraus' business card.

Alone, she looked around the unimaginative, ordinary office with chrome and glass furniture, a couple of plants and several trade papers strewn around wherever people left them after reading. She stopped at the open door leading to the man's private office and glanced in. The inside was crowded with oversized furniture, walls cluttered with photos of a man in his forties with short cropped salt and pepper hair, posing with famous actors, musicians, politicians and some tennis court jocks all of whom looked equally well built. Buzz Kraus was at least younger and better looking than the others she met and manipulated before him. Strangely, Linda felt a kinship for the man surrounded with photos of himself.

The tired looking man arrived and Linda produced her cheerful smile.

"Oh, you're here." Buzz Kraus forgot that he agreed to seeing Linda Reese, *a new face,* sent to him by a casting director who knew where his bread was buttered. Introducing Linda would get the casting director some brownie points and strengthen his position with executives at the studio.

He didn't break his stride. "I'm the associate producer of *Positano*." He loosened his shirt collar, walked into his inner office and glanced at papers on his desk. Linda followed.

"We have a large cast and rarely use outside actors. One, here and there. We usually hire star names. Otherwise just bits."

Then he turned to face her. "I've heard about you and wanted to meet you," he said.

"Thank you."

"Well, not about your acting, if you know what I mean." Then he caught himself, "actually, good stuff… I mean, what you do. Being a bad girl is good."

"Thank you."

"But personally I'm not interested," he continued. "You see, it's the married guys who play those games. I can give you a reading without any games."

"Thank you."

"So, you see, you didn't have to stop by." He picked up a script from a pile on the floor.

"Here. Unless you have one already?" Linda nodded 'no.'

"You can take this one. It's a bit. The reading's tomorrow."

"Thank you," Linda said, putting the script in her bag.

Buzz stepped into his bathroom to wash his hands and rinse his face. To his surprise, Linda got between him and the wide marble sink, lowered herself to her knees on the plush carpet, self-confidentially unzipped his fly, reached for his penis and unceremoniously put it in her mouth. She closed her eyes, recalling the faint remnants of chocolate. It didn't take long. Buzz was a mere man.

"Thank you," he said, straightening himself. "Dinner?"

Linda looked him over like merchandise in a meat market before saying, "Thank you."

It was during other dinners and other random acts of sex that Buzz realized Linda's singular value was sex. She didn't have star presence, the presence that commands the screen that makes an audience take notice. She was quite unremarkable. Her voice was high, although pleasant, but what put her over was her huge, beautiful smile. That was pretty much it.

A strange, easygoing friendship formed between Buzz and Linda. There was little to find out about Buzz besides that he had been a policeman who became a technical advisor on TV shows. He was divorced because his wife had thought his work in television would make their lives glamorous. His becoming an associate producer was not enough for her. She didn't understand that he had no creative talent to contribute. He was a logistics and practical procedural expert. That was all.

"She thought I was boring, refused marriage therapy, just wanted the money."

"You're kidding," Linda said, with eyes laughing.

"You're putting me on. That's not nice."

"Nice? Me? You know better."

During one of their conversations Linda learned that Buzz would leave *Positano* and had a new contract with Michael Gaston's production company. Buzz and Michael had known each other for a long time and Buzz was moving over to Michael's new show, *Pioneer Trails*, to be its associate producer. What caught her attention was the divorce of Michael Gaston, a writer-producer of television shows. Her face lit up.

"Sounds very interesting." After a beat, she continued, "This Michael?"

"Not for you. He's seeing someone. A pretty divorcee outside of show business."

"You don't know me well enough to know who's for me, Buzz." Linda spoke softly but she was annoyed.

"You're right. I just want to save you some trouble. He has a regular girl friend."

"Regular?"

"Regular," Buzz said. "I play tennis with them sometimes. She's an elegant woman. And charming. I think the word is 'vibrant'."

Linda never worried about rivals. She was prepared to protect herself.

"Vibrant?" She said, smirking.

"Are you coming to my house? I have some new grass and stuff," he said, and signaled for the bill.

"What about the *Tootsie role*, Buzz?"

"You know about *Tootsie roles*?"

"I've done a few of them," she laughed. "I'm sure it's no surprise."

Buzz thought for a while and finally said, "You know, maybe you can read for *Jessie*. A pioneer woman, her husband dies on the trail. Not many lines but a few weeks of work on location… If he ever gets the green light."

"Works for me, Buzz. I'll do Jesse." Linda turned back to him, "If he ever gets the green light."

Buzz paid the waiter and they walked out of the restaurant.

"Maybe after," she said.

"Maybe what after?"

"I'll go home with you again after I get the job," she said.

"OK." He didn't seem to care either way. "Then I'll hit on some unsuspecting female. Check out the AA."

"The AA? Alcoholics Anonymous? You're weird." Linda got out of the car as he stopped in front of her place. "Thank you, Buzz. I'll make it worth your while," she said.

"I know."

He drove off. Linda knew she lied. Even if she got the part, she would never bother with Buzz again. He bored her too.

And, indeed, the role of *Jessie* turned out to be so small that no real actress wanted it. The definitive *Tootsie role*. Linda had no trouble getting the reading and the part based on Buzz's recommendation.

She was packing to go on location.

CHAPTER THREE

"Take the money, Carol, you've earned it," he said, laughing.

"That's so ugly," Carol said, slamming the desk drawer closed. Jerry's runoff, the way the roads have runoffs for trucks, was full of bills, fives, tens, twenties mixed in with who knows how many singles. She walked away from the antique desk in the study loaded down with law books and moved closer to him.

"Jerry, so many times you've said that we fit together perfectly."

Carol Livingston, a dead ringer for Grace Kelly, her porcelain white skin shining in a black lace teddy, knew that Jerry's eyes followed her every move. Although nearing forty, she was striking in many ways, her body trained to be watched.

"We do. We're good together. As is." His gruff voice belied his gentle smile. His nearly fifty-year old face was still handsome, except for the multitude of crow's feet around his eyes and the slightly too deep laugh lines around his lips. Carol used to like his bedroom-tousled hair but his amused attitude irritated her.

Wearing high heeled, open toe boots, onyx jewelry, she was remindful of a dominatrix. The white polish on her pedicured toes matched long acrylic fingernails. She pulled on an ankle-length, gauzy black skirt, topped it with a white tunic then checked her make-up in the bathroom. She didn't mind Jerry leaning against the open door, watching as she repaired the mascara and false eyelashes. Carol was not from the *school of natural*.

By the time he returned to the study with a freshly lit cigarette, he saw that Carol had packed everything.

"You're not leaving the new teddy I bought you?"

"No," she said without looking at him.

"For next time?"

"Next time? You must be joking," she quipped.

"Would you like me to get you another. Crotchless? Maybe red?"

"You get a red one and you know what you can do with it." She piled her blond hair on top of her head, fastened it with an elaborate hair-clip and glanced around the room to make sure she had everything.

"Angry?"

"I'm not angry, just disappointed. Tired." Her voice was low, thoughtful. She walked close to him. "I love you. You said you loved me. What are we waiting for?" She took his hand, kissed it. "We could be even better."

"The black and white used to appeal to me," he said, pulling his hand out of hers.

"You called it my distinctive signature," Carol said.

"Well, I did. It was. It used to be." His voice went flat. He poured himself a drink. "Not anymore."

"You'll never get better loving, you know." When he did not respond, she helped herself to a vodka tonic from the wet bar.

"Are you telling me that no one else would ever love me?" He chuckled, making light of her.

"Yes. We only get one true love per life. I'm yours and you can't see that."

"You're drunk. Talking stupid."

She headed through the antique-filled living room, toward the foyer. He followed, lighting another cigarette.

"The longer I know you the more I see why Sammy's father didn't want to keep you around. You're too clingy. An albatross."

"That's a low blow. I never thought you'd get this low," she said from the open door, slamming it behind her.

Tears welled in her eyes but nothing came out. She drove in pain-induced trance, never blinking, hardly breathing, completely unaware of the short ride through the quiet of the night to her apartment on Carmelina Avenue. The old section of Los Angeles was populated with U.C.L.A. employees, teachers, workers, students by the dozens. She liked that her place, as most apartments in old structures, were spacious but made cozy by her unique homemaking touches. Although the black and white pieces represented her taste and attitude in life, somehow, this was a cheerful home. She was aware of her own image and the message it sent. Things are black and white and that's that.

She opened the door to her son's bedroom. She had given up long time ago on stopping him from hanging weird posters all around, using strange color bedside light bulbs, doing odd things beyond her understanding. Seventeen-year old Sammy, his longish red hair mussed over huge green eyes, was uniquely good looking. Another teenage boy and two teenage girls were drinking and smoking on a messed up king size bed. They were mostly dressed. Sammy was not embarrassed as he jumped up.

"Ma."

"I want to see this room clean and smelling like a rose before you leave for school."

"Yes, Ma," came the answer as Carol closed the door.

"See, that's all she cares about," he said sadly, looking at his friends. The girls put their arms around him and the four fell asleep.

CHAPTER FOUR

The abortion was quick and over. The pain remained. Wang Xiùměi, a young Chinese woman, was let out of the cramped basement apartment by some kind of medical person, who performed the secret wretched act on her 35-year old body. The door closed behind her. She was in agony as she slowly took the three steps up to the street and began walking back to work. Her lunch time almost over, she had to hurry. Trying to ignore the excruciating pain piercing through her, making her break out in heavy sweat, her clothes were drenched, her feet weighed her down yet she had no options but to keep going.

Xiùměi was tall and big boned, reminiscent of the ape family before its evolution. Her nose flat and wide, eyes unusually small and lips very thin. She knew early on that she was nowhere near the famed *China doll* look popularized worldwide by petite Chinese beauties. She knew she had to get a job because no one would ever take care of her. Working hard paid off when she became a school teacher in charge of five and six-year old elementary school children. Small people had respect for someone that tall. She spent long days at school into the night after everyone had gone preparing for her classes, studying, browsing on the Internet.

Long Wei Hong, the school principal, a married man some twenty years her senior, noticed the young woman. He came into her classroom, expressed interest in her work. She was eager to prove herself worthy but shy about his questions of personal nature. Each time he stopped in on his way out of school she became more relaxed, more friendly. He knew she was lonely. He assured her of her high value and she let him enter her body. She knew that becoming pregnant right away was punishment for being with a married man. She interpreted the bloody pain that followed as further punishment for her sin.

He gave her the abortion money, and bowing, he backed out of her life.

Xiùměi was empty beyond her comprehension. The walk back to school was long under the grey sky filled with heavy rain clouds about to deluge the city. Xiùměi gritted her teeth to gather all her inner strength. A clean, shiny car stopped next to her.

"Get in, Wang Xiùměi," she heard Long Wei Hong's voice. "Get in the back seat," he said. "You'll be late for class."

Xiùměi got into the car. In the front passenger seat sat an expensively dressed gorgeous young woman.

"My wife," continued the man as he started the car, "permitted me to stop for you when I mentioned that you were a teacher working under me. My wife is very gracious."

Xiùměi said "Thank you." She perceived that the man was married to a young beauty who gave nothing of herself, taking all until he was drained. Now she understood his needs, but no longer cared.

At home, that evening, Xiùměi fell asleep quickly. Afterward, for several days, she went to work while running a low-grade fever. She chose to suffer more pain by riding to work every day on a bicycle.

Xiùměi was one of ten children in her family. At age thirty, she was considered a spinster. They lived in what was considered a small town with a population of about one million in the Yinchuan region of northern China, landlocked in the middle of the vast country. None of them traveled. There was one television set on their block which everyone watched on special occasions.

She made up her mind to change her life. Being highly proficient on the Internet, she started a daily search for a man. Finally, the American, Allan Burke, believed everything she wrote about herself. The translation was loose, her photos were not very sharp, her size was camouflaged by clothes and scenery. She sold herself and now she had to make it reality.

———◆———

Allan Burke, 45, was an average looking man whose entire life had lacked purpose. If he had been a dreamer, he would at least have had an interest, maybe a goal. But he had no dream, no curiosity, no discipline, he relied on luck. As it turned out, he had none of that either. Although he came from sizeable money, following the death of the patriarch of the family, his grandfather, all the money was badly managed, misused and in general, it was gone. Allan's father moved away after he divorced his mother when Allan was still in his teens. Without guidance, Allan's life was spent drinking, smoking and partying with a bad crowd. His mother, once a princess of the mid-west, was reduced to waitressing.

Allan dropped out of school, dealt dope and worked some odd jobs, mostly painting houses. He felt inadequate about fitting into the Americana dating scene. He didn't like any of the bad girls who hung around with his crowd. Drinking and drugs were his major expenses and he would work just enough to buy what he needed and to maintain a hole-in-the-wall rental apartment with its only redeeming quality being that it was steps away from the beach. Nevertheless, Allan realized that he did want something seriously. A woman, a family. He proceeded to research foreign countries. Everybody would want an American, he believed. It'll be a piece of cake with the added benefit that he could keep secrets from an unsuspecting foreigner.

He started with Russia when it was still the Soviet Union. Girls were willing to send him nude pictures of themselves and encouraged him to visit. Allan spent all his savings on trips over there until he had to admit that he was not rich enough for the savvy Russian girls. He had no idea about the ring of agencies trading in matching up Russian girls with wealthy American men who paid high agency fees. That business was huge but some of the girls boldly took a chance on going around the rules, meeting Americans on their own. If they did not succeed, they could always stay on the roster of an agency. Naïve, Allan didn't know any of this.

Once again, he went back to house painting and Internet browsing in search for a wife. After connecting with Wang Xiùměi , he saved enough money to visit China and meet her. She and her large family lived in a one bedroom, kitchen and small bathroom unit in a city that looked strange to Allan in every way. No one spoke English and they used old dictionaries to communicate. He could not use chopsticks. They had no silverware. They took turns feeding him, which he considered pampering and kindness, not pity. They treated him like royalty. Xiùměi did everything she could to make him feel loved. They were chaperoned the old fashioned way and no physical contact between them was allowed. Allan enjoyed that and the idea of getting a virgin. He thought he could outsmart his lonely situation back home, take a shortcut and create a new life for himself. He determined that he was in love with Xiùměi. He proposed marriage, asking her parents for her hand.

She immediately stopped working. She told him that once her country knew that she would marry an American and would leave China, they fired her from her job. Allan had no means of finding out if any of that was true or whether this was simply her way of asking him for regular support money.

Through Internet communication and a great deal of miscommunication, Xiùměi and her family prepared the wedding. Allan was stunned to find some two-hundred of her friends and family in attendance at his own wedding. Strangers to him. He was informed that he had to pay for it. He promised that he would send the money. To his surprise, he could not take Xiùměi with him from China even though they were married. She told him she could not get a visa. Allan left China without his wife and with a large debt.

Back in California Allan asked his father, Victor, for money. Victor Burke was a self-made old man who refused to continually enable him. Allan felt cornered by the Chinese family and Xiùměi's demands that a husband must support his wife. Allan was a good enough house painter to get jobs but now he was under a lot of pressure to find more and more work and send more money.

Allan didn't like his father's second wife. Nevertheless, when Xiùmĕi finally arrived to the United States, Victor and his wife offered to visit the bride and Allan, *to make her feel welcome*. Bearing gifts, they drove the long trip from the retirement community in Santa Barbara for a short dinner on Manhattan Beach. Victor's wife purchased a nightgown ensemble for Xiùmĕi. Assuming that Xiùmĕi would be petite, on meeting her, she was embarrassed. The set did not fit. The moment was awkward.

It was a hard evening of loud, nervous laughter, and gesticulations, as four strangers tried to understand each other and act happy.

Xiùmĕi didn't try very hard. She had no command of the English language even though she knew for over a year that she would be living in America. She didn't study to prepare for her life in America, just took Allan's money and got heavy. Early on she agreed to everything Allan said. She agreed to help him paint so together they would be able to double his business. That was not to be. Turned out Xiùmĕi did not like painting. Following that attempt, she got a job at a Chinese restaurant. The 12-hour days on her feet also went against her grain. But Allan proudly reported to his father that Xiùmĕi kept trying different things. She started to work as part of a house cleaning crew and liked learning about such a business. Her interest peaked. She had a goal, a plan and a reason to rapidly learn English even though she was constantly on the webcam and mike talking with her family and friends in China. She was nice to Allan and he was no longer lonely. He didn't know that she was driven by the taste of making her own dollars. Working as a hotel cleaning woman she found she had a better chance for even more money and tips. She liked it when the male customer would return to the room for something he forgot and she could be alone with him. She had read about American men's fascination with Asian women. She would unbutton her uniform and cradle a man's penis between her ample bosoms. She knew how to get a large tip.

Xiùmĕi opened her own bank account and sent monthly checks to her family. She didn't tell Allan about her plans or how much money she sent home and Allan didn't tell his father the amount she contributed to the household. Xiùmĕi didn't care about Allan being broke often and told him to ask his father for money.

Once Allan binged out on booze and drugs. Xiùmĕi got sincerely upset and called Papa Burke, expressing clearly that he had to talk to his son. She knew that Victor was impressed by her eagerness toward improving his son. She felt she had the old man wrapped around her little finger and she could get away with anything. Finding out that his son was drunk and stoned again, as in his younger days, was terrible for the old man to hear. She saw that Victor was concerned for Allan and told Victor that Allan has to stop doping. Xiùmĕi was learning fast. Victor impressed upon Allan that unless he went on the wagon and cleaned up his act, he would lose the only woman who had agreed to marry him.

When Allan started Alcoholics Anonymous, Xiùmĕi decided to go with him. She was curious about it. A new thing to her. However, she said to him that she wanted to make sure he did what he was supposed to do. A loving wife.

Wanting to feel useful, Xiùměi gradually got involved with preparing and serving food snacks, cookies and coffee at the meetings. She bowed to everyone politely and people unthinkingly bowed back as they took bites off her tray. Xiùměi became part of the regulars whose group leader was glad that he didn't have to be in charge of the kitchen any more. At the end of each meeting everyone got up and applauded her for all her help. They ceremoniously *Christened* a jar as her tip jar. She thanked them but that was not important to Xiùměi. Sitting in the back, she listened to everyone, watched everything. She heard her husband give his talk about how he had improved himself since Xiùměi agreed to marry him and left China and her family to come live with him. She watched the well-dressed women who were attractive, well spoken, and who, without alcohol, were pretty and interesting. Xiùměi was learning how to dress, how to hold herself, things that were not available to her as a maid at the beachfront Hilton.

She had ideas.

CHAPTER FIVE

Marla liked the concept of being *the woman behind the great man* and in order to achieve his greatness, she would support Warren's every aspiration. One night she and Warren went out for dinner at Dan Tana's, a fine Italian restaurant on Santa Monica Boulevard. A popular hangout among the show business crowd, regardless of the level of success, everyone was checking out who was there with whom and who was worth networking.

Marla and Warren ordered cocktails, took the menus, looked around. When Eugene Romany and his wife entered, Marla recognized them from the SAG dinner. A tall couple, Eugene was showing a reasonable sized beer belly. Sherrie's angular face and wide shoulders made her the ideal look for a female science fiction character. She was Eugene's second wife who lured the father and family man out of his first marriage and proceeded to wear his power as if she had earned it. In her own way, she did. Warren had worked for Eugene on one of his shows, and waved to him. Sherrie saw the attractive young couple, gave Eugene the signal and ignoring the maitre d' attempting to show them to their reserved booth, they walked over to Marla and Warren.

"Warren?" Eugene asked with a grin.

Warren's face lit up. "Yeah, man. Warren Traynor. I didn't think you'd remember me. This is my wife, Marla."

Without waiting for an invitation, Eugene and Sherrie sat down, sandwiching them into the booth, Sherrie next to Warren and Eugene next to Marla.

They ordered appetizers and decided they would share some of the bite-size delicacies. Marla thoroughly admired Eugene, the writer, and Sherrie, the actress, who had a regular role on her husband's television series. Sherrie suggested to Eugene the idea of getting something recurring going for Warren on the show. The sweetest word to an actor's ears. Recurring. The promise that could enslave them. The conversation was all about the Romanys, people stopped by to say 'Hello' to the Romanys and they clearly enjoyed their celebrity. Warren was introduced a few times to various people saying *Hello* but not Marla.

At the end of dinner, Marla went to the ladies' room. She looked in the mirror to see why she went unnoticed. Did she look so terrible? She heard two women whispering in the toilet stalls.

"Sherrie's rule, do not mention another woman in her presence," said one voice.

"She's got it made. I'd hate to be the other woman in her group, ever," said the other voice.

When Marla heard them come out to wash their hands, she quickly slipped into another stall without being seen. By the time she returned to the table, Warren and Sherrie were gone. Eugene explained to her that they thought it would be fun to have another drink at their house in the hills. Marla was surprised that the decision was made without her.

"Warren told us how much you enjoy seeing different homes. Ours is pretty unique. You'll like it. "

"I'm sure," she said. "It's just that we could have come over some other time, not this late at night."

"Sherrie pretty much dictates those things," Eugene said with a smile in the corner of his eyes. Marla was ill at ease, but polite.

When they arrived to the hilltop home, Warren's car was in the driveway. They went inside. Sure enough, the combination foyer and living room was mind boggling, endless, with glass walls to the terrace that straddled the hill and looked at all of Los Angeles. The kind of place where on a clear day you can really see forever, to the Pacific Ocean, even to Catalina Island.

"Would you like another Tia Maria, milk and rocks?" Eugene asked, already mixing it at the bar. "That's your after dinner drink, right?" Marla nodded. She noticed the indoor pond filled with a variety of rare exotic fishes dominating a conversation area in the great room. She fell for the three dimensional op-art Mural and almost walked into the wall. She laughed out loud and turned to admire the ever-changing light beams shimmering against the reflections of the pond.

"Well, where's everyone?" she asked, accepting the drink.

"Upstairs." He pointed to a huge flower camouflaging a periscope. "Would you like to see?" He gestured to her. His look told Marla that her husband and his wife were having sex. "Would you like to join them?" he asked matter-of-factly.

Clinging to the cocktail, she walked out to the terrace, gazed at the city lights without seeing them. She was dizzy. She heard Eugene behind her and sensed that he was about to touch her. She stepped away.

"No," she said in a tone of finality. It was her *No* to everything.

————◆————

Marla and Warren drove home in silence. She felt the gravity of quicksand. Sinking fast.

"Warren," she said once inside the condo. "I love you beyond belief. I've stopped doing my life to be able to fully support yours."

"I know. Thank you."

"That's it? Thank you?" She walked away from him but then returned with new force. "I can't trust you." She shook him by the shoulders. "I don't know how to trust you again. Do you understand?"

Warren pulled out of her hold and poured himself a drink.

"Want one?"

"Are you asking if I want a drink at this moment in my life? That's bizarre. Why did you marry me when you knew exactly what kind of life I wanted? What were you thinking? "

He flashed his boyish grin. "I was thinking that you've the hottest body I ever saw. That's what." He moved toward her, like before, like always, to once again disarm her with his sexy charm. It wasn't easy but she stepped back, tears in her eyes.

Finally, after a long silence, she spoke. "My mother told me never to ask this of my husband, but here it is. Warren, what do you want? What do you really want to do?" Her eyes pinned him to the couch where he sat, casually crossing his legs and taking another swig of his cocktail.

"I want to find myself." He waited for an answer. There was none.

"I think I should rent an apartment. I saw one on Aqua Vista. A duplex."

Marla's stunned look froze on her face.

"You've been looking, then?"

"Yes."

"Aqua Vista?"

"Yes."

"Isn't that where Carolyn Shipley lives. Another one of your friends?"

"Marla, I work with lots of beautiful actresses."

"But this one is different." Marla sat down across from him. "Isn't she? Ms. silicone boobs, mini skirts and thigh-high boots?" Marla got up, started pacing. "Isn't she the social-climbing showbiz mother of two showbiz brats?"

"They need a father."

"And what do you need?"

She went to the den, closed the door behind herself. Warren packed a few things and left. Everyone was happy. Except Marla. She did not understand anything. Her life grew dark. She grabbed her chest as if trying to hold her spirit from slipping away, leaving her and diminishing into thin air. How can love turn meaningless? How can love just disappear? Is that reality?

CHAPTER SIX

Some women go shopping, some women eat chocolate fudge. Marla's anger and frustration awakened in her the wanderlust, paired with a high degree of recklessness. South America called. Magical colors of far away Rio de Janeiro danced in her brain with wondrous stories about the madness of *Carnivale*.

The flow of free drinks on the long international flight formed a rich deep pink *smoothie* cushion around her body, mind and probably even her soul. She was unaware of sitting amid six young Spaniards, wearing identical sports gear. Couple of them watched the movie, another was bobbing his head to the music on his headset, while the others were reading or sleeping.

On arrival, Marla managed to walk off the plane and spot the *BAGGAGE/EQUIPAJE* sign.

"Hello, Señorita," one of the Spaniards, a clean-cut man in his twenties, said smiling his seductive best. "I am Pablo."

"I am three sheets to the wind, Pablo," a glassy eyed Marla answered.

Pablo and his group walked with her. One of them watched carefully to see whether or not she would trip.

"This is David," Pablo said, placing the accent on a long "a."

Getting onto the escalator, Marla swayed. One of the young men grabbed hold of her until she was steady. He shyly pulled away.

"Oh, that is Ernesto, Miss Three Sheets. We call him Nesto."

Marla kept nodding and smiling. She was pretty much out of it. They reached the baggage carousels and within minutes their airplane's luggage was circling on the conveyor belts.

"The luggage is dancing," Marla said to Pablo.

Pablo gave her a puzzled look. "Dancing? Did you say the luggage is dancing?"

"Yes, yes. And there is my bag. See, the cute little bag next to the cute big bag. They're dancing. You know, like boy meets girl."

"Boy meets girl. I like it," he said. Once all their bags were collected, Pablo turned to Marla.

"Where are you staying?"

"I don't know yet. I'll have to call some hotels."

Pablo had a specially wicked smile on his face as he and his group huddled. They took her bags and walked her into their waiting van. The driver wore tennis whites, loaded the suitcases and they were off. The conversation was in Spanish, maybe Portuguese. Marla couldn't tell the difference.

"You're going with us," said Pablo. "Tomorrow we will call some hotels."

In the van, David asked her, "Is your name really Three Sheets? It is very, very maybe unusual?"

"Yes, it is." Marla leaned back and nodded off. A few minutes later, she awoke, somewhat re-energized. Squinting, she turned to her host.

"Pablo," she said.

"Yes."

"Are those uniforms you're wearing?"

"Yes. Tennis team. We're a tennis team from *España*. Spain."

David, with more of an accent than Pablo's but also with more enthusiasm, began an explanation. "Our team won *Bilbao Open*!"

"What's *Bilbao Open*?" Marla asked.

"*Vizcaya*," said Ernesto. The other two young men became animated.

"Miss, don't you know, *Bilbao* is the capitol city of *Vizcaya, España,* Spain."

They all looked at her. There was silence for a moment. Marla studied their faces and suddenly, as if the lights had come on, she said, "Oh, so your capitol city has an 'Open.' That's wonderful."

The guys were ready to celebrate the possibility of having gotten through to her.

"We won, OK. You follow? Three Sheets," Pablo said.

"I follow," Marla said.

"The prize, free trip to Rio de Janeiro," said Ernesto with an accent that was hard to discern.

"The trip was for any time."

"No dates," Pablo said. "Any time. So, we found tournament to make more money here and came on free trip. The Brasil Open. *Costa de Sauipe Tennis*."

They worked hard at trying to make her grasp the importance of their mission.

"Tournament has good prize money," Pablo said.

"Maybe free trip back home to *Tolédo*," Ernesto joked.

"Toledo?" she asked.

"No, Toledo, Ohio, America. *Tolédo, España*. Spain. Home."

One of the two nameless players gave her the brochure of their tennis club, their home base outside *Tolédo, España*. The Spanish language flier opened up to two pages. It depicted beautiful photos of the tennis club as well as a handsome man, who, whimsically, in the pose of *Atlas the Titan*, with arms stretched wide, was holding up the entire club in his two hands, as if holding the globe. She smiled without knowing what she was reading.

"One of us will go to quarter finals," offered Pablo. "That is plan."

"That is enough money for our trip," explained Ernesto. "Then, if any of the others get placed, there is more money."

"What is the money? The currency?" Marla asked. "*Cruzeiros?*"

"No. No. *Cruzados Novo.*"

"David, that was long time ago." Pablo held up the travel book and pointed to the Currency page. "It is *Cruizeros Reais.*"

"The bank knows," Ernesto added, pulling out a couple of credit cards from his pocket. "The bank knows."

"Who cares? We do not need money." David spoke like a wise old man. "We have sponsor."

"But we like money," Pablo laughed.

"We are the underdogs here, at this meet. We fool everyone. We travel without coaches. Nobody thinks we can win here." David laughed and the others joined in as they shared their secret with her.

"Nobody," Ernesto said.

They arrived to Hotel Gloria. Inside the lobby, they dropped their luggage and walked up to the desk. Copying them, Marla dropped her bags the same way, next to theirs. Pablo talked to the registration clerk and they found an additional room for her. She didn't need much convincing to join them.

"We go to dinner in two hours." Pablo was the leader.

"We break bread. That's what my mother called dinner," Marla said.

"Yes. In our country also. We break bread. It is special. Any time. Dinner, Lunch," said Pablo. "Friends are special."

The bellman had loaded his cart with all of their luggage from the front entry of the lobby and they followed him. First stop was Marla's room. "We go check in with the tournament and come back," said Pablo. Marla nodded. She was tired.

"Fine. Good. You come back. Two hours?"

"Yes." They all kissed her on her cheeks and left. She stood for a moment then set the travel alarm, undressed and crashed. An hour later she awoke, showered and like clockwork, the boys called to meet her for cocktails in the bar on the mezzanine.

After dinner in a Copacabana Beach restaurant, they walked on the silky sand carrying their shoes, they laughed, ran around, played under the starlit sky. A few feet behind the others, Pablo grabbed Marla by the waist and squeezed her to him, making her feel every muscle in his strong body. She shivered as her skin involuntarily responded to his masculine touch, then pulled out of his arms, ran to catch up with the group.

Back at the hotel, moments after she closed the door behind her, there was knocking. It was Pablo, with a bottle of champagne in a bucket of ice. She didn't mind having a nightcap with him.

"You come with us to tennis club in the morning, if you wish," he said.

They lifted their glasses.

"To victory," he said.

"To victory," she said. "Yes, I'd like to go with you in the morning."

"Good. I am happy. You are beautiful."

He put down his glass, took the one away from Marla and kissed her hand. This caught Marla off guard, still, she didn't pull away, didn't step back, yet her body would not yield. He kissed her lips, soft and long. Same results.

"Am I desirable? Yes? No?" he asked.

"Oh, very, very. Yes. You are," she said.

"I can make love. Good love. Easy. You are beautiful." He was trying his best. His face touching hers, he whispered into her ears and thought he felt her body relax. But no, she could not give.

"I'm so sorry, Pablo. I love my husband."

"Married?"

"No. Not anymore. But I still love him. My ex-husband," she said dreamily. Pablo's bewildered stare called for an explanation.

"My body's still in love with his." She sat down on the bed. Pablo moved for her again but the look in her eyes might as well have been a huge red STOP sign. Head hanging low, he started for the door.

"The champagne?" she asked.

"Yours. Gift."

"I'll change to another hotel tomorrow," she said.

Pablo walked back to her. "No. Not necessary. You go with us to club." He kissed her on both cheeks. "You bring good luck. You go with us to dinner, to club, to *Carnivale,* every place we go." He kissed her hands again. She could feel the heat of his lips burning her skin. "I am gentleman," he added, heading for the door again.

"If you come to my home, *Tolédo*, you be honored guest, I will be gentleman." He left Marla and the champagne.

———◆———

Ten days rushed by. She was one of the boys. She spent her time at the tennis center watching them play. One of them lost the first round. Ernesto injured his leg during the warm-ups and had to withdraw. Pablo was really hot and advancing with each game. The odds were with Pablo and David.

Marla walked around between matches. People talked to her in Spanish since she was wearing the Spanish team badge. Her name on the badge was Miss Three Sheets and thanks to the foreign land and lack of meticulous English, no one questioned it. They smiled politely and called her Miss Three Sheets. She saw the local aristocracy who played tennis and attended tournaments. She went to the closing ceremonies with the team and joined in celebrating Pablo as the second place winner.

Marla fit so well into the group she was perceived as part of the team and covered by their prepaid costs. She spent no money. She got to hit some warm-up balls and she was having fun. They were taking dozens of pictures with and without her. She maintained a continuous champagne glow hoping that she would forget her pain over the divorce. But Warren's memory was far reaching. She could never completely get away from him. She would hear his voice out of nowhere, or feel his eyes gazing at her as she walked. Unsettling. Her love for him was so all-encompassing, that it wouldn't simply end in spite of her decision to stop loving him.

But, eventually, when the tournament was over, she felt she had to sober up. She thought about the pros and cons of facing reality and decided that she was not ready. She said *goodbye* to the team at the airport and chose to take the long flight to Mexico, not Los Angeles.

Mazatlan and Cancún, Mexico's exotic jewels, had just started to light up her life when word reached her about the divorce proceedings. She had to go back to Los Angeles and participate in finalizing papers, attending the court hearing and, specifically, seeing Warren again, face-to-face. Warren's mother was at the hearing and gave Marla a long, pitying stare. Marla turned away, still the heat of Warren's presence made her tremble, as when he first kissed her. She broke out in cold sweat. She could hardly speak. Even now, being in the same room with Warren had an enormous numbing effect on her. He was deep inside her psyche. She was still not at peace. She was not over him. She could not focus on her future. Restless, scared, angry, lost, she felt negative and so helpless.

The champagne memory of the tennis team, the foreigners, became a recurring vision in her mind. Spain. *Tolédo?* Should she? Should she not? Was it that she wanted to find another party, another friendly crowd in which to hide from her life? Or, perhaps, return to the group of strangers who didn't care what stories she told about herself. Was it that she was so scared to be alone in a routine of normal living that she wanted to flee into another fantasyland? Her credit card charges would be paid by Warren for another six months. She was glad he had to pay penalties but she wished the whole thing had never happened.

Impulsively, she took off again.

She inhaled the scents of airports, airplanes, crowds of travelers, and got high from them, *adrenalin-curdling* in a way. Never liking the jeans and tennis shoes look, she traveled in August Silk, washable separates that were easy to wear and pack and somehow, always looked stylish. Outside the airport, she handed the note with the address to the taxi driver and it wasn't much later when he dropped her at the tennis club, her destination.

Artistic wrought iron fencing surrounded the club, a two-story building in modern Spanish architectural design. As she got out of the taxi, she entered the clubhouse, dropped her bags inside the entrance as the guys did in Rio.

The comfort zone of a tennis club always had a grounding affect on Marla. She hoped that here, as elsewhere, there would be members looking for roommates and that she could find lodgings. Better yet, she hoped to find Pablo and the others.

Quiet, the interior of the reception lobby whispered low-key elegance. There was none of the raucous noise typical of the American clubs yet it was just as active. Players were coming and going. She looked at them closely to find her buddies of her Brazilian escapade. No luck. She asked the receptionist, who recognized her from the pictures on display on the photo wall in the lobby. The receptionist informed her that the silly little team of semi-pro Spaniards got invited to play in Melbourne, Australia. Then they unexpectedly qualified for some high paying tournament and were working their way up in rankings. No hurry to return.

When Marla heard that story, she laughed out loud. Maybe too loud?

"Good for them. Too bad for me," she said and headed toward her bags inside the entry door of the lobby.

The receptionist, however, stopped her from leaving, acknowledged the team's invitation to Marla and immediately honored it with outstanding hospitality. Marla was guided into the grillroom and served Port with Stilton cheese, followed by light samples of *tapas*. When she asked for the bill, she was told that a foreign friend of the team was automatically a welcome guest.

And the man stepped out of the flier. Very Spanish, very handsome, very polished, very storybook. Wearing tennis whites, his smile came with what appeared to be three-hundred sparkling teeth and the brightest blue eyes she had ever seen. Short cropped black hair topped the lanky frame.

"I have that *If my friends could see me now!* Feeling," were the first words out of her mouth. She chuckled. "I might break out in dance." She was unashamed, and why not?

"Word is that you're a friend of our underdog team, my semi-pro ringers," he said in flawless English.

"May I introduce myself, Sebastião Emanuel de Pombal y Martín. *Sebastian de Pombal*. This is my unique establishment and I own the somewhat nomadic team as well." He gleamed with pride and mystery. He could not have been more appealing.

"Marla Hayes." She looked at him, shrugged her shoulders. "Marla. I am here, sort of nomadic, not an underdog, and far from being smart enough to be a ringer." Her voice trailed off. "I'm here. That's all."

"Then you're not Miss Three Sheets?" he smiled gently. "You look like her," he said pointing toward the pictures.

"That was a joke. No one got it. I had the wrong audience," she grinned.

"Three sheets to the wind," Sebastian said. "I know that expression. If three sheets or ropes are loose and blowing in the wind then the sail boat will lurch about like a drunken sailor."

"Oh, is that how it is?" Marla asked. "Pretty interesting. I never knew that."

Champagne was served. Sebastian leaned closer to her as he lifted his glass. "And did you take special fancy to any of my studly players?"

"I don't do that."

"What does that mean?"

Marla took a sip of the champagne. She was annoyed. "It means, Sebastian Emanuel whatever, de Garibaldi for all I care, that you are way out of line. Didn't anybody teach you that prying is poor manners?"

Sebastian was entertained by the fiery comeback. "It's *de Pombal*, Portuguese blue blood. *Sebastian de Pombal*." He smirked.

"Excuse me." She reached up with her arms, imitating the *Atlas* pose on the brochure.

"You shouldn't be mocking me, but do you think it's too much?" He also raised his arms as in the brochure.

"Not really. It's memorable."

"That was the purpose."

"Then it worked." Marla didn't care.

"A match?"

"Now?"

"Now."

"One condition," she said. "You'll stop asking for personal information."

"Which is?" he tested once more.

"Not for sale."

She was shaken, but held her own. "I travel alone. I am looking for lodgings for a few days. I intend to pay in U.S. Dollars not by bartering personal information or spreading gossip."

"I don't like people who ask no questions. People who don't want to know anything, I don't want to know. It's my nature," he said.

"Then we're opposites."

"I don't want to be your opposite," he said.

"Truce?" she looked into his bright eyes.

Sebastian's smile was almost angelic, if a man can be macho and angelic at the same time. She knew he was playing and she played back. It felt more like a buddy thing than a flirt thing. She smiled.

"I'll show you to the locker room," he said. Marla followed. Out of nowhere, appeared a uniformed staffer who did, in fact, carry her bags from the lobby to the locker room.

"How much time do you need?"

"Ten minutes." She went inside.

The ladies' locker was luxurious. The Attendant's corner blended into the well-appointed set-up. Showers, spa, steam, sauna, towels, slippers, lotions, hair dryers and lots of privacy. Always ready, her beach clothes and tennis gear were at hand, the top layer in her bag. When she took out what she needed, the Attendant pointed to a private dressing room, then placed Marla's bags in a closet-sized locker.

Dusk was setting in when they walked out to the courts. The two-story building sprawled in a U-shape around the string of tennis courts. Bleachers were cleverly incorporated in the side of each building so that everyone could watch practically every game from anywhere.

Sebastian took Court 7. "Court 7. My lucky number," Marla said just to say something. She really didn't have a lucky number.

Other players were passing by, saying *Hello* to Sebastian. He looked incredibly fit. The sparkling whites accentuated his smooth olive skin and sky-blue eyes. He had several rackets for Marla to test until she picked one.

Marla's getting off to a slow start was graciously ignored by Sebastian. Although Marla wondered whether he was just being patronizing, she didn't say anything. It was that thought that motivated her. She believed that patronizing was on the same level of being judgmental. Hateful characteristics. She'd rather be flying by the seat of her pants and burn her butt than give in to the phony well-meaning remarks of others. And by the second set she was getting better, anticipating his moves better and returning with good placement. She won the second set.

"If you win the next set," he said jovially, "I'll let you stay here free of charge."

"And if I don't?"

"I'll let you stay here free of charge."

"Then I'll win," she said with a playful giggle.

After the match she was surprised that he invited her to be his guest. What made her say *Yes?* She was drawn to Sebastian and took a wild chance. A reckless chance.

She learned that besides being a tennis nut, running a super-private racquet club was the fun side of his life. On the serious side, Sebastian was a financier in *Tolédo,* aware of business nuances on every level, locally as well as on large scales. She liked smart people.

Marla stayed at his incredible estate and met his older sister Emanuella, a major modeling agent in Barcelona. Emanuella was tallish, not thin and seemed even masculine because of her deep voice. But as she got to know her better she found out that Nuella, as everyone called her, was an extremely feminine being. Favoring no-frill elegance in her appearance, she became increasingly attractive to Marla. They clicked with ease. Nuella left after spending a few days with Marla and Sebastian. Marla continued her stay and traveled with him all over the country and to Portugal.

Without a doubt, *Cascais* by the seaside became her favorite. The small town, more like a village, rolled down to the main highway by the Ocean, or rather, by *Cascais Bay*. They stayed at the *de Pombal* family home, a small castle just outside the city limits. Although it was a tourist attraction, a well maintained residential wing was available for their use. They were honored by the Curator and the staff, who made her feel like royalty. From its tower, one could see the ocean and *Capo de São Vicente*, Europe's most south-western point, once considered the edge of the Western world. They made that side trip before heading to the many historic sites of Portugal. Another highlight was their stop at the Porto Santa Maria, an upscale seaside restaurant. They sat side by side, gazing at the ocean. Grilled appetizers were followed by *Dorado en Sal*, a golden fish smothered in salt. Marla's expectation of salty taste did not come true. The fish was wonderful.

Sebastian cradled her hand in his. He was attracted to her and did not understand why. She was pretty but in a different way. Everything about her was somehow different. She gave the feeling of being an open book but he could not read her. He wanted to give her the world. He wanted to hold her the way he held up the tennis club on the flier. She kissed him. His lips were soft and warm. Almond in velvet. She wanted to kiss him again.

"I know this is a public place."

"Yes," he said. "We should not embarrass other guests."

"Sebastian," she spoke very slowly. "You're the best thing that ever happened to me. Ever."

His face lit up as she stopped for a sip of wine.

"But yesterday, all that's yesterday, is still with me."

"Don't run off. This is fine." Sebastian took things in stride. He respected her boundaries. He showed her around the historical as well as the contemporary. She found herself trusting him. He helped her rationalize her anger with herself about her mother. He had a vast understanding of human nature and in a short period of time peeled away some of her façades. Sebastian also commanded respect. She liked being around that. Respect. But she could not give herself to him. Warren's touch was still in her system. Her first love had a hold on her. Sebastian understood when she decided to return to Los Angeles.

CHAPTER SEVEN

Empty, unfilled, Marla looked for grounding on the familiar terrain of her comfort zone, the tennis courts. The future ahead seemed so far away, she couldn't formulate it in her mind. She had a hard time formulating only the next day in her mind. Luckily, the next day was Sunday. A balmy, pleasant California Sunday. She arrived early to the Westwood Tennis Club, waited courtside while watching a match. She knew she looked good in the short tennis skirt and light top. There was no extra weight on her anywhere. As if sensing someone watching, she turned to face a pair of twinkling eyes on an otherwise average face of a man of average height and hair. But his eyes had it, compelling her to smile back.

"Waiting for your court?" he asked.

"No, not yet. I got here early," she answered. "Too early."

"Are you any good?"

"I think so," she laughed. "Are you?"

"Tennis is my best trait," he said.

"A trait? That's new."

"I've been playing it so long, it is part of my thinking, my body language."

"Don't tell me you're a pro?"

"I ought to be," he laughed. "But I said trait, not talent, remember?"

"Got it." Her coach arrived.

"Marla! Ready? Court 7," he yelled toward her and she turned to follow him to court 7.

"My lucky court," Marla said. "My lucky number."

"A lesson?" Michael said.

"Just in case I run into someone with a tennis trait."

"You did."

"I did."

Michael was shouting after her. "Doubles, tomorrow? 8 o'clock?"

"A. M.?" She asked before closing the gate to court 7.

"A.M.!"

The next morning, they learned each other's names, Marla Hayes, divorced, Michael Gaston, divorced. Buzz Kraus, a clean-cut man in his forties with salt and pepper hair and a pleasant smile, came to play the mixed doubles and brought a lady friend with a long weird Slavic name. Everyone called her Sally, or *Sally the Slav*. She answered. First generation from Slovakia, she spoke with an accent, laughed loud and displayed the vivaciousness of a person who, after a great deal of hardship in her youth, finally discovered that life was good. She was a decent tennis player. In fact, the foursome turned out to be well matched. They made a date for the following Wednesday. 8 o'clock.

"I don't like to play at night," Marla said.

"This is morning. Can you make it in the morning?" Michael asked. "Or do you work?"

"I don't work," Marla said. "Do you?"

"I do but I can go in after 10. So can Buzz," Michael said.

With that, the entire schedule of tennis playing was set. Marla didn't ask questions. She now had something to plan for.

As she came out of the ladies' locker room, Michael was waiting.

"Can you do dinner some night?"

"I don't know if I'm ready," she said, curling up her lips, making a funny face.

"As they say, it's only dinner. No big deal," he said, eyes smiling.

"Breaking bread is a big deal. Not just with anyone. It takes special people."

"I thought I could say 'We all have to eat sometime' and you would say . ."

"I was joking. I like to eat. When?" she laughed.

"Tonight. How's tonight?"

"I'll meet you."

"Where?"

"You tell me. I live in the Beverly Glen."

"La Sere, Studio City? 8 o'clock."

"A.M.?" she asked with mischief in her eyes.

"P.M."

She got into her car, waved at him and drove off.

At dinner, they didn't talk about the past too much. They knew they each had the baggage that formed his and her thinking. She learned that Michael was a television writer and Buzz was an associate producer who worked with him on some shows. She was impressed by his sharp min and quick thinking. Through writing about others and about relationships, Michael realized that his marriage had reached a dead end. He had already moved out of the family home and his divorce was final. He appeared to Marla to have a handle on his life. She would not admit her shortcomings in that area. They enjoyed each other's company. It was an easy fit. Comfortable with himself, Michael took the lead and started to ask her to screenings at the studios and included her in some professional functions as his date. Michael liked that she was not star struck.

They went to an open-air jazz festival one afternoon. Marla got into the music and started to sing the words as they came to her head more in the paraphrased form than as written.

"I'll disown you," Michael said pulling away from her. "If anyone asks, I do not know who this woman is. I bought her a hot dog and she broke out singing—badly." They laughed.

She invited him, for the first time, to her home. The fresh, sweet scent of assorted cut flowers welcomed him, as he entered the high-ceilinged spacious living room. Attractive melding of peach and rust was the base of the condo's décor. Marla recognized Michael's curiosity. "It was professionally done. Susanne Currie. You might have heard of her."

Michael walked around and nodded *No*.

Marla continued. "She's supposed to be some big time decorator, a friend of Warren's." She was setting up snacks on the wide breakfast bar. "Probably more than a friend, I think," she said, putting out wine glasses. "It took me a long time to figure things out. I was very trusting then."

"And now?"

"I still am."

"I knew that. People don't change. Not their core," he said, looking around the home appreciatively.

"It was a wedding gift," she offered.

"I'm impressed."

"From his parents."

Walking around, Michael appeared interested in everything, art on the walls, coffee table books on the coffee table, nothing eluded his attention.

"And you left him because ?..." Michael turned to face her.

"He couldn't keep his pants on. And that's enough of him, Michael. I'm glad he paid the price of sin and I got the condo and, oh, yes, the tennis club. Prepaid for years," she added.

"Little revenge is healthy," Michael said.

"Feels pretty, pretty nice," she grinned, then pointed Michael toward the bar.

"Would you like some wine? Kendall Jackson?" she said, then turned to him. "I noticed your weakness for Smirnoff." She bit her lip realizing she was too obvious. "Anyway, I got some."

Michael started to pour.

"I never knew how good cocktail onions were until I tried them soaked in vodka," she said.

"OK, coming right up. Have you tried it with a splash of Vermouth? A Gibson?"

"That's too sophisticated for me," she said. "Vodka and onions will be just fine."

In the kitchen, she prepared snacks of melted brie, sliced apples and pâté de fois gras on water crackers.

"Cholesterol city. From me to you, with love." She laughed.

"Isn't this illegal?" Michael asked.

"Cholesterol, should be."

"No, the goose liver."

"It's illegal to force-feed the geese in this country, but you can get imported pâté. Warren got some as a gift from another actor who had been shooting in Canada. He forgot about it, so it's mine. Do you like it?"

"I love it," he said. "I know so much academia, Marla, but I don't know much about real life. The delicacies I know from research. The sites and sounds I know from research. So much I haven't done. So much I want to do."

"I know about food," said Marla with some pride. "I love food, but I don't know much else. Guess we're pretty dumb."

"Yup. We are," he laughed.

They were silent for a while, sipping on their drinks, munching on the snacks, pondering their own thoughts.

"Come to think of it," Marla said, "I know a little bit of French and I'm good with computers and software and especially with computer research."

"How is that?"

"I wanted to be a translator at the U.N. before Warren. I studied speed talk, speed write, speed listen, speed French, speed computer search in the nick of time. Speed, speed, speed."

"I admire that."

"I'm sure I lost it by now."

"Lost what?"

"Speed," she answered. "The most important part of simul-translation. Speed. Which reminds me, I'm starting a job tomorrow."

"What kind?"

"I think it's advertising."

"You think?" he asked.

"Well, this man remembered me from some function."

"What do you know about advertising?"

"Nothing," she laughed.

"If I were a writer, I'd set this up so that the man doesn't care what the woman knows, the man remembered her beauty and wanted her around."

"That's very romantic, Michael. If I were a writer, I'd say someone is ready to throw a bone at the ex-wife of the son of a rich family. Something like that."

"My scenario is more realistic." Michael finished his drink. "Either way, I hope it'll work out."

When he got ready to leave, she walked him to the door. He leaned to kiss her but did not go further.

"Not ready yet. Do you mind?"

"I'm not ready either." She laughed and patted him on his shoulder as he was leaving. "Maybe by Christmas. A gift, perhaps?"

———◆———

Two days later Michael came over unannounced. She buzzed him in and was happy to see him. An impromptu light kiss *Hello* was just right.

"I couldn't wait to tell you, Marla. I got the green light for my pilot. We start shooting next week." He hugged and squeezed her, full of youthful energy. They were laughing and kissing. His excitement was sky high.

"We're leaving for location Sunday."

"Location?" She looked at him. He nodded with a wide grin.

"Location?" she asked again. Michael did not understand her apparent concern.

"You're going out of town?"

"Yes. To shoot the pilot. Not very long. Couple of weeks, maybe three."
She stopped kissing and changed the subject.

"Are you hungry? Would you like a snack? I could whip up something."

"Oh, no, not at all. I'm too excited. Just wanted to remind you we have a date."

"A date?" she asked.

"Christmas. And don't forget, I want it gift wrapped," he said.

"Excuse me. What gift wrapped?"

"The body," he said. "How soon we forget. Your body. Christmas gift."

"Could we go a little slower?"

"Did you say 'shower'? Shower-mates?" He held her close, feeling jubilant. "Christmas shower date! Keep it clean!" He laughed at his own pun.

"Not exactly," she said, blushing.

"Dirty? Pretty racy, I'd say."

"Stop it, Michael. You're embarrassing me." She suddenly looked like a confused little girl.

"Oh, I don't mean to do that. We'll have it all, Marla. A great Christmas! You just get the ribbons and bows."

"Ribbons and bows?"

"Gift wrap. Ribbons and bows in every color. Will you?"

"Who says?"

"Your man."

"MY MAN. Sounds kinda' funny."

"It doesn't sound funny at all. Sounds just right."

One more gentle kiss on the lips and he was out the door.

Location, the perfect place to binge out on the forbidden. Some things never change. Some changes are never planned but happen. Linda felt completely at ease showing up at Michael's hotel room with a picnic basket.

"I heard you like the simplicity of Smirnoff but I am proposing a taste challenge. My bottle of iced Grey Goose against your Smirnoff."

She walked in, set the basket on the wet bar. Opened a jar of cocktail onions, a jar of jumbo olives. She had already prepared a small platter of cheese, walnuts, tangerines and set them out with napkins, silver and the ice bucket on the side.

"And you are?" said Michael.

"Linda Reese, Michael. I read for you and Bernie for the role of Jesse, wife of…"

"I know who Jesse is,… Linda."

Linda proceeded to twirl the cocktail glasses in ice and pour the drinks. She seductively handed it to him. Wearing a little bit of expensive Carolina Herrera worked. He displayed no resistance. In fact, after many years of marriage to his high school sweetheart, this sort of thing was necessary, needed, inevitable. He knew he had missed out on a lot and deserved all the good things life had to offer. There she was. One good thing. An eager-to-please, expensively semi-naked, trashy female, wet and juicy. He went for it. Why not?

Michael and Linda's party on location never stopped. Shooting all day, Michael re-writing half the night and Linda getting high on grass and doing wonderful things to him the other half. Linda was cute and cuddly when toasted and made a man feel like the big boss. Based on the results, she already recognized that her father taught her well.

And now, she was on track. She never compared herself to other women. By this time in her life she knew she was the best at what she did. When she left Michael's room in the wee hours of the morning, she was certain that Michael was not thinking about the other woman back in Los Angeles.

But the other woman had a way of not disappearing. One morning Michael was having breakfast at the hotel with his director, Bernie McAfee and the male star of the show, Marshall MacIntire. Marshall was a hunk in every sense and a man's man whom women wanted to take care of. During their serious discussion of the upcoming scenes, a package was delivered to him. He opened it. Ribbons and bows of every color burst out, leaving behind in the box a fabulous blue mohair sweater. A Christmas gift. The charm of the elementary poem that accompanied the hand-made card hit home, gave him goose bumps. He missed her. He actually thought of Marla as the special woman in his life. Linda was a mere interlude. A location thing. He was looking forward to seeing Marla. In an unspoken fashion they were making plans for the future together, plans of traveling and gathering international story ideas for him.

And then came Linda. How could that happen? How could that NOT happen? He was just a man.

———— ◆ ————

And now? What now? He kept putting off calling and telling Marla how sorry he was about not being there for Christmas and New Year's Eve. *The life of a writer* would be his eternal cry. The production company was, in fact, taking a few days off so that everyone could go home for Christmas. Michael couldn't tell Marla that he chose to stay on and keep re-writing. Or was it the services of Linda that kept him from going back to L.A. Now, even though he loved the sweater, he couldn't call her. He was full of guilt. What would he say?

By the end of the shooting day, he decided he had to make the call. OK, he was THE writer. He would adlib something. He dialed.

"Marla," he said. "How are you?"

"Very busy at work and missing you very much when not at work," came the simple reply.

"I like that you speak your mind." He stopped for a moment. "You're easy going. There're too many pushy women around."

"Try to avoid them, Michael. You'll live longer." They laughed.

"And how's work? Two weeks and still on the job, hm?"

"Almost three," she said.

"What are you doing?"

"You'll never believe this," Marla said. "I'm a copywriter."

"Whoa!," was all Michael had to say.

"I'm a writer. Don't you just love it? Advertising. Still a trainee, though."

"You like it?"

Marla's voice was buoyant, "Love it. I love what I'm learning. I miss our tennis."

"Yeah. I'm getting soft in the belly," he said. "By the way, the sweater is great. Thank you."

"Then it fits?"

"Oh, yes. Perfectly. And the hood is great on these cold mornings." At least he didn't have to lie about that.

"It's blue. Matches your eyes."

"I don't know what to say. I didn't get you anything."

She laughed. "I'm glad you didn't lie and have your secretary run out to buy something in your name. It's better when I see you."

"Yes." He eagerly agreed.

"And the ribbons? Bows?" the words involuntarily escaped her lips.

"A nice touch. Like an inside joke."

"A joke?"

"No, Marla, I don't mean the joke part, only the inside, just between you and me."

She took a while before speaking. "Will I see you?"

"Of course, you will." He sounded definite.

"I sometimes wonder if you're still *my man*."

"I am. Don't worry. It's only the life of a writer. When you have a job, you have no life."

"That's too new to me."

"You'll get used to it," he said. Why did he drag this out? He knew he liked talking with her and wanted to finish on a high note.

"We have to get the pilot and some episodes and some exteriors shot and in the can in time for mid-season replacement, just in case a spot opens up on the network schedule. "

"Oh, I understand," said Marla. "Just don't want to. I don't like having to wait for you until after Christmas, maybe even until next year."

"I feel the same way," he lied.

There was knocking on the door. Michael headed to open it.

"I'm working long days, I will miss New Year's Eve without you, but I'll make up for it. I am your man…." His voice trailed off as Linda entered. She threw her long coat on the bed revealing a flimsy teddy and high heel *fuck me* sandals.

"Hello? Michael?" he heard Marla but could not get a word out for a long beat.

"Uhmm… yes, yes. I'm here."

"Well? What happened?"

Linda was grabbing his testicles and gently rubbing them.

"Oh… nothing… really. Just someone came in." He took a deep breath. "I had to let someone in."

"OK. You're not alone. You sound preoccupied. Go and do what you have to do. See ya."

Michael thought he heard her voice get teary but, indeed, he was preoccupied with the wonders of Linda. She picked up the ribbons and bows from the dresser and gave him a promising smile as she began to tie him to her with the soft satin ribbons.

"You naughty, naughty boy," she whispered. "Would you like to be tied up?"

Linda was working hard, building a future, one-orgasm-at-the-time. She could not be more serious.

CHAPTER EIGHT

New job! A job! Here I come!

The heavy rain of the rush hour clogged up the already overwhelming morning traffic reminding Marla of driving through walls of water only weeks earlier on her way to her first day of work. She will never forget that day and the feeling of relief on getting a real job. She recalled how, after all her travels, she faced reality, accepted the necessity of having to work.

With Warren out of her life, things were a mess. Just enough money left to keep the fees on the condo going, no practical skills, no friends who would hire her. Yet she tried. She called everyone she knew through Warren, but they didn't want to insult her by offering her menial labor. They simply didn't want to deal with her. Then she called everyone whose number she could find whom she knew before Warren, but only some men remembered her well enough to offer her jobs of a personal nature. Definitely not her cup of tea. But what could she do? She didn't qualify for anything.

If it hadn't been for Michael, loneliness would've closed in on her. The solitude she sought all her life became a friendless existence. Financially, she was bottoming out, ready to apply for jobs as dishwasher or cosmetics sales woman. One more name came up on Warren's Caller ID list left on a forgotten working unit. Apparently, Warren was considering hiring a publicist to make his a household name. She had no recollection of ever meeting the publicity man, Jonathan Kaplan. She called him. She was surprised that he remembered her.

Jonathan told her "I never forget a dignified woman. It's the way you carried yourself at the Screen Actors Guild dinner."

Marla had no idea that she had made such an impression on the man. She didn't care about what he looked like. Sight unseen, she jumped into an entry level job he could offer. Anything was fine.

"No, you didn't insult me," she assured him.

By the time she related this to Michael, the details of her search were minimized. Michael never knew of her struggle although he was dating her. Her mother's advice of being her own counsel prevailed. Everything about privacy suited her.

When she arrived on that rainy day at the Santa Monica office of The Kaplan Group, Jonathan was on his way out to a photo shoot. A stocky, balding youngish man, he quickly turned her over to Carol Livingston, the head copywriter, and left. Carol, a cool blonde, dressed in crisp black and white, was distant.

She showed Marla to a cubicle, gave her tools and a test task. Using her normal logic, Marla passed the test. It was after the test that Carol walked her around the loft office.

The Kaplan Group occupied the entire third floor, the *penthouse* of a commercial building in the heart of Santa Monica. They jokingly called themselves the High and Mighty Kaplans since there was no one above them. The spiral staircase to the roof from inside the loft was actually Carol's idea and Jonathan installed it. This way, they had their own access to the rooftop where tables, umbrellas, chaise lounges and plants created a restful garden setting. When rainstorms were predicted, everyone pitched in to bring things inside.

The elevator's arrival was marked by the enthusiastic traditional baseball fight-song that sounded like *tralala LA tata, charge!* Could have been a *call of the wild*, in a way. An inviting reception area in the elevator lobby was partitioned by an artist's divider wall that nearly touched the ceiling, a whimsical yet functional replica of the Berlin Wall. There was a natural flow of space and air on entering the premises. The skylight tube also enhanced nature and moved automatically from soft to intensified as the world changed outdoors. This office was the epitome of an ergonomically state-of-the-art creation that actually came together.

The reception entry featured an innovative row of narrow mirrors allowing the person at the desk to see behind herself, to the side and see the entire area without twisting and turning. This was a variation on *Feng Shui* where you can never be surprised by anyone behind you because you have eyes everywhere.

The general office concept was a large onion with its layers peeling away. It started with the center of the loft that held a marble-top conference table for 16. Drop-down screening panel was coordinated with the projection system built into the other end of the table. Carol explained to Marla that Jonathan had three and now with her included, four copywriters lined up in adjacent cubicles on one side of the loft. *NanaWall* transparent room dividers did their job as intended. Flexible, movable smart space that reduced the sound yet captured the outlines and movement of the person in the next cubicle. Carol's black and white theme carried over to her coordinated cubicle, reflecting her cut-and-dry thinking.

The introductions started. First, the receptionist. A woman of age but one could not tell the age even on close scrutiny. Somewhere between Jane Fonda and Teresa Heinz Kerry, was Penelope.

"Penelope, this is Marla Hayes," Carol said. "Jonathan's new find."

"Jonathan has a knack for finding employees who complement his style," Penelope said. "Including you, Carol."

"That's sweet," Carol answered dismissively.

"What do they call you for short, Penelope?" Marla asked.

"Penelope. Don't even think about Penny." With that, Penelope returned to her work on her desk.

Marla met Becky, a short, pixyish middle-aged woman and Walter. Walter was proud of being THE ladies' man and carried himself with self-assurance. An old fashioned *Dapper Dan* whose time has come and almost gone.

"Sorry, dear lady, but I cannot give you my best at the moment. Deadline, you know," he said with affectation. He looked up and on seeing Marla, changed his tune. In an obvious attempt to endear himself to her, he continued, "But I promise to correct that sooner than later." Finally, he whispered to her that he can get her the best grass this side of Tijuana. His wink was pathetic. He was so full of himself, Marla almost laughed.

"I am a cop," she said.

"What a way to go," he said with a second wink and returned to his work.

"Guess I'm not too scary." Marla looked at Carol, who ignored the entire moment. She went on with the introductions. The others were Grizelle, the bookkeeper and a tired looking man, Edward, the illustrator.

Opposite to the row of cubicles was Jonathan's office, with a door, and a small conference room, with a door. Otherwise, there were no doors. The mail room and copy center were open spaces as was Jonathan's assistant's area. Carol walked over to Jonathan's office. Its front door was guarded by a husky woman, Connie, who looked more like a nanny than a professional assistant.

"Connie is the clock that makes Jonathan tick," Carol said.

"I'm his assistant," came the humorless reply. "I'm the only one around here who doesn't buy into Carol's attitudes." Connie gave Marla a small wave of her hand as she continued working.

Carol ignored Connie and walked on.

"No doors, no secrets," she informed Marla. "Everyone knows everything about everyone. One big happy family."

And Marla's learning curve began. She followed the instructions of the streetwise, hard-edged beauty. Carol had been very pretty since childhood. Blinded by her own beauty, its inherent benefits and pitfalls, she never had a real sense of who she was. Her feelings were camouflaged by an exterior she had designed for herself.

She put Marla in a cubicle next to hers.

"I'm the official bitch around here and everyone's scared of me," Carol announced

"Joke?" Marla asked.

Carol smirked. "I hope not."

Although Carol was some ten years her senior, Marla wanted to hit it off with her and with everyone. She wanted to be liked. To fit in.

The elevator music was heard. A minute later, it was heard again, as it was going back down.

"Carol," Penelope said and came over, placing a small spring flower arrangement on her desk. Carol's *gag me* grimace belittled the gift.

"Didn't you perform last night?" Becky joked.

"Didn't you dazzle?" Walter dug deeper.

Carol walked to the conference table and put the flowers in the middle. She removed the card. A ribbon attached to it pulled a small jewelry box out of the flower container. She opened it as the others watched. Carol took the bright coral earrings in the sparkling white gold setting and held it up for everyone to see. It was heavy and beautiful.

"You performed," Becky said.

"Dazzled," Walter added.

"The idiot bought me COLOR. Can you believe that?" She tossed the jewels back in the box. "He had never seen me wear any color. Never. What's wrong with him? Is he blind?"

She picked up the little box. "You can have it," she said to Becky. "Unless you want it, Marla."

But Marla stepped back. She didn't want to deal with something she didn't understand.

"Coral is a great gem. First night?" Penelope said.

"And last," Carol said.

Penelope returned to her desk. Becky took the earrings.

"Thanks, Carol. It'll go perfectly with the blouse I just bought. Same color."

She turned to Marla. "Carol never keeps these things. Only from Jerry, right? The love of her life."

"But why?" asked Marla.

"Just passing time. Love'm and leave'm. I don't want to remember them," said Carol, heading back to her desk.

"Them?"

"Means more than one." Carol sat down and continued, "I sleep around. I'm easy, but not cheap."

"Cheap is relative, isn't it?" Marla said.

"Are we the little philosopher?" Carol's sharp tongue charged into Marla. Becky and Walter rose up again.

Marla withdrew. "No, not really. I just meant to say that the earrings didn't look cheap to me," Marla said. "I never got anything."

"You got the ring."

"Never again!"

"Lighten up, Carol. It's her first day," Becky intervened.

"I forgot. I'm sorry," Carol said, seemingly genuine.

"She's testing you. Don't mind her," Walter said.

But Marla did mind. She couldn't handle feeling small and helpless. She got her things and started for the exit. Penelope watched as she got into the elevator and left. Carol appeared in the reception.

"Where is she?"

"Gone," Penelope said.

"Oh, God. Jonathan'll kill me."

Carol ran into the stairwell and ran all the way down to the street. Outside, he rain had stopped. She saw Marla walking to the parking garage. She ran after her.

"Marla!" She watched Marla turn around, tears running down her face. She walked over to her, reached out her hand for a handshake.

"I'm sorry."

Marla accepted her hand. "I need this job," she said.

"C'mon upstairs. I can give you some instruction books to take home and study," Carol said.

They went back to the office. Penelope looked very busy and the two of them walked by her.

"I'll read them over the weekend," Marla said enthusiastically, and watched Carol fill a canvass tote bag with pamphlets, DVD-s and other materials.

"Go ahead," Carol said. "Go home. We'll start fresh on Monday."

She pointed Marla back to the elevator, nodded reassuringly and watched as she disappeared with the music of the stadium *fight song*.

Carol turned around. Becky, Walter, Grizelle and Connie were standing behind Penelope's desk.

"It's OK. It's OK." Carol looked at them. "I'm a bad person. Flog me."

They gave her a nasty look and went back to work.

"Don't hassle her again, Carol," Penelope said, her voice rolling throughout the office.

———•◆•———

That night, Marla's den became *information center*. She plunged into studying the unfamiliar craft, some call it art, of advertising. She wanted to impress them on Monday, to prove herself, to be accepted. She would have to do whatever it takes.

CHAPTER NINE

The days rushed by. Marla loved her job and was told by Becky and Penelope that when Jonathan says nothing about your performance, he is satisfied. No comment is good. She noticed the passing of time only in reference to Michael, not hearing from him for two weeks. When he finally called, she was happy but in the end, somehow the conversation left her uncomfortable. She couldn't put her finger on what exactly had her puzzled. After she hung up with Michael, she tried to relax. The evening was endless. There was no way she could go to sleep. Fear filled her at the thought of the possibility of losing Michael. She was a one-man woman and she was right for him. After all, their five or six-month relationship was incredibly deep, smart and funny. Marla was looking forward to enjoying sex with someone other than her first love. Michael seemed to fit the bill in many ways.

She remembered, through her unpleasant experience with Warren, that life was different on location when away from the routine of home. Although she didn't think anything of Michael's sudden departure from their conversation, something was gnawing at her. She told herself that he was busy. That's that.

The evening was wearing on. She couldn't get Michael out of her thoughts. She couldn't fall asleep. May watching a little Jay Leno would help. Maybe another glass of wine? She wanted to find a point of relaxation and get some sleep. Marla curled up in the settee filled with too many decorative pillows that used to give her a feeling of security.

The doorbell rang. Carol was downstairs. Marla pressed the buzzer. When she stormed in, Carol's eyes shone with a wicked gleam. She was out of breath, headed for the bathroom.

"I need some wine," she said as she rushed by Marla.

Marla didn't have to be told. She was already pouring, wondering what was up. Carol returned, somewhat calm, but her grin implied something sinister going on in her mind. With a grand gesture, she emptied her purse on the dinner table. A mountain of one, five, ten and twenty dollar bills graced the white pine wood. Carol unzipped the side pocket of her purse and a lot of coins, quarters, dimes and nickels rolled out onto the table. She circled it a few times sort of like victory laps, took a gulp of the wine and stared at Marla with satisfaction. Marla waited. After a few more sips Carol settled down.

"I robbed Jerry." Her voice was perfectly calm.

"Do I want to hear this?" said Marla.

"I went over to his place. Unannounced."

"I thought that's a no-no."

"All's fair in love and war," said Carol.

"Are you sure you want to tell me about your escapade?"

Carol continued. "Macho, his dog, loves me. Didn't bark. He followed me around to the bedroom window. I saw Jerry with a woman." Carol looked at Marla, but Marla was hard to impress.

"Anyway, they were going at it hot and heavy. The back door was unlocked, as usual. I walked in, went to his money stash and *Voila!*" She gestured at the money on the table.

"I can't believe it!"

"Oh, yes, you can. He doesn't know who he's messing with! C'mon, help me count."

They sorted and counted and sipped wine. They chuckled, screamed and sipped wine.

"Three-thousand Dollars." Carol grinned from ear-to-ear. "It's better than an orgasm." She laughed, threw herself on the floor and rolled around on the plush pile.

"Three-thousand Dollars."

"Do you think he'll figure it out?" Marla asked.

"Well, depends on how many people know where he keeps his pocket change."

"He knows you know."

"Aha," Carol lifted her index finger. "Then he knows I was there and saw him with the woman. Will he ask me?" They laughed even harder.

"But why, Carol?"

Carol walked around, helped herself to more wine, appeared to be thinking.

"He takes me for granted. I want more." She gulped down the wine. "But that's enough about me."

"Michael just called," Marla confided. "Something weird about it."

"When's he coming back?"

"He didn't say. He was vague. I think this might be over and done with." Marla's voice cracked a little.

"Don't get morbid about it," Carol said. "It's just a man. Another man in the entertainment business. When will you learn?" She looked at Marla. "You couldn't trust your husband. Why would you trust Michael?"

"Actors are different. They're too attractive, too easy. But a writer?"

Carol laughed. You seem to have forgotten about Eugene Romany. He was a writer and obviously a fucker."

"But his wife" Marla said. "What about her?"

"She's a joiner. Keeps the marriage young. Maybe you'd have stayed with Warren had you joined in the games."

Carol felt righteous. "That's why I don't fuck anyone who means anything to me. And I stay away from show business."

"I have a lot to learn." Marla was deep in thought. "Are you happy?" she asked.

"Please, no philosophy tonight." Carol prepared to leave.

CHAPTER TEN

"I didn't douche. Wanted you to remember me until next time." Linda held two lace panties in her hands.

"I've been wearing them for three days. Here, smell them." She passed the panties by his nose. "My farewell gift."

Michael didn't know things like this could happen. He was sure it was a manly thing to like and appreciate what she had done for him. Or was it gross? It didn't matter. One last grope of his balls and she was out the door, heading for the company transport to the airport.

Michael walked off his erection. He thought about how he was really out of action before his divorce. He and his ex-wife barely had any sex. She never did anything to excite him. She just expected that no matter what, he would get hard. It was getting more and more difficult. Getting drunk did not help. A little alcohol sometimes would get him there. But Linda! Wow! She knew every trick in the book. Well, Michael wouldn't know what every trick meant only that she knew many.

Now, however, location work was running overtime and Michael had used up all legitimate excuses to keep Linda with the company. The *Tootsie role* payroll had been exhausted. She had to leave. He had to concentrate on his job.

As he stood in the shower, stretching and brushing his back, he thought of Marla. He hadn't called her since before Christmas. He forgot. That made him feel foolish.

Wearing a bathrobe, he fixed himself a cocktail, lit a cigarette and settled down to his duties. Re-writing, checking on pick-up shots, reviewing charts, graphs, making sure that they had everything they needed from this location and would not have to spend more of the budget on a return trip.

Suddenly the hotel room seemed dreary. Life left with Linda. He was surprised at his strong feelings toward her. He was wondering about what he was doing? What did he want? "Why do I let Linda happen to me?" he spoke out loud.

As he got calmer, he called his two kids directly on their phone to avoid the ex. The kids were OK. They sincerely missed each other, the daily interaction. But at ages 9 and 10, they had some sense of understanding that people did not always like one another forever. Talking to his children made him feel better.

He finally decided to dial Marla. Maybe she would be out. He could leave a message.

"Hello," came her soft throaty sound.

Michael understood the many contrasting feelings experienced by his written characters, but those which he himself was experiencing at this moment, overwhelmed him.

"Marla, how are you?" Hearing her voice felt good. Peaceful.

"Oh, Michael. It's great to hear from you. Are you back?"

"No, afraid not. Not just yet." As casual as he could be. He didn't want his voice to give away his apprehension about seeing her.

"Well, then, I'm glad you're thinking of me. I think about you often." She slowed down. Michael sensed that she was going to say more.

"Sometimes, absence does make the heart grow fonder," she spoke slowly.

"And other times?" Michael interrupted.

"And other times, who knows, we just have to step back. Re-think things."

"Will you let me know the results, Marla?" Michael was weighing her words and feeling his feelings.

"Am I still your man? It hasn't been that long." He had no idea what got into him to be saying something like that. Where did this come from?

"Don't answer that," he continued. "I have no rights to you." Deep down he thought he should try to distance himself from her, yet he wanted to conquer at the same time.

She laughed. He was relieved. "I haven't heard that laughter in too long."

"Well, Michael, any time you're ready, you just come around and we'll laugh. Again. Nothing has changed. I don't flit around, you know that." It was important to Marla that she didn't show her insecurities. She wanted to appear positive not to scare him away.

"I'm sure of that. Talk to you soon."

He heard her say, "Oh?"

"Bye now."

He hung up. He knew it was an unfinished conversation and was upset with himself. Was he upset about being at a loss as to what to do? What did he want now that he had choices? Before, when he had impregnated his sweetheart, he had to marry her. Now, he had a 9-year old and a 10-year old boy and girl. He loved them but he could not continue the boring life with his wife. There was no sex, there was no friendship, there was no connection, there was no laughter, there was only writing, writing, writing and taking the kids to their classes, and having the same vacations with her parents every year. Never with his parents. Although his parents said they forgave him for *knocking up the girl*, his father remained irate about not having had the father-son birds-and-bees talk with Michael in time. For some strange reason, they chose to remain angry.

While they liked when the grandchildren traveled to northern California to spend long weekends with them, they discouraged Michael and his wife from personal visits. Michael hoped to find a way in the future to overcome their rigidness and reconcile with them.

They did not reject his gifts and he found out from his children that they kept a scrap book titled "About Michael." They were just unable to get past their puritan *id*-s. He used this painful fact of his life in some of his writing hoping that he could get it out of his system.

But now, it was all about his cock. How did that happen? Marla seemed to be a lady of quality. Unless he was missing something, he thought, she could round out his life. A writer needs a lot of time for writing. Career-wise, he could not afford to be dating on and on, getting to know women and trying to determine their long-range potential. Why was longevity on his mind? Must be in his middle-class roots of planning ahead and securing the future. To him, every woman he would date would be a potential wife. Marla? Linda? Marla? Who?

CHAPTER ELEVEN

Marla worked long and hard, learned from Jonathan, listened to Walter and Becky, and followed instructions closely. She was fascinated with the logic underlying creativity and how she instantly felt at home. She would let her imagination soar and things *advertising* began to make sense, things *visual* began to speak to her. Combining that with her computer savvy and common sense, Marla found her niche.

She framed a copy of her first paycheck after which she received automatic deposits. Pride in her ability to take care of herself began to fill her mind. Before, she didn't think she could get anywhere with her formal education unfinished. That has changed. Learning new skills in advertising she knew she would do whatever she had to in order to remain self-sufficient and never to depend on anyone.

Unbeknownst to Marla, one of her sixty-second commercial spots was entered by Jonathan and Becky into the annual *Clio* competition. She never heard of *Clio* awards and found out that those were advertising's highest recognition by peers, the only people who really knew what went into the creation of a powerful ad campaign. Marla's spot was actually nominated in the writing category. By the time she heard about what was going on, it had already passed the hurdles of various levels of panels of judges and made it to the top of the heap of finalists.

The next few weeks at the advertising agency were filled with excitement. It was an unusual occurrence that a novice copywriter would show so much promise. Jonathan sold this concept to Reed Rhoades, the host of *FRIDAY SEGMENTS*, a local TV magazine show. The *handle* of the interview of Marla would be a comparison between an actor being nominated for an Oscar in his first-ever film role, and how it feels to get started in advertising and catapult to the top the first time out. Big. Very big.

Reed was over six feet tall, with a *Dick Tracy* jaw and lean enough not to worry about the camera adding the crucial ten pounds to your look on the air. His sleek hair cut, no tie, jacket with elbow patches and a full-face toothy smile made him appear more casual than he really was. The cameraman, Marty, an *Under Armour* aficionado with longish hair and unobtrusive attitude, stayed on at the Kaplan office after the initial interview to get candid footage on the rookie copywriter. When Reed and Jonathan shook hands over the *Marla segment*, she felt like the white slave who was just sold by her owner. Jonathan was drooling with joy, happily giving his permission to let Marty follow Marla around in her daily activities, all the way through to the awards event.

Marla never liked being the center of attention and Becky, whom she trusted, had to assure her frequently that she had earned it; she was smart and she would go places in her new career.

Penelope brought Marla a cup of herb tea. "Let's grab those free radicals," she said and sat down in Marla's guest chair.

"It's all right to be better than the others, Marla. I've been living it for years." She laughed.

"You were born that way. Better, I think," Marla said.

"Yes, I was. And modest." Penelope's soft laughter traveled through the quiet office. "There are always more people against you than for you. It's just the way life is."

Penelope got up, patted Marla's shoulder. "But there is also always somebody who cares. Remember that." She went back to the front desk.

Marla accepted direction well. She did not look into the camera and forgot about Marty around her at every turn.

"Carol," she stopped over at the next cubicle. "Isn't this exciting?"

"Yes, yes. Whatever."

Marla's need for and anticipation of Carol's camaraderie fell on deaf ears. "What's wrong? Aren't you happy for me?"

"Oh, let's not get carried away. One of my ads a couple of years ago was almost nominated."

"But it wasn't?"

"It's all politics. Nothing else."

"What does that mean?"

Carol started to dial the phone. "You'll find out. You're still new in this game. You know the stuff about *all that glitters* and so forth. It can lead nowhere. Top, bottom, nowhere. Wait and see."

"Aren't friends supposed to be happy for each other?"

Carol's sly look was unsettling to Marla. "Friends?"

"We shared your secret," Marla said.

"Whoa, you're naïve."

Carol turned her back to Marla and got on the phone. "Jerry, Hi." She laughed flirtatiously. Marla went to the kitchen for coffee. She was not comfortable with what just happened. She had a lot to learn about trusting people.

She found the boss helping himself to fruit juice and crackers in the kitchen. Before even swallowing, he gestured her to sit.

"I'm tickled pink about this nomination, Marla. I'm very proud of my agency!" Jonathan spoke rapidly as if he had to crunch 48 hours into 24. Everything was doubled up. "I've been out on my own for only five years and every year someone or something puts us into the limelight. This year it's you. You have to admit I have an eye for talent." His wink was not characteristic of him and surprised Marla.

She kept nodding, sipping coffee, knowing she couldn't get a word in edgewise.

"At first I didn't think you could reach the top and now, look at you, not only beautiful but brainy. By the way," he rose, gulped the rest of the juice and started for the door. "I didn't ask for your permission about the documentary coverage on you and your spot because technically you belong to me, your product is written for hire, so I'm in control. You see?"

He was at the door. "You'll understand all this when we know each other better."

Marla grinned. "Better? Why?"

"It's good for you. Both of us. You'll see." He was gone.

Carrying a cup of coffee, Marla returned to her cubicle where she found Carol sitting in her chair, waiting for her. "You'll never guess what he said."

"Who?" Marla was miffed.

"Jerry. Finally I returned his calls. He has been leaving messages but I didn't know what to expect. I wasn't sure, you know my motto about leave'm wanting more."

"What makes you think that I care?" Marla gestured to Carol to get out of her chair.

"He wanted to let me know that he was robbed and had since put in an alarm system. He has been calling to give me the combination so that I could come and go as always." Marla was bewildered.

"Did he say who, what was stolen? Anything?"

Carol's mysterious look turned smug. "He didn't say that he was at home at the time; he didn't say if it was anything other than money; surely, he didn't want to get into details."

"Then, it looks like he feels guilty, doesn't he?" Marla asked.

"And doesn't want to lose me."

Slowly, as the rising roar of the summer thunder, Marla and Carol started to laugh. Their laughter got louder and louder, until it rocked the office. Becky and Walter stuck their heads in. Without knowing what it was about, they couldn't help themselves but join the contagious laughter. Jonathan walked out of his office.

"People! This is not a good day to wake the dead. We're expecting outsiders, real humans here, any minute." He closed the door behind himself.

CHAPTER TWELVE

The Kaplan Group was small and close-knit. They often shared lunch in the conference room regardless whether or not Jonathan could join them. They ordered in, talked about everything, enjoyed their relaxation together until it was time to clean up and get back to work.

"Hello, children!" Carol's voice followed the descending elevator's *stadium fight song*. "Momma is back from a back-breaking weekend."

Sporting a necklace and matching bracelet, she walked past Penelope.

"See, this is at least 10.6 carats Black Onyx in white gold. I have to have it appraised." She leaned down to Penelope. "What do you think? I have the whole set, necklace, bracelet, cocktail ring and the earrings!" She was excited.

"See, this idiot noticed my taste and really, really wants to see me again."

Penelope put her hand on Carol's. "It's not the same, though, is it? Without love." Carol pulled her hand back. "It's more like work," Penelope watched as Carol's steps slowed down and she disappeared in her cubicle.

"Can we see it?" Becky said, her head popping up above the cubicle wall.

"Can you see them," Carol corrected, getting up and looking at Becky over the partition. She held her necklace with the ringed finger, waved the bracelet and mimicking a jewelry model, she pointed at the earrings.

"Them. Plural." Her accompanying smile was grand. Walter's head showed up.

"Whoa!" Walter said. "Are you giving those away?"

"You can tease me, Walter, all you want. These will be fine for Mondays, don't you think? I'll call them my Monday jewels."

Carol felt good. Looked into Marla's cubicle. It was empty. Carol found her in the kitchen having coffee and writing on a pad.

Carol, once again, paraded the jewels and helped herself to coffee.

"Well, how do you like these, Marla."

"Nice. Very pretty."

"That's it?" Carol was dissatisfied. "Nice? Pretty? You're working too hard, Marla, if you can't see that I'm wearing a few dollars here."

"Oh, Carol. Those things don't mean the same to me as to you, that's all." Marla was busy.

"Why? Oh, I forgot, you were married to a few dollars." Carol's tone was sharpening. "Why would you leave him?"

"See, that's what I mean. Same things have different meanings to different people. I didn't marry the money or the family. I loved Warren."

Marla spoke in a dreamy tone, "People fall in love and you know, by now I know, that there's nothing like your first love. Your true love. I can't get past Warren. With anyone else the feelings are not the same. Don't you agree?"

"I wouldn't know, Marla. I never felt any love like that. Sammy's dad, you know, my son, Sammy, kept saying we would get married and we only did in a civil ceremony about a week before he was born. It was a sad experience. And I didn't know how to hold him. I didn't know anything. I was one of those pretty girls from the wrong side of the tracks, easily intimidated. Well, no more!" Carol stopped abruptly, punctuated her statement with a thump of her foot.

"Isn't it time to stop dwelling on the past?" Marla asked, heading out the door. Carol followed.

"You're running hot and cold on me," Marla continued.

"Hot and cold? It's called unpredictable, if you want to know," Carol said. "You think your past was so much better?"

"It's the past," Marla said.

"So, no one since Warren?" Carol asked.

"No, not really… Well," Marla said.

Carol listened up. "Well?… Well?"

"No one."

"Well?" Carol pursued.

"Oh, in Spain. I met someone I liked."

"Who?"

"Doesn't matter. I didn't do anything about it."

"Good sex should often be left to one night," Carol said.

"Oh, it's nothing like that." Marla's tone turned to a whisper. "Nothing like that."

"Oh, come on," Carol prodded.

"Leave it alone, Carol," Becky interjected. "She doesn't want to talk about it."

"Yeah, some imaginary Spaniard. Maybe she had too much port."

"Port is from Portugal not Spain and no, I didn't." Marla was getting uncomfortable.

Carol didn't sit down. Penelope could hear all this and had enough.

"Doesn't anybody have a deadline?" she spoke out loud.

"The voice of reason," Becky said.

"Who elected you official watchdog?" said Carol.

"Not you," Penelope said.

Carol ignored this and continued her earlier topic. "So, there's an imaginary Spaniard. Then there was Michael, maybe is. Almost… maybe."

Carol laughed. "Don't you see being a one man woman doesn't work. You're always waiting. Well, I don't wait. Let them wait for my call."

Carol laughed out loud. "When will you ever learn, Marla? From actor to writer?"

"Carol is just testing, Marla. See what her quasi-superiority complex can do. She's about to run out of material. She'll leave you alone soon," Becky said, trying to soften Carol's digs. Marla looked lost.

"I like friendly banter," Walter said.

"Doesn't sound friendly to me." Becky turned to Marla. "I've been married for ten years and my vicarious sex life through Carol's stories is more interesting than the one at home. Her laughter put a smile on Marla's face.

"I'm grateful to Carol because based on her escapades I learned to handle the ladies better," Walter grinned.

"Thank you for the credit, Walter." Carol asked.

"May I keep my private life private?" Marla said.

"Not if you hang with showbiz men. They're trash."

"And lawyers?" Becky interfered.

"Don't even start me on Jerry, OK? I'm done with him."

Marla sat down. She was at a loss for words. She didn't know how much of this was in fun or in malice.

"Carol is really not as bad as all that," Walter said. "She has a pretty good handle on everything. Except, no computer savvy. None at all," Walter said. He was trying to change the subject and soften the hard-nose image Carol was putting out.

"I get everything done that needs to get done," Carol said, her head dipping out of sight, below the top of the partition.

When the elevator *fight song* marked its arrival, all heads disappeared. Jonathan was back. As soon as Jonathan's door closed, all heads reappeared at the top of the partitions.

Marla turned to Carol. "You know, if I can help you with any computer work or information, please let me." She walked around to Carol's cubicle.

"Don't go out of your way for me, Little Mary Sunshine. No one expects that," Carol said.

"I don't mind."

"She's a nice person, Carol. Let her," said Becky.

"I'll bring you up to speed," Marla said.

"It's that word, *speed*, that I hate the most. Everything is fast, now, immediate. The faxes, the e-mails, the scanners. All that speed makes for mistakes. People are rushing, you know. People are relying too much on computers." Carol looked up from her desk. "What was wrong with regular mail, telephone conversations, real live messengers?" She threw her hands up into the air. "I miss those days."

"Well, they are gone, Carol. That's all we know," Marla said and returned to her desk. "I'm a natural when it comes to mechanical or technical stuff, so, just don't forget, OK?" She looked around. "That's for everyone." She sat down and the cubicles were quiet.

Penelope buzzed Marla and asked her to meet in the kitchen. She was fixing fresh squeezed juice in the juicer. "It's cantaloupe," she said to Marla. "I had it at a Lebanese place and just loved it." She handed a glassful to Marla.

"Mmm, it's good. It's different," Marla said.

"Marla, I have only known you a short while, but you're a straight shooter. It's a good way to be." She topped off Marla's glass. "Here's just a little more."

"Thanks," Marla said. "You're right about me. What you see is what you get," she said, laughing.

"I just wanted to say that it's good. Don't let anything influence you."

"I have, before," Marla said, "but I'm getting stronger."

Penelope nodded and headed for the door. "That was good juice. We must do it again, hm?"

Marla smiled back. "We must."

CHAPTER THIRTEEN

Hollywood! The capitol of awards dinners, awards shows, people celebrating themselves. Designed by the film industry and copied by every other group, the advertising community also threw an annual bash. Marla had only been to the SAG dinner before with Warren and she was genuinely overwhelmed by the grandeur of the black-tie gala dinner affair at the Beverly Wilshire Hotel. The biggest names in advertising were interviewed in the lobby area of the banquet hall. Television cameras and paparazzi surrounded the recognizable celebrities as they arrived. They were product spokespersons, endorsers, narrators. This was a mini-Oscar night. A night of magic. Marla's name was on every program as one of the nominees. Amazing. One sixty-second television commercial took her to the next level in advertising. She got a raise. She now knew that she would never go hungry, she would always have a job with Jonathan or in the field.

Jonathan's entire company filled the round table for ten; Jonathan, his assistant, the creative branch, one bookkeeper, one receptionist. Nine. No dates, no appendages.

Jonathan ceremoniously looked at his people and the extra seat. "On some Jewish holy days we set an extra place setting and wait for Elijah, the Prophet. Tonight, we are waiting for Buzz Kraus, my friend."

Jonathan enjoyed hearing himself talk. In fact, he enjoyed everything about himself. He looked toward the entry and waved.

"I invited Buzz. He was my mentor when I worked in television."

Marla looked toward the entrance but couldn't tell who Jonathan's guest was until Buzz walked directly over to their table. She laughed out loud as Jonathan started the introductions.

"Buzz and I played mixed doubles a few times," she said as she reached to shake his hand. "Tennis. Mixed doubles."

Buzz remarked about also knowing Marty, the camera man who was still following around Marla, the nominee. Old home week for the guys.

Jonathan turned out to be a former writer for some police shows where Buzz was involved as technical advisor. The two of them never lost touch with each other.

"Why would you go from television to advertising? That doesn't make sense to me," Marla said to Jonathan.

"Television IS advertising. Some TV shows are just long ads. I liked the idea of *less is more* and getting a thought out quickly, and don't forget getting paid quickly." Jonathan was clearly proud of himself, of his decision, his accomplishments.

Buzz didn't agree. "There's a simplicity to advertising copy versus the real writing in episodic TV."

"Are you serious?" A fired up Marla presented her point of view and was captured on the video.

"I don't know anything about television writing but I think advertising copy is as creative as any writing and much harder. Sixty-seconds? Thirty-seconds? You have to deliver in an instance. The audience has to remember what you're selling. You have to be clever to do our work." Marla's eyes were gleaming with excitement.

"I don't want to argue, but if you want to try TV writing, you should," Buzz said directly to Marla.

"Are you offering me a job?" she looked toward Jonathan with a grin.

"I can't do that but I can make some introductions." He was not exactly flirting with Marla but Carol's sharp edge surfaced.

"Don't you have to go to school or something, study screen writing, or something?"

Buzz laughed. "School is fine, but it's whom you know. That's much better. You've heard about the *right place, right time.*"

"Are you the right place, right time for Marla?" Carol asked, seductively leaning close to Buzz's face.

Marla was thinking out loud. "You know, I'll give it a thought. What if I have some talent? One of those latent things." She looked at Carol. "You showed me the ropes when I first started in advertising. I can learn anything."

Carol, knowing that the camera was on Marla, leaned close to her and practically purred, "There's a lot more I can teach you."

Buzz was thoroughly entertained. Jonathan rose to move around and work the room, stop at other tables, shake hands and air-kiss some women. Marla watched him for a while.

"Are you a good teacher?" Buzz asked.

"She's nominated for an award," Carol said coyly and looked into the camera. "Could she have done it without me?"

"No. Working with you made the difference. I really appreciate it." Marla was sincere.

Lights dimmed. People settled down. The ceremony started. A sense of anticipation heated the air. Penelope put her hand on Marla's. Suddenly, Marla realized that winning was really important to her. Her fists tightened and nails dug into her palms. Lips quivering, beads of perspiration settled on her forehead. She forgot about the camera on her. She only knew that she wanted to win.

No. A tie for the Bronze to Marla Hayes of The Kaplan Group and Anthony Osherow of the B B K & K agency.

How to be cool and collected? How to appear strong? She looked around, squeezed her eyes closed tight, then opened them slowly. The face of a lost little girl on the verge of tears was captured by the camera.

She walked out of the banquet building, took a deep breath, looked at the star-filled sky. After a beat, she pulled herself together, turned around and was surprised to find the cameraman close by. Marty smiled, pressed the off button and went over to her.

"Thank you, Marla," he said. "I have some great stuff."

"Most of which will be on the cutting room floor," she laughed. "I don't mind. It was a good experience." She reached out to shake his hand.

"Tell your boss, Evelyn Baker, right, that I'm looking forward to seeing it."

The cameraman started toward the parking lot. "I think, unless some major news breaks, this will be on the next 'FRIDAY SEGMENTS.' Thanks again."

More handshaking, then he was gone.

Penelope found her outside. "I've been around the block a few times and I know a few things about people. Marla, you're going places." She hugged her lightly.

"Now be a big girl, come inside, have a ball!"

When they returned, dinner was being served. Carol moved next to Buzz. Jonathan was talking with the president of the organization. Marla felt lonely. Walter cut a piece of ribbon off his invitation, used it to cover up the other name on Marla's *Clio* statue and jovially presented it to Marla.

"No one will be the wiser. It's all yours. A little something for your mantle." Marla needed a good laugh.

CHAPTER FOURTEEN

Michael's face lit up on seeing Linda waiting for him at the airport. It was a nice surprise. He didn't really mind her independent action. The other members of the crew were more interested in being picked up by their own families than watching what Michael was doing and with whom. She had hired a driver who put Michael's luggage in the trunk of the limousine and had a cocktail ready for him.

They drove to Linda's townhouse. It was *tastefully busy*. Lots of nick-nacks. Maybe too many. The master bedroom and bath upstairs were spacious and also over-decorated. In the living room Michael noticed a wrought iron bowl, or strips of wrought iron in the shape of a bowl, suspended from the ceiling. She explained to him that it was a handcrafted Indian candle holder and when the candle was lit you would lie down under it on the floor, smoke a joint and watch the slithering movement of flames shoot through the openings, dance on the walls, transporting one to the *land of psychedelia*.

The heavy aroma of honey-cinnamon lulled him deeply into a sensuous high. As comfortable as he was, the fragrance of fresh cut roses, lilies and exotic flowers of Marla's condo flitted through his elevated mind.

Linda had the evening designed for love and games. The cocktails and hors d'oeuvres were ready. The Jacuzzi tub bubbled invitingly. Being a writer, he was keenly observant. In the bedroom, while undressing, he noticed that some of her furnishings were really drug paraphernalia cleverly blended into the décor. She joined him in the soothing Jacuzzi, rubbed and massaged him with scrubby bath gloves, bringing his skin to tingle all over. Her smooth, firm body against his gave him goose-bumps. He felt rejuvenated. He was a boy again. Linda knew her customers. Michael was easy.

The night of lovemaking ended early morning when the driver returned to take Michael to the studio.

———◆———

No matter how early in the day, the studio was always humming with life and activity. Cars were coming and going, actors and crew were preparing, some soundstages already had camera rolling. Michael went to the bungalow that housed his office. This reception office, as most, also had the usual glass and chrome motif and sparkled in the faint early morning light, brightening a cloudy day. The smell of fresh coffee, brewed by the timer-controlled machine, filled the air. Michael was home, was regaining his footing. He could always count on Judy, his secretary, to get him grounded. He helped himself to a cup and disappeared behind a one-way mirror sliding door—the entrance to his inner sanctum. By invitation only. In contrast, his office resembled that of a scholar's home base *circa* 1970. Mahogany bookshelves reached to the ceiling with a professional rolling library ladder resting on the side. The dark wood mood dominated and blended easily with the earth-tone fabrics of the chairs, ottoman, lampshades, picture frames, desk accessories. It was a well designed, calming, even enriching environment for him as well as his visitors. He glanced at the pile of notes organized in order of importance, waiting for his attention. One of the items was Marla's office number with a reminder to call and make dinner arrangements. He checked his watch and as he looked out the window saw Buzz appear on a golf cart. He went outside and jumped in.

"They're ready with the rough cut," Buzz said, while backing out of the parking spot and heading toward the three-story building that housed most of the screening rooms.

"I don't know, Buzz. I'm worried." Michael was wearing his professional producer hat.

"We have plenty of time to make it right," Buzz said. "In case anything is wrong. I have been following the daily progress. It's a good show, Michael."

"Hope someone will drop out mid-season. I need a new series. I need to make some real money. You know, ex-wife, two kids in private school… yes, you know." Michael chuckled. "And this dating thing isn't cheap, either."

"You know how to pick'm." Buzz laughed. "But, what else is there?"

They grinned and nodded in agreement.

"Well, in case you're interested in a change of pace, come with me Friday night. I'll stop in at the AA meeting. Great place to meet chicks."

Michael laughed out loud. "Yeah, as if I weren't in enough trouble."

"Yeah, I heard. Linda. Is it serious? What you want?"

"I don't know what I want," Michael said. "Got too much of a good thing, or two good things. I think."

Buzz's sleazy smile was his answer. "Never too much. Two? Who? Anyone I know?"

"Marla."

"Are you saying that Marla is more than tennis?"

"Much more."

"Let me know if I can help out?" Buzz felt smug. He'd better not tell Michael about him and Linda. Could be a career-breaker.

"You mean with Linda?"

"Linda had a chance with me and blew it. Guess you swept her off her feet," Buzz said convincingly.

"Well, Marla isn't up for grabs."

"That's OK by me, Michael. She doesn't want me. She's too hard to get."

"Isn't that how you like them?"

"You know, Michael, I'm getting too old for those games. The challenge isn't there."

"Do you want to be alone?"

Buzz thought for a while. "I think I'd like to marry my best friend. Sex is getting less important. I'm sure you're not ready to understand that."

"Understand, yes. Buy into it, no." Michael laughed. Somehow, Buzz helped him see things he hadn't seen before.

They arrived, parked and headed up the stairs to one of the smaller screening rooms. Michael and Buzz waved *Hello* to some of the projectionists whose doors were kept open until they started screening.

"You know, Buzz, I have to decide how to end this flimsy affair and get my life back on track."

"Are you sure? End it with Linda?" Buzz questioned him. "She's lots of fun." Michael shot him a puzzled look. Buzz thought he said too much.

"I'm guessing. When you kept her there after her shoot was finished. What else could it be?"

Buzz and Michael entered the screening room. The small room had fourteen rows of plush seats, five across each. The rows were elevated stadium style, the seats had wide spaces between them with small desk lights for note taking. Michael headed for the producer's seat in the center with the telephone and stop start buttons at his disposal. On one side of him sat the director, Bernie McAfee, and on the other side was Buzz. Unexpectedly, he saw Linda in the back row. He was not happy about that.

Bernie turned to him. "Michael, Linda said you had agreed to her joining us."

Michael was not about to make a scene. That would be all over the studio lot in minutes. He smiled at Linda, waved to her, then sat down.

"Yes," he said. "Linda is studying production and this is one phase, the rough cut, that really interests her." With that he pressed the speaker button on the console and spoke to the projectionist.

"Any time you're ready."

The room went dark and Michael forgot about everything but his work. The film that they had sent back to the studio on a daily basis was pieced together roughly by his editor. It followed the continuity of the story. Without music and sound effects, they were able to mark the sequences of the visual moments that would make up the entire pilot.

Hours later, when the lights came on, Linda was gone. He and Bernie went back to his bungalow. Judy, Michael's, roly-poly secretary, was thanking Linda for a huge bouquet of flowers.

"Hi, Michael," Judy said. "Your messages are on your desk, your sandwiches were just delivered. Should be fresh. Bernie, I ordered for you, too. OK?"

"Great. Thanks," Bernie said and headed into Michael's office with his note pad sticking out of his unzipped tote bag.

"What are the flowers for?" Michael asked.

Judy shrugged her shoulders. She didn't have an answer. Linda jumped in, "Just a note of appreciation for her holding down the fort so well while you were away."

"Oh, then it's from me?" Michael smiled. "I must be a nice boss."

"You are," Judy and Linda said at the same time.

Michael waved it away. "Please set the answering machine and no calls until Bernie and I are finished." He turned his back and closed the office door behind him.

"Well, I think that went well," Linda said with a sigh of relief.

Judy got her purse. They headed out the door.

"Better than well. He was calm. He didn't argue, just accepted the facts."

Judy and Linda walked into the constant murmur of the busy the commissary. In a film and television studio, someone is always out to lunch.

"I really appreciate your help, Judy. I'm doing the right thing for Michael. Trust me."

Judy wasn't sure of all that she had heard about Linda and Michael on location. Judy had a duty to her boss and while she loved gossip, she would never take sides, she would never expose her boss of six years, she would never divulge any of his private life nor his business life. She had planned to stay working for Michael for a long time. She had never met Marla, only knew her by voice, but sensed that Michael was really fond of her. She had known Linda from a distance and as many actresses who wanted to get close to producers, would often bring gifts and take the secretaries to lunch. Linda was a little overdoing it, but Judy wouldn't complain. She would accept gifts happily. Why not?

CHAPTER FIFTEEN

Friday night. The advertising agency had all but cleared out. Carol grabbed her purse and stuck her head into Marla's cubicle.

"How long are you going to be? Do you want me to wait?"

"No, no. I want to finish story-board and then look at it again after the weekend," Marla said.

"Well, in case you want some fun, I am going to AA. Last time I went I met a famous actor. Married, of course. He never called me after a great night of sex. I'm going to follow up on that. You should come. That's where some of the best men are on a Friday night. They've stopped drinking. They can get a real hard on unlike the drunk ones. Here is the address if you change your mind." Carol handed Marla the slip of paper and left.

Penelope appeared, dressed for evening. "Marla, still here?"

"Yes, Penelope. What are you up to? You look fabulous!"

"That's what I wanted to hear," she said, sitting down. "I'm a donor at the Shubert Theater. Tonight, the artists are honoring us for a change. Black tie, of course." She let her low-key laughter roll throughout the empty office.

"Besides, do you want to know the truth?"

"Yes, yes," Marla said. "I do."

"Tonight, my dear, I'll meet my next husband. I can feel it in my bones. A man who doesn't have to impress women half his age. I man who is secure in his own generation."

"Bravo! Go girl!" Marla said.

"Do you want an older man?"

"I don't want any man, Penny."

"Penelope," she corrected.

"Penelope. I've given up one career for love already. It didn't go well."

"Some husbands take the easy way out and die. Others can't stand living with a perfect woman, so they leave. I had both kinds." Penelope's self-deprecating words rang true.

"Did you give up anything?" Marla asked.

"A little bit of me went with each affair. But, as they say, for better or for worse, I'm still standing. I still like belonging with a man. It's that simple."

"I doubt that I can do it again," Marla said.

"You'll know when the time comes. You will."

"But is that what I want? I wonder about it. Is that all there is to life?"

"For me, love and family was all I wanted," Penelope said. "I was raised for that."

"So was my mother. And she raised me in her own image." Marla was searching for words. "No malice intended, but she raised me for her own time. I am still trying to climb out of the life for which I was raised and find my own."

Penelope intently listened. "When did you first have this thought? This concept you just told me?" she asked.

Marla had to think about the answer. Her face lit up. "Actually, I've never seen it this clearly before now. Never verbalized it."

Penelope looked at her watch, got up and headed for the elevator.

"And that, my dear, is step one. Your first step." She left with the *fight song* of the elevator.

------- ◆ -------

Carol arrived at the mid-meeting break which gave her a chance to mingle and mingle she did. Nobody did it better. Coffee cup in hand, she moved around, checking out the men.

Xiùměi bowed to her, offering a tray of snacks. Carol, as everyone, automatically bowed back and took a bite-size cookie from her. Carol, as everyone, instinctively liked the quiet immigrant.

"Nice idea that you come with your husband. More families should do that."

"Thank you," Xiùměi said meekly.

"What do you do?" asked Carol.

"I am cleaning maid at Hilton. I will have cleaning maid agency my own one day soon." Xiùměi was definite as she looked into Carol's eyes.

"It's this ambition that built this country. Let me know if you need any advice. I'll try to help you. Here's my office number."

Carol handed her card to Xiùměi and turned away. She kept looking around for the actor from the previous meeting and saw him sitting with another woman. She leaned close to his ear and whispered, "I could report you, my dear. Dating within."

"I could report you for being a fake alcoholic," he said, looking straight at her.

"Touché." Carol walked on.

She sat down but couldn't get into it. She was getting bored, fidgety and ready to leave. She looked around. Toward the exit door of the meeting hall she thought she recognized Buzz Kraus coming in. What timing, she thought, or was it planned. Is he an alcoholic or is he a fake? Only his hairdresser knows for sure. Or was it Memorex. Carol chuckled to herself. The meeting was about to end. Buzz helped himself to refreshments. He knew the ropes. Obviously, he had been there before. Xiùměi eagerly poured him a cup of fresh coffee. Her thigh rubbed against his as she moved around him. Allan Burke saw this, or thought he saw this. Buzz smiled at Xiùměi and she snuck him a note with her work number at the Hilton.

"Lunch?" she said. "Sucky-you? Sucky-me?" Then turned away when she saw Allan walk toward them, eyes burning with anger and jealousy.

Carol realized that a fight was looming. She didn't believe in that kind of violence.

"Buzz!" Carol shouted across the room. "I'm glad you could come. Thank you so much."

She watched as Allan and Xiùměi shared a smile, both relieved for different reasons. Buzz turned to Carol, kissed her on the lips and said, "Let's go. The show is about to start."

Laughing hard, Carol and Buzz ran outside, heading for Buzz's car.

"I really need a drink," Buzz said.

"Ditto."

They didn't see Marla pulling into a parking spot next to Carol's car. She watched them leave, then continued on her way.

Buzz drove to his favorite restaurant, Le Sere, in Studio City. He noticed that the Valet parked his Mercedes convertible next to Michael's Mercedes coup. Everyone knew him and Michael. They were frequent guests together and good tippers.

Inside, the Maitre D' was happy to see him, knew him by name, asked if he was expected by anyone or if he and his guest wanted a booth. Buzz saw Michael and Bernie at a table in the bar.

"C'mon. We'll say a quick 'hello'," Buzz said. She followed him.

"Michael, Bernie, this is Carol," he looked at her for a last name.

"Livingston," she said quickly.

"We keep running into each other so we thought we should at least know each other's names." Buzz laughed.

"That sums it up pretty well," Carol said.

"Would you like to join us?," said Michael.

"It doesn't look like that to me," Bernie said, laughing.

"Right. Some other time," Buzz said and they walked over to the booth that was readied for them.

They ordered drinks, toasted and grinned at each other, feeling a wicked connecting.

"Are you going to see the Chinese Missus?" Carol asked.

"Not if you preempt it," he laughed. "Although, they are not mutually exclusive of one another now, are they?" He was smug.

"Well, let me assure you, my interest in you is strictly platonic."

"Is that why you saved me from a bloody encounter?"

"I saved you because you're a friend of my friend and of my boss."

"You mean Marla Hayes?" he asked.

"Yes, Marla. We can't have you in the news as the victim of a brawl at the AA."

"You think I'd make the news?" The idea tickled him.

"AA would make the news," she laughed.

"In case you're interested, Marla is tennis. I am not seeing her."

"But you will."

"How can you be so sure?" he asked.

"Marla is the sweet thing every man is fascinated by. They want to know what's underneath all that sweetness. Could there be a raw sexual animal?"

"See, I'm not every man. The thought had never crossed my mind."

"You're lying."

"The Chinese Missus is another story. I've heard amazing stories about the sexual prowess of Asian women."

"Good thing I just want a studio tour from you. A VIP tour, of course."

"That's a great idea. It's been a while since I escorted such a beautiful woman. I'll be the envy of everyone. Maybe we'll have dinner afterwards."

"Maybe."

CHAPTER SIXTEEN

The next Friday afternoon at the office, the projection screen was dropped out of its recessed casing in the ceiling and the entire Kaplan Group watched *FRIDAY SEGMENTS*, the magazine show, hosted by Reed Rhoades, and including the piece on Marla. Marla liked the natural ease of Reed's on-the-air attitude that brought her, his audience, into his living room. He had charisma and his deep voice had an underlying softness to it that pleasantly caught the listeners' attention and were the main elements that made *FRIDAY SEGMENTS* a Los Angeles staple.

There she was. Marla on the huge screen, *warts and all*, as they say. She watched herself, her heart palpitating. She was animated some times and at other times she seemed frozen. While she knew she was frozen because of fear or loss of her footing, it came off as one of those *Betty White double takes* that translated to either *Who? Me?* or, *Of course, I know what I am talking about.* Marla was embarrassed but the colleagues liked the interview and all in all the experience made Jonathan glow with pride.

Kudos and congratulations went to Marla. Jonathan gave her a hug that was more than brotherly. Amid the accolades Marla sensed Carol's openly bitchy attitude revealing her real green-eyed monster. Everyone applauded Marla. Carol said nothing.

"You know, since you did teach me so much, I would like to hear you say that you're happy for me," Marla said. "It is, after all, a team effort."

"I see they edited everyone else out," Carol said.

"You mean you?"

Carol left without an answer. The others were happy for Marla, especially Jonathan.

"I have plans for you, Marla." Then he spread out his arms like a priest would toward his congregation, and said, "This agency, the High and Mighty Kaplans, will become the biggest little boutique advertising house in the country. I tell you, millions of dollars are within our reach."

"Hear, hear!" came Penelope's applause from the front.

Jonathan walked Marla to her cubicle. "We'll have dinner one night this week, Marla. You tell me when."

As Marla settled down at her desk, she heard Carol say, "Been there, done that. Not much in the bedroom," she said.

Marla couldn't take any more of Carol, got her purse, headed for the elevator.

"Are you sure you want to celebrate without us?" Becky teased.

Marla's thoughts were distant.

"Call if you need help!" Walter said. This was followed by laughter, cut short by the elevator *fight song*.

———————◆———————

As if on automatic pilot, Marla went to the tennis club. Carol hurt her once again and that took the joy out of the celebration. She knew she was too sensitive for the real world but she couldn't help it. When angry, as now, she needed to hit, run, sweat. She quickly changed, and looked for a game. Early evening games were not hard to find. Executives often worked off their day's tension with fast moving tennis matches. She was a pretty strong player and although she preferred to play singles, she jumped into a newly forming doubles match with three men. She didn't care if she would be overpowered. She needed to get a lot of frustration and anger out of her system.

Hours later she and her partners were coming off the court heading to the lockers. It was everyone's habit to look at the reservations board and see the names of people playing on the courts. She was surprised to see Jonathan's name since she did not think he was a member. Then she noticed that Buzz Kraus was the member host to Jonathan and two women, one Evelyn Baker. Marla recognized Evelyn's name. She was the manager of local television station KMRTV. Marla decided to go over and meet her. Surprisingly, she saw Carol, of all people, sitting courtside. Was she watching Buzz or Jonathan? Marla chose to stay in the background unnoticed. When Jonathan and Evelyn changed courts and stopped for a drink of water, Marla could hear them talk about, of all things, her, Marla.

"I would like to try her out. She has a great look and a lot of personality," Evelyn said.

"Marla, on camera? You're joking." Jonathan was cocky.

"Please have her call me. I want to meet her."

"No, way, José," came Jonathan. "I need her. She's blossoming."

"You don't own her, Jonathan. Don't be so selfish."

Jonathan stopped and looked Evelyn in the eyes. "Promise you won't approach her, Evelyn. I want you to promise."

"OK, OK," Evelyn acquiesced. "Are you involved with her?"

"Frankly, I like going to the office more since I know she's there. Is that involved?"

Evelyn wanted details. "Does she know?"

Jonathan didn't answer. Then, after a beat, he said, "I don't want to scare her away by getting personal. It's too soon. I need her absolute trust first and to know that she is over the actor. By the way, for her I am giving up trying to get him as a client."

They continued the match.

Marla was stunned at the attitude Jonathan took. She felt small, getting smaller, then disappeared as if she had never existed. Her head was pounding, eyes burning, breathing heavily, she was extremely disturbed. Could not believe that someone would unilaterally decide over her future. She thought Jonathan was her friend.

She headed out into the dark of the night unaware of the outside world, without looking for trouble she put herself in harm's way. She stopped at the first bar in Westwood and quickly downed a couple of cocktails. She thought about going home but wasn't drunk enough. She hated feeling helpless. She stopped at another night club. Was she challenging fate? Did she care? Strange looks came her way from the crowd of customers. She forgot she was wearing tennis clothes. Some male come-ons went in one ear and out the other. Her lack of reaction made people think that she was deaf, or a foreigner who didn't understand English. Her face had no expression. Her own world had closed in on her. She absentmindedly drove to Warren's old apartment in Westwood where he and she were first falling in love. Where she was the happiest in her life. She stopped in the alley behind the electric car lift and just sat. It was much later that the headlights of another car behind her, trying to drive through, brought her back to reality.

She managed to get home. She didn't remember how. Dropping her clothes on the floor one-by-one, she headed across the living room to the bar. Down to panties and bra, she fixed another drink. She sank into a drunken self-destructive revelation. She saw her mother the way she looked at her wedding. Dead in body, not in spirit, her things and memorabilia in the den called out to Marla. At first she stared at the beautiful trunk decorated with carvings and inlays. Marla sensed that an artist of considerable talent made it for her mother. She lifted the cover slowly, reached in and without looking, took out an envelope that was on top. She let the trunk cover fall closed.

She opened the envelope that housed her mother's letter to her, the last communication before she died, and read it over and over. By the third time, she recited it as if for an audience. On her knees, she looked up at the sky and talked to her mother.

"Nobody cares. No one loves me. What's to become of me?"

She had another slug of scotch, lay on her back on the floor and continued talking to up there, somewhere.

"Michael is finished. Why? What did I do wrong? Why? Why couldn't I hold him?"

The drunker she got, the closer she felt to her dead mother.

"*You can do anything you want to do.*" She heard her mother's voice. "*You can be anything you want to be.*" Over and over again, it echoed in her head.

She didn't leave the house for days. She could not bring herself to face anybody. What should she do? Why doesn't anybody respect her? Why can't she fix her life and make it livable?

Marla watched movies around the clock, went from wine to vodka, to scotch, to tea, water, juice and back to wine. She drank and remained in a general devastated daze. She wanted to disappear, self-destruct. It didn't happen. Restless sleep overtook her.

She was climbing up a steep hill of gravel and rocks. Suddenly, Christopher Walken appeared at the top, short blond hair moussed to a straight reach for the sky. He was wearing a navy blue suit and, in a Moses Moment, was shouting down to the people on their climb up, advising that they turn around and rush to the sea.

Marla slipped and slid downhill. Small rocks around her rolled under her feet. She found her balance and saw a Ten Dollar bill to her left. Without making a full stop, she picked up the money and continued her way down to the sea.

No one paid attention to her or the money. She saw an easier way down and edged to her right. There was another Ten Dollar bill, which she picked up without missing a beat or without looking around. It was hers for the taking, no doubt.

Working her way down, an earthquake rearranged her track. Before, she was ahead of the crowd. Now, she was inside a room with glass walls all around and a few pieces of heavy garden furniture painted deep red. Some kids, boys, were looking in at her, talking to each other and pointing to the furniture. She understood. She picked up a chair to throw it through the glass wall and break it open. The boys continued pointing. She turned around and behind her found an opening in the glass labyrinth. Found the way out.

She was completely under the spell of the strange images of her fantasy when the telephone's customized melodic ring reverberated throughout the place. She let the call go to voice mail. She did not care. She was trying to figure out her dream. She thought she could analyze it and find some hidden message about strength; find some direction about how to go upward and not down. Maybe to break out of the box. The glass box. Money was there. Find the way. Her mind was swimming, her world was spiraling into the nowhere.

The doorbell rang downstairs. She heard Carol's voice on the intercom but did not buzz her in. Same for Jonathan when he came by. She told them to go away. She told them to see her when she wanted to be seen.

Holding her mother's letter, she returned to the trunk. She opened it again. She hadn't dared to open it fully before. Now she needed to. She wished she had let her mother get closer to her after the death of her father. Not only did she leave her mother for Warren, she also reduced communications with her to far less than normal. She hurt her mother by adopting her father's casual attitude toward infidelity. Making light of it. Now that it had destroyed her own marriage, she mourned the loss of the woman, the only person who may have truly cared about her.

Marla had already begun to recognize that her mother had lead a different kind of life when she saw some valuable signed art work, decorative sculptures and memorabilia in her home. After her mother's death, with the exception of the trunk, Marla had hurriedly stored everything at a nearby commercial storage house and never even thought of them again.

But this was another time and place. Time to look inside the trunk and peruse the various items. She grew fascinated as she realized that her mother had known some truly talented artists and famous people. One tip-off was the range of books autographed to her. The author and illustrator of "Misty," James McQuade, besides declaring his love, even made a sketch of her mother. Jazz composer and musician Chick Sponder of Stan Kenton fame, along with Pete Rugolo, left their marks. Pete Rugolo set to music her mother's poem, "I'm A Real Woman." Marla tried to sing it, hum it, but mostly she liked the words. She decided to try to find a vocalist to perform it one day soon.

The composer, Vic Mizzi, primarily of The Addams Family fame, apparently also passed through her mother's life, although Marla noted from a one-page memory piece that his time was very brief. Maybe just one dinner. Her mother wrote, *"After listening to his bragging about Carol Linley's great body and Eva Gabor's promiscuity, I lost interest. Was he talking about things he knew first hand or was it only hearsay. Was he trying to impress me? Either way he was out of line. Clearly, this is a rich man. I should connect with him. But, when he asked about dinner next week, the words 'In your dreams' came out of my mouth on impulse. Why? I'll never know. I'll figure it out. Maybe. If I want to."* Marla laughed out loud. Her mother had integrity. On the other side of the page was a reminder to thank Patricia Dubin McGuire, the daughter of the talented Al Dubin, most famous as half of the songwriting team of Harry Warren and Al Dubin, for making the introduction.

There were personalized autographs from other writers, but the most impressive were Sid Sheraton's early bestsellers. "The Other Side of Time" contained the famous man's handwritten words *"For Kathi who's not afraid to dream—Love Sid Sheraton, March 18, 1974."* Marla also found some notes by her mother stating that both of the leading female characters were based on herself. The dreamer was even named Catherine and the dark side of her mother was named Noelle. The 1976 book, "A Stranger Looking Back," was autographed *"For Katherine with more affection than she knows—Sid Sheraton."* On "The Naked Masque" on November 19, 1970, he wrote *"To Kathi—A delight to know—warmest regards, Sid Sheraton."* That must have been at the beginning of their romance or affair, or whatever it was. By the time "Descendants" came around in 1978, there were no words—apparently her mother had purchased the signed book herself. Was that about the time Sid's wife died? When did that happen?

A separate manila envelope contained stubs of Carnival Cruise Line tickets for her and 14-year old Marla. *"Remember the cruise that Sid bought, i.e., he said here's a Thousand Dollars, spend it on something silly, not on paying bills or rent. Do something fun!"*

There was a box full of floppy diskettes from her mother's computer. Marla decided she should search for the real story between her mother and the renowned author.

Driven by nostalgia, she became certain that finding out more about her mother's life, about how she discovered her own strength within herself, might give Marla some sense of direction. Something obviously she did not allow her mother to do during her lifetime. Marla felt stupid about that, as if there was a hole inside her. Some dark black hole.

She walked around naked. Night after night she stared at the sunset from her bedroom window. Her mother's voice rose to a crescendo. *"Be yourself. Rely on yourself. Count on yourself."*

Slowly, she felt her core rise out of her solitude. She felt centered. Her defining moment delivered her to euphoric relief. She felt life. She took an ice cold shower. Standing under the three-showerhead waterfall, she scrubbed herself with the large loofah until her skin was raw and nearly turning blue. She turned off the water, wrapped herself in her peach colored deep pile terry robe, picked up the phone and dialed.

"Evelyn Baker, please. This is Marla Hayes."

CHAPTER SEVENTEEN

Michael couldn't sleep. It was nearly four in the morning. He looked around the one-bedroom and den condo that he bought in a hurry in Encino, near enough to the studio. He gulped down a V8. He paced around and agonized. He couldn't talk about his personal dilemmas with anyone. He didn't have a close friend, a true confidant. Suddenly, Marla came to mind. They used to have good talks. But there was no way he could call her now.

He sat down at the computer. Didn't turn it on. Didn't want any e-mails from Linda or anyone. He didn't know why he was restless. He hated the feeling of being in a limbo with every aspect of his life. At least when he was married, things were in place. Wife, kids, everyone was accounted for. The only recurring question in his life had been whether or not a show got picked up, whether or not he got a writing assignment.

"That's it!" he yelled out loud. That's what woke him up. It was about time for the new network schedules to come out and be disclosed. Wondered whether his pilot would go to series. He was anxious and he hated to admit that one of his reasons for his anxiety was the security of the solitude of writing. He loved writing. That was his soul, his companion, his fulfillment, his entire life.

He got dressed and headed over the hill to *Nate 'n Al's* deli in Beverly Hills. The place where somebody always knew you. You had people to be with. There were other early risers, writers, producers, old timers, has-beens, newcomers, studio suits and a variety of groupies. You could walk in any time and find someone with whom to bullshit.

Frank Prince from The Hollywood Reporter, the show business trade paper, waved to him. Michael glanced around to see who else was there then sat down with the short, dark haired man.

"Hello, Frank. How's the Hollywood Reporter?"

"You tell me. You read it!" Frank said.

"You write it," Michael laughed.

"I know your pilot was a winner," Frank said. "I saw the numbers."

"That doesn't mean a thing, Frank," Michael grinned, sipping on a cup of strong black coffee. "Unless you have inside information. Has the network announced anything to the press before they would tell us? Would they do that?"

Frank smiled. "You've been around long enough to know that there are no rules. No scruples."

"You're kidding. Then you know? Well,…?"

"I can't tell you. You still have to get it through your official channels," Frank said. "You know, your network bosses in their designer suits."

Michael jumped up and headed out the door. "Thanks, OK!"

"Call me later," Frank added as he waved after the disappearing figure.

All the way to the studio Michael beat himself up for going to breakfast in Beverly Hills instead of his usual, *Jerry's in the Valley*, which was much closer to the studio. As he tried not to speed over the canyon, his mind raced ahead of him. What could it be? Frank would not say anything if it were bad news. Or would he? Michael just didn't know any more.

He was waved into the studio by the gate guard. He parked in haste but as he entered his office at the early hour, except for the rich smell of coffee that filled the air, there was nothing. There was no note, no e-mail, no voice mail, nothing.

This was the first time in his career that he had had no executive producer over him. Michael, himself, was the executive producer of the pilot and would be of the series, if it went.

Realizing that he hadn't eaten breakfast, he walked over to the commissary, sat down and ordered a lot of food. Before he could begin to eat, his cell phone rang. It was the network suit calling. "Yes, Mike, you've got it."

Michael didn't like being called Mike, but this was not the time to point that out.

"What, Buddy? What exactly have I got?"

"Thirteen episodes and depending on how the first five do, you may go to 22. Not too shabby, hm?" The voice was cheerful.

"Oh, God." That's all Michael could say. He looked up and standing at his table was the network suit, Buddy. Bluetooth in his ear, he clicked off his phone conversation with Michael and sat down at the table across from him. Michael also put his phone down and grinned. Just grinned at Buddy.

"I'll make this series the best ever," he said.

Buddy poured himself some coffee but there was no time to eat. Other suits came over to Michael to congratulate him. Michael was beside himself. Finally, he had his first series created and exec produced by him, and to be written mostly by him. Real money.

Back at the office, Judy started the day. When Michael informed her of the happy news, she almost cried. They spent the next several hours accepting faxes, flowers, gift baskets, congratulations and preparing for the arduous schedule ahead. Everyone in Michael's tried-and-true core team which included Bernie, his main director, and Buzz, the associate producer *cum* jack-of-all-trades, were in a celebratory mood. Buzz was the *go to* guy when no one else was available. There was also his main Film Editor and a newly hired Story Editor.

Judy buzzed. Michael pressed the speaker phone button. "Please pick up the phone, Michael."

Michael was in the greatest mood. "I have no secrets in front of these guys," he said, laughing. "This is my family, Judy. Let's go out and celebrate, OK? Guys?" He did pick up the phone.

"Linda will meet you at the Ivy at seven," Judy said.

"Is she on the line?"

"No, her phone is turned off. She went to confession."

"Is this a joke?" Michael worried.

"Well, she sounded serious to me," Judy said.

Michael nodded in bewilderment, hung up and was about to share with the guys then he thought better of it.

"OK, then. Let's have a champagne brunch Sunday, bring the wives and dates, whatever. Then Monday, eight o'clock, the chapter begins." He said all the right things but everyone could tell that his mood had sunk considerably. One-by-one they got up and taking Bernie's lead, left.

In spite of the good tidings, Michael was weighted down by helplessness. He wanted badly to get away from all that he could not control. He wanted to get away from being ruled by sex. Linda was the top of the list, and the only one on that list.

------------◆------------

When he entered the secluded Ivy restaurant that evening, he saw an unusually radiant Linda sitting at a specially private table. Champagne and caviar were the order of the night. As he got closer and closer to her, like *Lorelei, the siren*, she was luring him into her will. By the time he leaned to kiss her *Hello*, he was smiling. He was at ease. She had him hook, line and sinker. She handed him her glass of champagne and poured herself a new one.

"Then you heard?" Michael said.

"Oh, this is too too marvelous. You're THE MAN," she said sweetly. Being around Linda, made him lighthearted. He had to be and was THE MAN.

The waiters poured champagne, brought appetizers that Linda had requested. She had always been attentive to his likes and dislikes in food and drink, and easily pre-ordered everything the way he would.

"This is my last weekend before the madness begins," Michael said, more to himself than to her. "I'm hosting the team for Sunday brunch and then we'll say *Good Bye* to free time."

"I don't know about Sunday. I had other plans."

"Why do you make plans without asking me first?"

"Because it's time that everyone knew that I am not just your significant other but your wife." Linda was dead serious.

"That's what you discussed in confession?" Michael was sarcastic. "I'm sorry." He stopped to think. "I'm sorry. I didn't mean it like that."

"Well, then," she rolled her eyes. "How?"

"I'm not ready for that. I am just barely out of a marriage that wore me out. I'm going into six months of around-the-clock writing. I have two kids…"

She looked at him lovingly. "Three."

"What? Three what?"

"Kids." She took a long sip of her champagne. "The third one is on its way, dear. July. Sometime in July."

"I need time to think about it."

"Think about providing this child with everything your first two have, the schools, the nannies, the vacations, everything." Linda's face grew tight as she was centered on Michael.

"I'll need a hundred episodes and a syndication deal before I can afford all that you want, Linda. Could you just hold off," he pleaded.

"Do you want me to abort, Michael? Do you want that on your conscience?"

"Never. Never in a million years," he said.

She got up, went to the ladies' room. He was alone. The happiest day of his life. Alone.

CHAPTER EIGHTEEN

Carol, wearing a sporty black and white outfit, took the grand tour of the studio. Her regal carriage, demure behavior, brought out the best in Buzz. He enjoyed practicing the role of gentleman. It came back, like bike riding. They watched a couple of scenes on a soundstage. Carol had never seen film being shot, movies being made. She made him feel like a big man who knew a great deal, who had all the answers. As a VIP, Buzz's guest tram was let ahead of the tour groups. Besides seeing the entire tourist attraction, she was exposed to some of the inner workings of a great, well-oiled machinery. This was more fun than she had expected.

Dinner on Venice Beach at Primitivo Bistro, a place known for its tapas and wine, was an excellent choice. They shared muscles, lump crab cakes and an amazing potato salad. It was all simply delicious. Buzz was glad he introduced her to a new restaurant and she loved feeling pampered. Without any hesitation, Carol lied to Buzz about how her husband died in an accident just days after their wedding, how she raised her son, Sammy, now 17, by herself, and how she never found a new love she could trust. She chose to repeat Marla's words, "People fall in love and you know, by now I know, that there is nothing like your first love. Your true love. I can't get past my husband. With anyone else the feelings are not the same. Don't you agree?"

"I wouldn't know, Carol. I never felt love quite like that. Maybe one day I will."

"Maybe," she said and produced a fresh smile.

Buzz drove her home. They kissed and said good night. Carol made no gesture of inviting him in. She was reserved and sexually unavailable. She did not come on to him as all the others did. Buzz told her how sad it was that so many women were so hungry that they would practically attack him and drag him to bed. He said he preferred a lady and he thought Carol was a lady. Besides being intrigued, Buzz was turned on.

Their dating began. Carol even forgot about Jerry, briefly. She was so happy with a real successful man who, in addition, also believed everything she said. She was boasting to Marla and everyone in the office about her dinners and outings with Buzz and the famous people she was meeting through him. Every morning and every hour on the hour she would look in the mirror, stare into her own eyes and unblinkingly she would recite her mantra:

"I am not going to mess this up. I am going to make this work.
I am not going to mess this up. I am going to make this work."

Every time she started to tell Marla about her relationship, Marla became busy with something that couldn't wait. Finally, she confronted her.

"You know, Marla, I listened to all the nitty-gritty about Michael and you'd just go on and on."

"Until you advised me to stay away from showbiz guys," Marla replied. "I stopped going on and on, remember? And now, where does your guy earn his living? Just say, 'show business, Marla'. He is in the business that I told you to stay away from."

"Now, now girls, stop the catfight," came Walter's voice from the next cubicle. "I can hear you, I can hear everything."

"Me, too," Becky said.

"We can all hear you." Penelope's voice traveled clearly from the reception.

"Well, thank goodness you're all my friends," Marla said.

"That's funny. I thought they were all my friends," Carol said.

Becky walked around her partition to face Marla. "Yes, that's what's special about this place. We're all friends of each other, through hell or high water, we stick together. We are not in judgment and nobody rules."

"Hear, hear," Walter said, rising above the partition with a gleam in his eyes.

"Well, I won't be around here much longer," Carol said disagreeably. "I hope you will find someone to fill my shoes." She also stood up, higher than the partition. "And someone who gets nominations."

Marla's head popped up. "You didn't get the nomination, Carol. I did."

The elevator *fight song* interrupted the moment. Like unruly schoolchildren, their four heads disappeared below.

Silence filled the office. Moments passed. The elevator *fight song* came on again—the visitor was gone.

"Just the mailman, children!" Penelope said with a smile in her voice. But the elevator *fight song* came again. In a couple of minutes Carol's phone buzzed.

"You have a guest, Carol," Penelope said. "I'll take her to the small conference room."

Carol was puzzled. She wasn't expecting anyone, just the same, she checked her hair and face in the mirror hanging on the partition above the computer monitor. Carol was stunned when she saw Xiùměi helping herself to water, choosing the right glass and coaster. Xiùměi was dressed in a seersucker suit with a soft pastel orange plunging T-shirt, high heel sandals and matching purse. She looked good.

"Well, what a surprise, Xiùměi. How are you?" Carol said. "I'd offer you some water or a soft drink but I see you've already got it."

Xiùměi bowed and Carol automatically bowed back. "Yes, thank you, Carol. I came with no announcement. I not very sure if you would let me come. So, I came without."

"That's fine, but please, stop bowing. You live here, you learn to Americanize."

"People help nice immigrants. Who bow," she answered with a surprisingly firm smile then sat down across from Carol.

"I have idea about agency for day-cleaners and day-cookers." She looked at Carol as if her eyes wanted to pierce into Carol's brain and see what really was going on. Xiùměi continued. "I have made many… much… research." She proceeded to open a large manila envelope. She pulled out a thin presentation binder and handed it to Carol.

"Once you said to ask you if I questions. Remember?"

Carol nodded. She was actually amazed at watching this self-composed woman. "Yes, I remember." She smiled.

"You meant?"

"Yes, I meant it." Xiùměi pointed to the binder. "All numbers, all research, license, and list of all things important and necessary." Carol took the binder from her. "I will read it and call you."

Xiùměi got up. "No. Please, No. I come back. Friday? Next week? Two weeks?"

"Fine, next week. Tuesday. Are you available on Tuesday?" Carol asked. "We'll have lunch here, on the rooftop."

Xiùměi was heading toward the door. "Thank you. Tuesday. OK." As they were at the elevator, Xiùměi cracked her first smile and said, "No Chinese food, please."

Carol laughed with her and the elevator *fight song* ended the meeting."

CHAPTER NINETEEN

Marla met with Evelyn Baker, the manager of KMRTV. The high-powered executive impressed Marla as *Earth Mother* in a tailored suit and a *Rebecca Minkoff* go-with-everything *Devote* bag nearby. Evelyn was a plain, unimpressive, slightly plump woman somewhere in her forties, easy to smile and eyes burning with warmth and life.

"I'm so glad you called. I can't begin to tell you how much I wanted to talk with you," Evelyn said.

"But Jonathan didn't permit it. I know. I heard you two talk."

"That's interesting. When?"

"At the tennis court a couple of weeks ago."

"He's smitten with you, you know." Evelyn leaned back in her executive chair. "He's not going to let you out."

Marla nodded in agreement. "I can't allow that, can I? I know he gave me a break when I was down and out, but I have to draw the line somewhere."

"You gave him a nominated spot. That's not nothing."

"Yes. True."

Marla, looking thoughtful, said, "You know, I was wallowing in self-pity, skidding to the bottom, to oblivion. I've always been ruled by someone and on my own fumbled a lot. Then I'd hide. But yesterday the lights came on, the brain kicked in. I realized this was my life, not a test I could re-take. This was the one I had to do. I had to stop watching myself from the outside looking in. I had to take charge." Marla rose out of the chair, captivating Evelyn with her power. "So, here I am. Do you still need a weather girl?"

"We never really needed one but when we saw your footage, we wanted you on our team."

"I told you too much about myself, didn't I?" Marla's insecurity surfaced again. "You probably don't even want me anymore."

"Are you kidding?" Evelyn's smile was reassuring. "You just knocked my socks off with your speech. You're dramatic, a natural performer. I want you."

"Not too much? Overkill?" Marla walked around then settled down again.

"I got carried away. I'm not looking for fame. I'm looking for balance. That evasive thing. Something my mother had tried to find. I was communicating with my mother for the first time since she died. I'm just so thrilled that finally she reached me. She did. The first contact. She knows it." With a little grin Marla pointed to the sky.

"Now you know I'm nuts. Are we still on?"

"I don't think there is anything you can tell me about yourself that would change my mind. I, myself, am an open book. Secrets are often harmful to your health." Evelyn laughed.

"Actually, I'm touched by the devotion you show toward your dead mother. My mother is alive," said Evelyn, "she has Alzheimer's. It's living hell for me, but I refuse to put her into a nursing home. Those are terrible places. The worst. They steal from the patients, they don't answer their buzzers when they are called, they don't keep them clean, they're horrible. I've not heard anything good about any of them."

Evelyn was looking through Marla or maybe just seeing past her. She continued. "I've hired nurses around the clock. I won't get rich but having the inner peace that most people never find is a form of wealth."

Marla told her that she was one of *most people*. A spiritual connection between her and Evelyn was immediate. Marla was compelled to trust the other woman.

Evelyn explained that KMRTV was independent of all networks and had refused for years to be swallowed up by a chain of any kind. They were the voice of Greater Los Angeles. That's all they wanted to be and that's all their audience wants them to be. They mean to stay small but carry a big stick and be heard. They are a wealthy operation, accountable only to the Board of Directors, and she, Evelyn, had all the authority of running the station.

Evelyn and Marla agreed that she would do weather on the weekends and not upset her job with Jonathan. Marla wanted just one weekend to give it a try. Evelyn told her that the first time she would be a mess, no matter what. Not to worry. She'll get it after a few attempts.

And so, without telling anyone, Marla went on the air as weekend weather girl. She wished Evelyn had been there, but it was the weekend after all. Marla was a mess in a way, as predicted by Evelyn, but it never came through on the air to the casual audience. She had an outer calmness as she read the meteorological report. The make-up woman placed a couple of thin mini-pads under her arms to absorb perspiration. It worked. She had to do three reports during the half-hour news and do it again during the evening news.

Evelyn was on the telephone as soon as Marla finished. "I think you have a future in TV-land, Marla," she said.

"Oh, I just love it," Marla said.

"Love what exactly, the weather?"

"The weather." Marla sat down, her energy drained.

"Don't let it get you. It's only a job," Evelyn said. "Part-time job. See you."

Marla removed the sweaty pads from her armpits and tossed them in the trash. She looked in the mirror. She liked what she saw.

———◆———

Monday at the office was different. Everyone seemed to have seen her on TV. In the lunch room, Becky and Walter gave her thumbs up. Carol surprised them by wearing a lilac scarf-tie over the usual black and white Chanel. She stepped in for coffee, announced that weather girls were usually some executive's mistresses, neither meteorologists, nor news people.

"Guess I broke the mold," Marla said.

"It's the general belief. I thought you wanted to know."

"I don't care about general beliefs, Carol."

"Well, you shouldn't do it. It's bad for your image."

Marla was annoyed. "You know, you are advising me against this and that and then you do the opposite. I used to think you were my friend. "

"Your friend, yes. But I'm not your mother. What are you talking about, anyway?"

"You told me not to date Michael. You told me that after Warren I should've learned my lesson about showbiz guys. What about you and Buzz?" Marla looked at her with newly found strength.

"Strictly platonic."

"I find that hard to believe." With that Marla walked around to her own cubicle and buried herself in work. But her mind was on Carol's statement. She got up and went back to Carol's cubicle.

"If what you say is true, Carol, then you have plans for this guy? Buzz? Serious plans?" They were almost whispering, but the more they lowered their voices the more the colleagues listened up.

"You're a good student, Marla. Now watch the master get her way."

"I'm through watching you, Carol. I'm too busy living. By the way, nice scarf."

Marla walked over to Jonathan's office and knocked.

As she entered, Jonathan's face lit up. He gestured for her to sit.

"Guess you saw me, too. Who'd think everyone watches the news on Sunday."

"Only the weather. Getting ready for Monday," he said.

"Then you saw."

"Can we talk about it over dinner?"

"Sure. What time?"

"I'll pick you up at seven."

"Great." She was out the door. She returned to her cubicle and didn't notice that Carol had gone for the day until she heard Penelope offering the voice mail to a caller for a message.

———— ◆ ————

Jonathan arrived early with flowers and a bottle of wine.

"I hope you don't mind that I got here so early."

"Of course not." Marla was cheerful, self-confident.

"We have time for a drink. Would you like me to open this Kendall Jackson. It's a vintage *Cab*." he said.

"I hope you didn't go out of your way for an expensive bottle."

"I want this to be a very special night," he said.

Marla was curious about the point of it all and not about playing games.

"So, what's on your mind, Jonathan?"

"I don't want you to leave. I have plans for you."

"I have plans for me, too. My plans. You don't own me."

"That's what Evelyn said. That I don't own you. But shouldn't I be able to expect loyalty?"

"I thought about it long and hard, Jonathan, and I don't mean to leave the agency. I'm only doing weekend weather."

"Weekend goes to weekday emergencies, then to weekday regular, then to news, then writing your own copy and becoming an anchor."

Marla started to laugh. "That sounds so great, but I'm really not interested. Besides, it's been only two afternoons. Aren't you getting ahead of yourself, like maybe two, three years?"

"You're too talented. It'll come to you sooner. In leaps and bounds. I can't let you do this."

"Why do you think you have a say here?"

"Because I told Evelyn that I needed you and not to go after you."

"I made the approach. Evelyn kept her promise to you."

"How do you know?" He poured more wine for both of them and helped himself to some crackers from a large bowl on the counter top.

"I was at the club that day. I heard your entire conversation."

"Then you know how I feel about you."

"I don't feel the same."

"I thought we could build the agency together. Build a life together."

"Won't happen, Jonathan. It won't," she paced.

"You wanted to take me to a fine restaurant so when you tell me all this I don't make a scene."

"Marla, I want the best for you. I'll make you head writer."

"I can do you a lot more good on the outside."

"Oh, yeah? Why would you?"

"You gave me a break." She looked deep into his eyes.

"I wanted you, that's all. You know, boy, girl, man, woman."

"What I'll always remember is that you gave me a break when no one else would. That's big."

"I need you. I'm not done with you."

"Yes, you are."

"Then you're fired."

"Then I quit."

"Fine."

"Fine."

He marched to the door, stopped and looked back. Marla did not budge.

"You want me to fire you?"

"You just did and I just quit."

"I'll sweeten your deal. More money." He couldn't stop himself from pleading with her.

"It's not about money it's about me."

"What about me. I'm in love with you."

"You know the saying about 'If you love someone you set them free?' Something like that."

"Final word?"

"Absolutely," she said.

"It's not over until the fat lady sings," Jonathan said and marched out the door.

"Yeah, like that's original."

CHAPTER TWENTY

Carol and Buzz's engagement party was well planned by Carol herself. Her black and white motif ran through Buzz's house, but a new color had moved into her life, purple and its many hues. Hundreds of dark and soft lilac-purple flowers accented the otherwise overwhelming two-tones. The backyard had groups of round tables, barstools and high cocktail tables scattered around for the guests. Napkins and table runners were filled with sentimental thoughts. Rows of strangely sculptured bushes partitioned different sections of the garden, bringing alive the bizarre land of Edward Scissorhands.

The caterers set up their stove and cooking stations in the garage open to the street. Their way of advertising when seen by the arriving guests, worked. Several people would take their business cards for their own future use.

Through Carol, Xiùměi got a menial job with the caterer. She and another woman who worked for the agency where Xiùměi worked, took on the job of clean-up after the guests and after the caterers. Měi Wong and Xiùměi became friends during her early days in the country when she worked at the Chinese restaurant. Měi Wong admired how smart and aggressive Xiùměi was and happily followed Xiùměi's every move.

Xiùměi was making friends with Carol's caterers. She was likeable, such a willing foreigner, it compelled people to help her. Xiùměi offered to do dirty jobs, odd jobs any time the caterers would need it and asked for their guidance.

More out of politeness than interest, Marla went to the engagement party by herself. Jonathan arrived with a cool, lanky redhead on his arm. She was an exotic beauty, a showstopper. He paraded her around as if some trophy. They were an odd pair, the short squatty man and the statuesque, striking woman.

"This is Missy Poole," he said to Marla. "Missy, meet Marla Hayes, my former employee."

"Oh, dear," she whispered. "Then you're my current employee." She reached out with grandeur to shake hands.

"I'm afraid you're mistaken," Marla said.

"Mistake? The 'm' word? No, no, not in my world," she said with a saccharine smile.

"That's a rhyme. Not a very good one. I'll have to work on it," she added.

Marla looked at Jonathan, wondering what this person was?

"Missy Poole, Marla, is the sole heir to the Poole fortune," Jonathan offered.

"For now the TV station is all I show, until everybody ahead of me dies, you know."

Her giggle barely concealed an overly developed superiority complex and irritated Marla.

"Ah, I must work on this one also," she cooed.

"If you'd excuse me," Marla said, wanting to move on.

"KMRTV. The station." Missy looked at Marla. Jonathan gloated. "I'm your boss. Happy to meet you."

"Evelyn Baker is my boss."

Marla had to get away. She turned and walked without looking back.

"Becky, is Walter coming?"

"No. He liked Carol better in her black and white period, with less color and more adventure, if you know what I mean."

They helped themselves to drinks.

"I am kidding. Walter went to pick up Penelope. They'll get here."

"And your husband?"

"On the road again. Business. I came anyway," Becky said.

"Good for you. And me. I needed company."

"Watch out for Jonathan," Marla said. "He's really over the top this time."

"You're the only one I ever saw him have the hots for. And I've been working for him since the beginning."

"Was I the only one who didn't know about that?" Marla asked.

"That's usual."

"Did Carol know?" Marla started to put two and two together.

"Duh?! Why do you think she is chasing this guy? Engagement, my ass. Jonathan was interested in you. You were dating a successful writer, not like her attorney who refuses to marry her. So, she wanted someone famous. Or at least, important. She wanted to outdo you."

Becky filled a plate with picture perfect food and they settled at a table of strangers, surrounded by big, sculptured bushes.

"I thought she was my friend."

Becky laughed. "She's no one's friend."

At the next table, behind an animal shaped bush, a bejeweled woman in overstated out-of-place evening clothes, laboriously arranged herself on a stool. Marla saw, from the corner of her eye, Michael bring the woman some tidbits and heard his voice speaking to someone.

"Yes, we're very happy. Baby on its way, new home, we'll give a wedding reception just to make it all public. You must come."

Marla turned to Becky. "Who is he with?"

"Who?" Becky asked.

"Michael," Marla said.

"I don't know Michael," Becky said.

"Right."

Marla got up and with her back toward Michael, slipped out to the patio. She went far enough to not be noticed when she turned around. Becky watched Marla, then followed her, bringing more champagne.

Marla took the champagne and slowly peeked to see Michael from behind another guest.

"I don't want him to see me" she said to Becky.

"Now, I've got it. Oh, my God," came Becky. "This is THE Michael? The guy you've dated?"

Marla nodded.

"You poor thing. And to run into him with a pregnant wife, happy and gleaming."

Becky put her arm around Marla. They both looked toward Michael. He turned and saw Marla. He froze. Their eyes locked. Michael made an apologetic gesture with his hand. Marla saw Linda turn, follow Michael's gaze and see that he was looking at her. Marla bent down as if to pick up something she had dropped. When she straightened out again, Michael and Linda had mingled their way toward another direction.

Marla reached for a fresh drink on the tray circulated by Xiùměi.

She looked at Becky. "I know the whole office knew about me and Michael but what I didn't know was that I'd still hurt. People don't change. I keep forgetting that. He married his first wife because she was pregnant."

"Are you uncomfortable? Do you want to leave?" Becky asked.

"Am I ready for some drunken driving? Is that what you mean?" Marla liked her joke. She wasn't drunk.

"I can't keep running from yesterday, can I?" she continued.

"It sounds good but you're just saying that, aren't you?"

"Yes. Yes, Becky. Just saying it." Marla got up. "Maybe I should get out of here."

Marla walked into the den to get her wrap. Sitting at the desk with her back to the door was Carol, on the telephone. "Jerry, I got your message. Yes, noon tomorrow is perfect. I'm quitting my job in the morning." She hung up, turned around and saw Marla.

"Well it could've been worse than you hearing me."

"That was not very nice, Carol."

"Since when do you expect *nice* from me?"

"My mistake. Sorry."

"Oh you think you know it all, don't you? Let me remind you that I like sex."

"Yeah, yeah. Jerry tides you over until the wedding."

"Poor Marla, that's YOUR Michael, isn't it? With the pregnant tramp who got between you two."

"I didn't know that was how it happened, Carol. I simply didn't know."

Marla got her wrap and headed toward the front entrance just as Eugene and Sherrie Romany arrived, bearing gifts. Warren and Carolyn Shipley, Ms. Silicone Boobs and obviously their new playmate, were with them. They practically ran into Marla.

"Well, hello there," Eugene said.

"Hello, hello," Sherrie added with a self-satisfied smirk.

"You remember everyone, honey, don't you?" Warren said.

"Why should I?" Marla said.

"Because, my dear, your husband now has a career."

"That's not my husband, Mrs. Romany. That's something of yours."

"True, I have some rights to him."

"And his chippy?" said Marla. "What does she do for you?"

Sherrie moved into Marla's face. "My genius benevolent husband has created a spot for Carolyn's little daughter on the show."

"What a happy family. All this benevolence. Little too much," Marla said.

"Oh, the impudence!" Sherrie was getting wired. "Just look who is talking. Weather girl!"

Eugene, Warren and the others anticipated a catfight coming on with hair pulling and jaw slapping. Sherrie was beside herself.

"And you really think you got your job, haha, job, for your brilliance!" Sherrie said with rising fury. "Just ask anyone about the nature of your services!"

Eugene put his arm around Sherrie. "Darling, she's got a *Clio*. It's probably the brain."

Marla looked at Eugene, smiled.

"Thank you."

She went around Sherrie and could see only the exit.

Carol reappeared in a glib mood. "I'm sorry about your ex being here also. I didn't know he was that close to Hollywood royalty."

"Carol, don't you ever look in the mirror? Your nose is so brown."

"I've never seen you jealous before. But here is more. Buzz and I have set our wedding date. It's a surprise. The invitations will go out next week."

"Well, you know what they say: How do you stop a Jewish American Princess from fucking your brains out. Marry her."

Carol wasn't laughing. "Guess what, I'm not a JAP. Besides, I am just starting to fuck his brains out. And I mean 'brains.' You know, engagement, prenup, wedding, fucking, postnup. My way or no way."

"I'm afraid I didn't know."

"That's your problem then. That's the problem."

"Problem?" Marla did not know where Carol was going with any of this.

"Anyway, my dear, now you've got it all. I'm officially handing over the flag of leadership of the agency to you. I'm quitting on Monday. Now you can have it all, Jonathan, the nominations, you can be queen bee."

"I hate to inform you that I've already quit."

"No!?" Carol was stunned.

"Yes, my dear. And by the way, I think I saw your son going upstairs with Sally. Remember one of Buzz's tennis friends, Sally, about 35 or 40, up the stairs to the bedroom."

"Well, what do you want me to do? Leave my guests?"

"I'm sure that was a rhetorical question, Carol. Now, if you don't mind, I'm through mingling. You go, celebrate yourself. I doubt that I can gather any more dirt at this "B" party." Marla's look could kill.

— ◆ —

The white Rolls Royce rolled silently through the gates of the Eaglesglen Country Club to the mansion Michael had bought on the golf course. That was the one! Linda simply had to have it. The three-level home had a screened-in lap pool, the latest rage, and a hot spa with a unique fountain facing toward the golf course. The tennis court was visible from Michael's airy, rambling office on the main level. Around from his office, sandwiched between the living room and the kitchen, was the formal dining room for sixteen. The guest wing jutted out to form an *L* shape and protected one side of the pool.

Downstairs, a screening room for ten and game room featuring a billiard table as well as the latest video games, complemented the wet bar. Powder rooms were hidden by doors the size of a painting, or part of the tapestry of the wall. The top level was off limits to everyone other than Linda and Michael. It was their private space, a little over-decorated, truly in the image of Linda.

Linda let Michael lock up the house for the night. She went upstairs to the master bedroom with his and her dressing rooms and his and her bathrooms. Linda looked around the beautiful home and nodded with appreciation.

"Yes, Daddy. Shy girls finish last," she muttered under her nose.

She remembered how her father had molested her early on but gave her so many gifts and rewards along the way that she equated the two. Sex and rewards. If she was a good little girl and made her father real happy, the gifts came endlessly. Linda became the sexual expert who liked being in control.

Mumbling to herself, she clumsily climbed out of her party clothes dropping them on the floor. Michael came in and heard her close the door to her bathroom.

"You're pregnant," he shouted, trying to intervene.

"Is the Pope Catholic?"

"That's not funny, Linda. Can't you stop snorting just for a few months?"

He was deeply concerned. Then she reappeared . She looked more desirable than ever in a custom-made maternity *teddy*. A smile came to his face.

"You're really something."

"How would you like to touch your baby on the inside?" She turned on the charm that always worked on Michael.

"The concept is intriguing," he said.

"I'll show you the way, but it will cost you."

This was a new one on Michael.

"What does that mean?"

"Put the money on the bureau, dearie," she said and lay seductively in the middle of the oversized king. Her stare ordered him to do what she wanted, while she gently swayed her full breasts, circling both nipples, touching them with her pinky.

Spellbound, he went for his wallet, pulled out some bills and placed them on the dresser. He looked at her victoriously but her stare did not break. He put down some more bills, and more. Finally, she smiled, cupped her breasts with both hands.

"Come and get it."

She moved him around and he did everything she wanted. He knew from experience that her kind of sex would bring him great pleasure. But it went too quickly. She was normally more game. Maybe her pregnancy made the difference. Well, he thought to himself as he waited for her to bring him a warm towel, his first wife never had sex with him after she knew she was pregnant. With all her faults, Linda filled an insatiable need in him. Before her, he didn't know how wonderful sex could really be, even at a high price.

He heard her reaching for the TV remote.

"What about my towel?" he asked.

"It's gonna cost you."

"Oh, not again." He got up and went to his bathroom. When he returned, she was watching late night TV, some juvenile, off color, vulgar show.

"Linda, honey. Can you put on your TV ears if you're going to watch. I'd like to sleep."

"Isn't this my house the same as yours?" she pouted.

"That's not the issue, honey. I need a little sleep every once in a while."

"Fuck off. You're not my Daddy." The crazed words rolled out of her lips.

"Your Daddy? What's this business with you and your Daddy?"

"He was the first and he was the best."

Michael listened up. He was stunned. "What are you saying? Was something going on between you two? Did he molest you?" Michael sat on the bed next to her, wanted to talk, to work things through.

Linda caught herself in the nick of time. "No, no. It's just that he was the first man I loved Michael. That's all. Don't go ballistic."

Michael left for his shower. Ice water prickled his skin, the back of his neck and pounded the top of his head through the oversized inset showerheads. Kohler at its latest and finest. He was calming down but still puzzled. When he returned, Linda was sipping a cocktail and watching television.

"I've been thinking. We need to put some order in our lives with the baby coming," he said.

"My life is fine, Michael. Just fine. You worry about order." She put on the TV ears and left Michael's world.

CHAPTER TWENTY-ONE

Marla arrived with a bottle of wine and a loaf of bread to Carol's apartment on Carmelina Avenue in an old building in an old section of Los Angeles. Due to the proximity to the University of California at Los Angeles, its Medical Center and Research Center, the area was densely populated with a great number of employees, teachers, medical personnel and lay workers, students by the dozens and others. Marla parked on the street and walked to the two-storey building. Carol's apartment was a downstairs unit by the entry with high French windows just a few feet above street level.

"The wine I understand," Carol said. "But bread?"

"Oh, it's an old fashioned tribute to an old fashioned woman, my mother. She taught me about breaking bread. Peace, bread, friends, dining. Maybe too mushy."

"Not for me. Nothing is too mushy for me." Carol smiled and poured from an already open bottle of wine. "I gave up on black and white after fifteen years. Haha," she said. "What do you think? How do you like it?" she asked as she gestured around the apartment.

"I didn't know what to expect."

"I know. I've lived in black and white for years."

"I didn't know that, either," Marla said.

"Things are different now. I like the way I look because Buzz does. I know I may be setting the feminist movement back some decades, but I am one of those women who is not whole without a man. I'd like to be whole for the first time." She looked almost delicate.

"At 39, I still have something to sell to the right buyer. Not baggage but knowledge."

Carol's place, as most old structures, was spacious. Her unique homemaking touches and sense of style made it cozy. At first glance the soft, gentle world of pinks, mauves, lilacs and purples seemed gaudy. Then it settled. Felt good. Carol would have been a good wife and would have made some man, maybe even Sammy's father, very happy. Maybe this time around it would work.

In the kitchen, Marla watched her put the finishing touches on dinner. Wearing perfectly coordinated hostess lounging pajamas, she toiled.

"You look marvelous, Carol," Marla said. "Women don't dress the way they used to. You know, color coordinated."

"Well, you know what I think? I am who I am. I dress my way. I don't go for fads unless they suit me. Old school mentality says I always have to look my best, always have to be coordinated, always have to be desirable, always have to be ready to be loved. It was the way to catch a man," she laughed. "Or not."

She refilled the wine, lit the candles and gestured Marla to come to the table. She rambled, and seemed to slow down. "The weekly hair appointment was a must. Before Vidal Sassoon our hair was not wash and wear. The only thing I wouldn't let go is the manicure-pedicure. But otherwise, I think I'm loosening up." She looked at Marla, waiting for confirmation.

"We do what we need to do," Marla said.

"I know it's another time, but I can't change completely who I am. You see?"

"Why did you feel you had to invite me? I'm not angry with you," Marla asked. "You have a good thing going with Buzz and like you said, if you keep him on a string… you will get what you want."

"It matters what you think of me."

"But, why, Carol? Your life is moving along well. You don't have to please anyone but Buzz."

"Me. I have to please me. Too many mean things were said. I know there is the ugly streak in me, Marla. I know it. It built up with life. My life. My baggage. I can't just shed it like a snake sheds its skin. Sometimes I don't even think that I want to. Can you understand that? It's this meanness that protects me."

"I wish I could have developed that," Marla said. "I need to protect myself."

"You're too young. If you stay alone long, it will come." Her thoughts were older than she, belonged to some earlier times. Marla had never seen her as natural, smooth, relaxed, effortlessly serving dinner.

"You are a homemaker. Look at you, it's the easiest thing. You'll make Buzz very happy."

"I like him. I think getting to know each other without the tension that sex brings will pay off." She seemed vulnerable, even dainty to Marla. She went on in a soft tone of voice which Marla had never heard before.

"This old fashioned courting is good. With all the free sex, which I give and take, I have forgotten how nice it is to simply get close to another person. Buzz and I talk about it."

"Frankly, I didn't think you could do it. You're such a sexual being," Marla said.

"Well, that's where Jerry comes in handy, so to speak." They laughed. "Sneaking around makes him a better lover. And it's daytime. I can spend the evenings with Buzz."

"Weren't you in love with him?"

"Jerry used me. He never wanted to get married. So, I'm using him. Why not?"

"This is pretty funny. I can't make love because Warren is still under my skin and you can't make love because you're on a mission."

"Two hot mommas," Carol said. "But I have my outlet. No questions asked, no lies told."

They ate the simple dinner of pulled pork and cabbage that cooked all day in the crock pot. It was tasty, not heavy, and beautifully served over fresh-out-of-the-oven steaming tomato-bread. The salad of tangerines, nuts, arugula greens, slivers of garlic and tomatillo, was an unusual accompaniment to the country-style main course.

"What about your imaginary Spaniard?" Carol asked.

Marla recalled her mother's letter—*'Be your own counsel.'* She smiled mysteriously and said, "Imaginary is the operative word."

Carol, unlike before, gave in.

The door flung open. Sammy walked in. Clearly stoned. He headed to his room without a word. In just minutes he re-appeared with an overstuffed duffle bag.

"I'm leaving, Ma," he said.

"For how long?" Carol asked.

"For good. Sally and I will travel. All over the country. Maybe the world."

"What about your education? Is she going to pay for college?"

"I'll make my own money."

"You didn't make that offer to me," Carol said.

"You're supposed to pay for your kid's education."

"Well, then. Will you call me when you sober up?" Carol's face was cold as ice. "I have a few bits of information that you will need as you become 18."

"I'm not stoned."

"Whatever. You call me."

"Aren't you moving in with Buzz into his great house?"

"When the time is right, Sammy. But if you leave now, there'll be no room for you in the great house."

Sammy walked up to Carol, all this time ignoring Marla. He kissed her on the cheek. "You'll never lock me out. You're my Mom. Later."

Slamming the door shut, Sammy left the apartment. Carol went to the window, looked out. Sally was in her car, waiting for Sammy.

"You might think I'm the worst mother and it's true. But I needed a break anyway."

CHAPTER TWENTY-TWO

"Knock, knock," Evelyn said sticking her head into Marla's little office dimply lit only by a desk lamp.

"Hey, c'mon in."

Evelyn switched on the main light switch by the door. "Let there be light."

"Gee, thanks."

"They told me you were here, but it's Thursday. What's up?"

"Oh, Evelyn, this seems to be the only peaceful place in my life," Marla said.

Evelyn's face lit up. She sat down opposite Marla, put her feet up on the desk facing Marla's, leaned back in the guest chair same as Marla was leaning in her chair. They were a mirror image of each other. "I'm so happy you said that."

"Because?"

"Because it's been on my mind and on some of the other execs' minds, that we should be able to do more with you. The camera loves you but we had this wild idea about showing off your brain as well. Hm?"

Marla nodded.

"Well?"

"OK, OK. What's the hook?" Marla asked.

"What if I say that we want you to try to develop a new segment for *FRIDAY SEGMENTS*. Something fresh. Local, interesting, maybe impossible? Just take a shot at it. If you think it'd really interfere with your day job, we'll understand."

"What would Reed say?"

"It was his idea, believe it or not," Evelyn said.

"I don't have a day job, Evelyn. Only the weather. I quit Jonathan."

"He came on to you?"

"Well, he told me his feelings and I told him mine."

"I'd be lying if I'd say I'm sorry. His loss is our gain. Agree?"

Marla didn't answer.

"I don't want to stop doing the weather. I like it."

"We like it, too. So, let's make a deal." Evelyn was almost jubilant.

"This is too simple. Is there a catch? I mean I know that people, highly qualified people, trained journalists, are dying to get on the *FRIDAY SEGMENTS* staff."

"Well, Marla, they're just not lucky."

"OK, let's talk this out. What do I do? Oprah? I hate Oprah." Marla's thoughts were businesslike, not emotional.

"I am on the same page. That show is sensational, patronizing and manipulative. It's a hit," said Evelyn. "But don't do Oprah. Do Marla."

Evelyn got up, went around the desk, patted her on her shoulders. "Go see Reed tomorrow, talk about what you want to do. We need your succinct advertising brain. I'll prepare a contract. Or, do you have an agent?"

Marla started laughing. "Do I need another hole in my head?"

Marla looked after Evelyn and then looked up.

"Thank you, Mom. You're the best agent!"

As Marla headed out of the building, she passed by Rhonda Smither's office. *Got Gossip, Call Rhonda,* said the sign on the door next to Marla's office. Just then, a petite blonde with silver highlights in her hair, wiggled down the corridor toward Marla.

"Oh, you're the weather girl, hello, hello," she said with a high-pitched voice. "We meet, finally."

"Who are you?" Marla asked. When she saw Rhonda's face curl up and venom about to spew out, she grinned.

"I was joking. Bad joke, Rhonda. I know who you are. Can you forgive me? Without you I wouldn't know who is sleeping with whom, who is eating where and what and when and all those earth-shatteringly important things. Can you forgive me?"

Marla reached out to shake hands. Rhonda's face relaxed.

"OK, OK, but somebody's got to do it." She went inside, then stuck her head out and yelled after Marla, "Hey, weather girl, got gossip, call Rhonda."

"OK, gossip lady. Got weather, don't call me."

Marla was still grinning when she walked out to the parking lot. Reed Rhoades drove in, stopped next to her and rolled down his car window.

"Marla, you got the news?"

"What news?" she was deadpan.

"Oh, did I jump the gun?"

"You mean the offer to work with you? No, you didn't," she grinned.

"Well, do you want to come in and talk?"

"Now?"

"Yes, now. Now's as good as ever, right? Just give me a minute."

Reed drove to his assigned parking, grabbed his briefcase and joined Marla at the back entrance to the TV station.

Marla was at a loss about subject matter. Reed suggested to start with something or someone with which or whom she is familiar so that her line of questioning would be natural. She should know the message she wanted to deliver.

"Remember, the reason *FRIDAY SEGMENTS* is popular is that it's a potpourri. The audience has no idea what will be next. It's like real life," Reed said.

"What about getting rid of a demon, an albatross around my neck?" she asked.

The host's face lit up. "That could be very interesting. Personalizing something, or is it someone?"

"Someone."

"Personalizing someone of importance and playing off the first-hand knowledge? This is someone of importance, isn't it?"

Marla nodded.

"Just don't know the approach," she said.

"It'll come to you. Important local person? That is too good. Marla, you're full of surprises. Let me see your notes whenever you're ready." He gave her a thumbs-up and she returned to her own office. She changed her mind about leaving. This unexpected window of opportunity that opened as if it were a bolt of lightning, was her new lease on life. New life.

"Let there be light," she said, flipping on the switch. "Let there be more light." She turned on the desk lamp. "More, and more." She moved around and turned on every source of light she could find, including candles, decorative storm lights, everything, until the room was glowing. She paced up and down. She sat, she got up. She pulled her hair, flexed her fingers. She knocked on her forehead and shouted, "Let there be light!"

Indeed, the lights came on.

Marla dialed the phone. "Hello, Judy. This is Marla Hayes. Remember me? How are you?"

"Fine," came the weak answer. "Michael is married, you know. Oops, I shouldn't have said that."

"That's all right, don't worry. I saw him at Buzz and Carol's engagement party."

"Oh, then you knew." Judy's voice was beginning to gain strength. "What can I do for you, then?"

"I'm calling in an official capacity, Judy. KMRTV, you know? I work there now and have an idea for Michael."

"I don't know," Judy's voice trailed off. "We're in production."

"You don't have to know, Judy. I want to arrange for an interview with him. Have him call me, OK?"

"I don't think that's a good idea, if I may say so."

"Just tell him he owes me one. "

Michael and Bernie came out of his office and heard Judy say in disbelief, "Michael owes you one? Are you serious?"

"Whom do I owe what, this time?" Michael was jovial.

Judy didn't know how to cover this up. "It's Marla. Marla H…."

"I know which Marla. Just get her number. I'll call her after this meeting."

He and Bernie headed out the door. Michael turned back, "Or have her call me in a couple of hours."

Judy delivered the message with a disapproving tone.

When Marla and Michael talked later that day, he immediately scheduled her interview with him the following Monday afternoon and blocked out several hours. He didn't see anything wrong with accommodating Marla this way.

Marla arrived home drained from mental exhaustion. A hot Neutrogena bubble bath was called for. She grabbed a notepad to start the list of questions for the interview.

"I'm the audience," she spoke out loud. "What do I want to know about your television series. What will make me tune in? Does the name of the writer matter? Does the executive producer and his achievements matter?" Soaking in the silky water relaxed her. She was making notes, trying to hit on an unusual selling point. "Aren't people more interested in actors? The faces they know?"

She decided to watch some of the more successful previously aired episodes in an attempt to learn from Reed. She climbed out of the tub, put on a robe and continued with the list.

"Why would this kind of show be of interest to me? What makes it timely for today's audience? What makes it historical? Is it really historical? What makes it emotional TV?"

The DVD player barely began to run when she fell asleep on the couch in the den, her feet resting on her mother's trunk, her notepad containing pages and pages of questions falling to the floor.

Marla had never been in a film and television studio before and when she drove up to the main gate, she was nervous as a child. She was expecting something other than an active business production area and that driving to a *producer*, Michael's office would have some special requirements. Still, her min d was racing a mile a minute. Her own personal time with Michael was brief. Through a great deal of revisiting memories she came to understand that they were both just out of deep relationships, looking for inner peace. Meeting each other brought on promising thoughts and feelings. She felt no malice for

Michael. Things happen the way they are supposed to happen. She continued to rationalize. She was thinking that her knowing him before will now help her career and future. It was a trade but not a bad one.

She knew what she wanted to do about the interview but was not at all sure if Michael would go along with her or if he would want to take control. Definitely *nervous-making* time.

Judy looked different than Marla had imagined from her voice. Her beautiful telephone voice suggested a pretty woman in Marla's mind. When she saw the overweight, middle-aged person, she thought better than to say anything about her disappointment. It was basic politeness that got them through the first few minutes until she could enter Michael's private office. She nodded with appreciation on the contrast in decorating flavors between the ultra-modern reception area and Michael's office. A clear expression of the man's individuality.

Michael's warm smile put her at ease, as always. She told him she came ahead of her crew to get a general feeling going.

"You're nervous, and you should be," Michael said.

"How did you know?" she asked.

"First of all, don't forget I know you. Well, not much, but enough to know that you're at a turning point."

Marla grimaced, making fun of herself. "Guess mine is not a poker face."

And a peaceful feeling settled between them.

"So, the plan is that if I come in with you as my first interview, it'll be BIG. I'll have set the precedent for the level of movers and shakers that I want to feature."

Michael started laughing. The two of them were chatting as if no time had passed between them.

"What's funny?" she asked.

"I looked in on the show Friday. Does the host, what's his name, Reed, have any idea of what you're doing? You'll make him look pretty weak."

"He knows I have a big gun lined up but he doesn't know it's you." A conspiratorial laughter connected two people who were never far apart.

"My cameraman will be here at 4:00, and we'll just roll through it like a tank."

"What about prep, Marla? Don't you want to give me your list of questions?"

"Don't writers start with *It was a dark and stormy night?*" she laughed.

"Got it." He went along with the kidding. "Then we continue with 'the wagon train struggled forward, horses overworked, men overwrought, women and children trying their best'."

"Really? That's deep."

"No, no," he said. "I'm teasing. Where's your sense of humor that I remember so well." They looked at each other with so much angst and meaning and yearning. The silence was suddenly thick.

Marla stood up. "This is harder than I thought."

"We can do it," came Michael's encouragement.

"Tell me out loud that you're not my man," she said softly.

Michael understood that it had to be said. "I am not your man, Marla. I am your friend."

She took a deep breath, looked out the office window and saw her crew arrive.

"They're here. Now, Michael, we'll talk about the show. Your show only. I am not looking for gossip or sensationalism. Let others do that. We'll talk about how the idea was born. What makes you think it's worth my time. I am the audience, remember?"

They were at ease. Marla listened. Michael was surprised to hear himself talk about the pride he found himself feeling for his new series. Marla made him comfortable. He forgot he was being taped.

"It's the idea of how history repeats itself. How we don't learn from our mistakes. That thought had been festering in me for a long time. Finally, I found a vehicle in which to explore it. Then I took contemporary attitudes, characters I know firsthand, and wondered how they would have behaved a hundred years ago. That's it, in a nutshell."

"There must be a great number of people who feel the same way, who have the same curiosity," Marla said.

"And who know the same people I wrote about," Michael interrupted. "The network wanted to do the series almost immediately. Why? Identification. Either the decision makers identified or they felt that there is an audience who would identify with the characters, their efforts, their attitudes, achievements and so on."

"Or who would be as curious as you are. Obviously, the old west and the battles that shaped it…"

"Is who we are today." Michael was really going. "The gangs, we had them then and now; the power struggles on many levels, then and now; the meek and the strong, then and now; the believers and the atheists, then and now. *Ad infinitum.*"

"Nothing changes. Love, sex, greed, envy, revenge…." Michael took a deep breath. Marla turned to the camera.

"Well, on this note, we say so long to everyone in the audience who stayed tuned. Thank you. Until next time…." She made a small waving motion almost under her chin. It was endearing.

"It's a wrap," the director said.

Unnoticed, Linda came in.

The crew was ready to pack up and go. Michael walked over to Marla. They hugged. "Well, what did you make me do?"

They laughed with great release of tension. "Nothing you didn't want to do. And thank you, Michael. Really. It's supposed to be on this coming Friday. And the name of the show is…."

"*FRIDAY SEGMENTS*. I know. Four o'clock." Michael leaned close to kiss her and their farewell kiss was on the lips.

Linda watched and frowned. Marla had no idea she was there and practically flew by her as she left the office. The crew was already loaded onto their van. They drove out of the studio.

"I didn't expect you here, Linda," Michael said.

"Do I know it. You're picking up with your old girl friend now that I'm pregnant." She was about to rage.

Michael gently took her by the arm and guided her out of the office. He turned to Judy, "If it can wait, I don't want to take any calls. Linda and I will be relaxing at home."

Linda's pregnancy wasn't showing much since she had always been a touch on the plump side. Michael gently guided her to the Rolls. As she settled in the passenger seat, she straightened her back and her posture took on a special pride. This was her car, Michael was her husband, it was his baby she was carrying and she was Mrs. Michael Gaston, none other. She looked at Michael behind the wheel.

"I'm sorry, Michael," she said sweetly. "Are you mad at me?"

"No, not really, Linda, honey, but don't be showing up unexpectedly, OK?"

"Then you do have something to hide." She probed, still sweet as honey.

"I have a career. A professional life. If I don't pay attention it can slip away. Younger guys with younger ideas can take my place. There'll be no Rolls Royce, no mansion, no house staff, nothing. So, if you want our children to have a great life and a great future…"

"Did you say children, Michael?" Her face lit up. "We'll have more than one?"

Michael smiled. "Yes, Linda, we'll do it all." He put his hand on her knee and patted it. "You can be so cute sometimes and a real monster at other times."

She reached out and massaged his neck.

"That feels good. Really good."

"Before we go all out, I mean, make a lot of babies, I need a tiny favor. I've been talking with this nutritionist. He's also a personal trainer."

"That would be good for your self-esteem, getting your shape back, maybe even realizing that there are ways to quit drugs."

She continued the deep rub with her strong fingers.

After a beat she spoke, "I need an orgasm."

"I can help," Michael volunteered.

"You can watch. That'll help." She gazed at him wickedly.

He grinned. "What will you think of next?" he said in amazement.

And she continued the deep rub with her strong fingers. Michael stepped on the gas.

Well, why not?

CHAPTER TWENTY-THREE

"How about breaking bread with an old friend? Me?" Warren said in a voice message to Marla. "I'd like to be seen with a celebrity. Call me... Please."

Marla felt goose bumps on hearing his voice again. She was afraid to see him, to listen to his boasting. She knew only too well that was part of what kept him going, part of the self-confident *persona* he had developed under the tutelage of his rich parents. But, he was now a working actor, a recognizable commodity. Pleasing Sherrie Romany paid off, kept him in a recurring role in her husband, Eugene's television series. Marla knew that what he was doing was no different from a street whore, but it served his purpose, he had fun and it was the way to go in Hollywood since time beginning.

They met at the Peninsula Hotel.

"You don't mind being seen with me, Marla? Do you?" Warren tried humor to get the conversation going.

"Since I know how 'being seen' in the right places is an actor's tool, I don't mind," she said.

"With the right people. Don't you forget it," he said.

A small loaf of bread was placed in front of them. He didn't bother with the knife and the butter on the cutting board. He lifted the bread, broke it in half. She accepted the piece he handed to her. The look in her eyes assured him that he got to her and once again, he was in charge. He appeared interested in everything about her. She liked that.

She told him that doing weather on the weekends was scary at first but she was becoming pretty good at it. As soon as she understood what happened behind the camera and in front, what the audience saw and what she saw, she relaxed.

"Weather is my real job. I can do an occasional interview if I come up with interesting subjects. I was lucky getting a major TV producer but now it's up to me to maintain the standard." She laughed softly. "I don't know how to top it. Someone has to be either but preferably both, fascinating or famous. Important but not obnoxious. Just don't know."

"An actor?" Warren asked.

"Not likely. I don't think actors should be let out without a script."

"That's pretty harsh."

"I don't think actors know who they are until someone gives them a character."

"OK, OK, I got it," Warren said, but she went on.

"A great number of actors can rarely talk without grammatical errors. Just because a good piece of writing in a good script brings out the best of their talent, interpretive talent, it doesn't mean that they know anything. Anything about issues. They can have an opinion, but that's just one person's opinion. They should not try to influence their fans' thinking. I can't give them a forum. You know what I mean, Warren?" She sipped on her drink and laughed out loud.

Warren was stunned by the strength of her conviction.

"My mother said actors are needy little children,"

"Isn't that too general, Marla?"

"Oh, maybe ten percent have innate intelligence."

"Ten?" Warren wasn't happy.

"OK, I'll give you twenty. Better?" Marla smiled.

"All that time I never knew that's how you felt. I thought you loved me."

Marla smiled. "Loving you has nothing to do with your work as an actor or my work as anything. You're talented and with a good script, who knows, you might be a star. In the meantime, you're working, you're getting recognition, you're signed for a co-starring role on a cops and robbers mini-series that should elevate your standing maybe all the way to the big screen. I am beginning to understand a lot more about your business than I did at first."

Warren thought about this for a while. "So, you think it's the script, not me?"

"What do you want to hear?"

Marla busied herself with the meal.

"I don't mean to hurt your feelings, you know that. But actors interpret."

"Honey," Warren said with his sexiest, most endearing smile. "Far be it from me to combine our family life with business. Just wanted to congratulate you. Wanted to help you celebrate. We were pretty good together once."

As they started to walk out of the restaurant, they saw across the lobby the paparazzi outside the hotel. They knew that at the moment even they were considered celebrities by some. Certain scandal sheets were known to hold on to photos in their stock file in case the subjects do become recognizable big names. Warren turned to the Concierge who took their parking tickets and arranged that their cars be brought around in the back, away from the flashing cameras.

Warren didn't think twice about inviting himself to the "old homestead." He wanted to see it, have a drink. Reminisce. Marla thought she was strong enough to withstand him. She was wrong. Lovemaking was inevitable. His familiar touch made her crumble. She had no reservations, no inhibitions, nothing to block the surge of feelings that overtook her senses, her body and mind, like a volcano's lava rush to satiation. Wow!

After a few minutes of rest, Warren got out of bed, went to the kitchen and prepared two wine spritzers, put them on a tray. Sliced some cheese and apples and headed back to the bedroom. As he walked through, he studied the home he once called his own, he inhaled the scent of cut flowers, closed his eyes and a genuine smile filled his face.

"Our picnic. The afterglow. Just like old times, remember?"

"I love it," she said.

"Marla Hayes on TV. I never knew this was in you, honey," Warren said, praising.

"Neither did I. I'm glad I made you proud and that brought you back home."

She went to sleep happy. During the next few days Warren accompanied her everywhere except when he had to work. They were at restaurants and sporting events. Some entertainment columnists showed interest.

At the El Torito Grill one restaurant they ran into Rhonda Smither, the *"Gossip Minute"* lady at KMRTV. She was friendly to Marla before but now she was going overboard.

"Marla, you're the hottest thing in entertainment news. And the weekend weather is *Must See TV*," she enthused.

"Not exactly, but thanks for saying so, Rhonda. I appreciate it."

"And you, Warren?"

"This is her time," Warren said. "I'm here to show my support."

"Rhonda, let's talk in the office, not here, OK?" Marla said. "We really would like to eat."

"Good idea. But before I go, would you scoop me about who your next interview will be? Could it be Warren?"

"Definitely not. I'll not scoop you, OK?"

"All right, Marla." She stopped and turned. "What about this?" Rhonda pulled the proof of an upcoming *In Style* magazine from her bag and opened it. Inside Marla saw Warren in his SciFi character costume posing as background to European Supermodel Carlotta Rainee. The following pages depicted each of the beautiful model's outfits coordinated with a fictional TV or film character in the background by the actor identifiable with that role.

"This is wonderful," Marla said. "Good exposure for Warren. He deserves it."

"I'm here, "Warren said. "Don't talk about me in third."

"You know, you're right. Maybe there's a little tension in the air," Rhonda said.

"No such things. We're starting new," Warren said. "A two career family unlike before.

Rhonda, a contemporary Hedda Hopper, looked at them with doubting eyes. "Wonderful, right." She swished away and returned to her table.

"That was pretty patronizing, Warren."

"I didn't mean to be."

"Are you sure?"

"I am," Warren said. "Just relax . We're starting new, right?"

"Right, honey. I'm sorry."

They ordered wine and munched on chips and salsa.

Warren looked as if his brain would burst.

"What's on your mind, Warren?"

"No, nothing really."

"Well, you can tell me. You have to tell me, if we are starting new," she insisted.

"All right then, am I your next interview?"

"For the last time, No. "

"But if Rhonda Smither implies that in her column, wouldn't it be warranted?"

"Are you going to go to work on her now? Or have you already been in her pants?"

Warren made an effort to let that one slide.

"Marla, everybody who sees us together probably thinks I will be the interview."

"Is that what you think?"

"I hope."

"You don't meet any of the criteria, dear. None."

"What is the criteria?"

"Are."

"What are the criteria, may I ask the scholar of the day."

Marla ignored the snide remark. "Local achiever—first time something; local achiever who turned his life around—who gives back to the community; local famous, intimidating, scientist in our midst. Someone I can admire and at the same time translate my admiration into identification. The stuff America is made of. Not an actor. OK?"

Warren was unhappy, ready to put her down, belittle her as in old times, except by now, Marla could hold her own.

"You used to love actors."

"Until I got to know them," she laughed. "Well, some. Just enough. Can we just leave it alone and be people together?"

Warren calmed down. "You're right. Maybe down the line I can change your mind."

"Maybe," she said just to be done with the subject. She reached out to hold his hand. His eyes searched around the restaurant to see if anyone was watching them. A photographer's flash-click let them know they were not alone. They smiled at each other for the public eye even though their conversation turned sour.

"What time do you work on Saturday?" he asked.

"Four. What do you have in mind?"

"Carolyn's son is in rehab. I want to go see him. Since you're working anyway, I thought you wouldn't mind."

"Whatever happened to Carolyn?" she asked.

"You don't want to know. Well, maybe you do. It'll give you a vicarious thrill. You can gloat. She pissed me off. She left me for Burt Ryan."

"Ryan? I thought he moved in with the singer, you know, Deborah something."

"Shayne. He lived with Carolyn first. Played father to the kids. My kids. I mean, I loved them like my own. I think that's when the boy got hooked on drugs. No one paid any attention to him."

"Like you did?" Marla was curious. "What did happen?"

"I was good for the kids. I encouraged him with his singing, I drove him to every recording session and he was never out of my sight. Then she left me."

"So, you say Carolyn is not a good parent?"

"Carolyn is not a good parent and the real father, somewhere in San Francisco, is uninterested. Ryan left her, then Ryan left Shayne, and I don't remember who was the next one but Carolyn was left out in the cold."

"But you always had Sherrie in your back pocket, didn't you?"

"That's business," he announced. "No more, no less."

The evening did not get any better.

———— ♦ ————

Saturday morning at the tennis club Marla and Warren beat everyone in mixed doubles. They were tuned into each other on the court before and now. They always enjoyed great satisfaction in playing tennis. Afterward, Warren went his separate way.

Marla was scheduled to work the afternoon and early evening shifts that Saturday. The weather was blistery hot in Los Angeles as had been all week. The official make-up person touched up her face. They laughed a lot. Marla's face coloring was so naturally balanced that powdering her nose was pretty much all she needed in those touch-up sessions.

The voice of the director came on the loudspeaker. "Well, folks, we have a big decision to make. Evelyn just called. She said if we want to broadcast the weather from some interesting location out of the studio, it's OK with her."

"Griffith Park," came a suggestion.

"Hollywood Bowl!" another one.

"Will Rogers Park?"

"I was thinking about the beach," the director said.

"I'm always ready for the beach," Marla said.

"How ready are you?" Laughter filled the studio.

"Have my bikini, skirt, hat, ready, you know."

"OK, then, Santa Monic a here we come." The director led the way to the van, then turned back. "Gotta stay with my monitors," he said as he saw the base crew run the remote broadcast check-list.

One of the news anchors wearing his make-up bib said, "Couldn't we do the whole show from the beach?"

The director yelled back, "Afraid not. Only the privileged few."

———◆———

Carlotta Rainee, the gorgeous European supermodel, was used to having some heads turning in her wake as she was coming out of a beachside condo building. Wearing a short beach wrap, holding hands with Warren, her first American conquest, she was strutting mischievously. Even though they hid behind huge sunglasses, the glow of lust in her eyes burnt right into Warren and he was cockily showing off with having such a beauty on his arm. They walked hand-in-hand toward the pier. His large-rimmed floppy straw hat made him blend in or at least unrecognizable. When they reached the pier they went down the stairs and continued to walk into the sand, moving slowly toward the columns under the pier. Once in the shadows, their sexual drive kicked in, their heat rose. Carlotta, uninhibited with a huge sexual appetite, clearly wanted it all, right then and there. She licked his suntanned neck, planted little kisses on his arm and worked her way toward his muscular chest. Warren didn't need much more encouragement. They went at it hot and heavy.

———◆———

Marla looked carefree and bright as she reported on the heat wave. Wearing a wrap-around beach skirt of flimsy see-through fabric over her bikini, she was at ease, having fun. The audience on the beach was hooked as were those watching on television. Never knowing what Marla will do next made the *KMRTV weather* a popular show.

The camera followed her impulsively heading toward the ocean. "Let me test these waters." She put one foot in it. "It is my duty to report to you that the water is fabulous. Come on down, you won't be sorry."

She gestured around with her arms. "Look at the fun all these people frolicking in the sun are having and," she glanced at the monitor in front of her showing the camera panning the fun-loving people on the beach. The camera stopped on Warren and Carlotta who did not look up until they heard applause around them.

"And look, we have a celebrity in our midst. Looks like supermodel

Carlotta Rainee, I believe, amusing herself with… looks like none other than TV star Warren Traynor, my husband… well, ex.”

She was back on camera again. “OK, back to you in the studio.”

She looked toward the pier but Warren and Carlotta had hightailed it out of there. Her cameraman *cum* driver came over and handed her the telephone. It was Evelyn. “You know your ratings will skyrocket after this.”

“Do people think I can top this?” Marla asked self-deprecating.

“I really care more about how you feel? Do you want to go back on the air for the next report?” Evelyn turned out to be the most caring person Marla had ever met.

“You know, I kinda’ have to. The old me would have curled up in a corner but that would make me a loser.” She stopped for a beat. “I want to do the next report. I’ll finish my schedule. But, thanks for asking.”

As Marla hung up the phone, a very pretty blonde, about Marla’s age, came over.

“Hello. My name is Cybill Dunn. My husband and friends are over there, see the fancy tent? Well, I think you could use a glass of wine about now.”

Marla thought for a moment.

“Maybe that’s the answer,” she said, laughing. “And my crew?”

“We have plenty,” Cybill answered. They followed her to the open tent set up by the ocean, with all the amenities of a fine picnic spread. A private party in the middle of a public beach party. So very California. Cybill introduced everyone, especially her husband, Marcus, a retired public relations man. There was no doubt, they loved being together.

After the six o’clock local news, when Marla was finished with her reports, she joined Cybill and her friends for dinner at Jeff King’s Ocean Avenue Seafood. During the course of the evening, Cybill gave Marla a note with an address on it.

“Marla, listen. Marcus and I are going to Lisbon next month. He has to work in Europe for about a year. Here is our address and number. Maybe you can visit. One never knows.”

“Lisbon? Cascais Bay,” she said dreamily.

“Oh, then you’ve been there. Maybe you’ll come back,” Cybill cheerfully babbled on.

“I would like to. One never knows,” Marla said.

It was almost ten o’clock when Cybill and Marcus dropped her off at the station. She got into her car and headed home.

Warren wasn’t there. She systematically picked up his things and threw them out into the street. And that was that.

Next day at the studio, Rhonda rushed over to Marla’s office, showing her a photo of Warren picking up his things in the dark of the night while Carlotta waited for him in a convertible.

“Courtesy of my friends at large,” Rhonda said. “Exclusive!”

“Congratulations,” Marla said, attempting to be busy at her desk.

"I'll use it on today's *Minute* even before it hits the papers. Marla, do you realize what this means?"

"That he'll be ridiculed in a larger public than before."

"No, no, my naïve little friend," Rhonda said breathlessly. "I'll make him famous! He'll be a star! Wait and see what I can do!"

She flitted out of the office, leaving a bewildered Marla behind her desk.

"Naïve. That's me," she said.

CHAPTER TWENTY-FOUR

Sebastian and his band of Spanish tennis players were on his private jet. The six young men were lounging, watching movies, reading, enjoying the long flight to America to play the circuit in the U.S. and catch the attention of tennis aficionados with their performance. They were glad Sebastian had come with them for a change and they could travel like kings. First stop, Palm Springs, California.

Sebastian carefully paged through computer printouts in his office in the front of the plane. One page had a small picture of Marla Hayes on the left top corner. The vital statistics about her were nothing new. What interested him was the page with photos of her in the bikini on the beach and the zoom shots of Warren with the model. He turned the page and on the back of the photo was the name and address of the model, telephone numbers, e-mail address, her agency *EMANUELLA 'S MODELS OF THE CONTINENT*.

Sebastian dialed. "Hello. Monique, dear. Is my sister there?"

"Just one moment, señor," said the receptionist in Barcelona.

"Ciao, Sebastião, where are you?" came Emanuella's masculine voice.

"How did you like Carlotta? Or didn't you catch the act?"

"Nuella, I don't appreciate what you're doing. I don't like you spying on anyone for me."

"What makes you think I was spying for you? It's Carlotta. I'm keeping an eye on my models. Coincidence, dear brother. Let it go."

"You didn't plant her?"

"No. It must be a sign from above. The Gods are working with me. We'll find you the woman of your future." She laughed at her own clever prophecy.

"Who took the spy shot?"

"Silva. You remember, Sylva, my lover last April?" Emanuella said with a satisfied gurgle in her voice.

"And you trust him with Carlotta?"

"I don't really care. I'm through with artists, photographers and such. You'll be happy to hear I have a new man. A banker. You know, president of the bank."

"I am happy to hear that, Nuella."

"Are you sure Carlotta is….?"

"All wrong. Even on a bad day I could not spend more than twenty consecutive minutes with her. Although, I'm guessing she liked this assignment as much as a lingerie runway show."

"The less clothes, the better. You know how kinky she is," Emanuella said snickering.

"We're only young once." Sebastian was still looking at the photo of the model and Warren. "You know, she looked really good even in that messy setting. All that mud. Under the pier. How gauche. Anyway, maybe you should put her in movies, hm?"

"Whatever you say, brother. I'll look into it. Anything else?"

"Not now. We'll be landing in Palm Springs in a couple of hours."

"Is that where Marla lives?" Emanuella was curious.

"You don't expect me to be that obvious, do you now?" Sebastian laughed. "She plays tennis, remember?"

"Yes, I've got it. Tennis is the key. You jocks make strange bedfellows."

"You say your models are any better? More valuable? Honorable?" Sebastian laughed.

"Of course not. Just commodities, that's all. Keep me posted, dear. Ciao."

Sebastian liked his privacy and liked his power. He didn't get involved in his sister's modeling agency although he always laughed at the way it got started. Emanuella, an extremely well educated, refined but unattractive girl, was possessed with the idea of marrying off her handsome brother. By becoming an international modeling agent, she had access to the most beautiful girls around the world. She would visit her brother carrying a portfolio of photos of those whom she considered worthy of him. Carlotta was not one of them. She was naughty, fun loving and couldn't care less about her future. When she smiled, she lit up the world and anyone in her presence knew that *life was good*. Her lanky body, daringly different haircut, flawless, glowing skin, radiated sex. Emanuella tried to give her some insight into class, but it didn't take. However, on her own, Carlotta developed a style of walking and moving that was uniquely elegant. Simple. She did not wiggle her bottom, she did not shake her shoulders. Her stride had the regal refinement of Audrey Hepburn. It was a good idea, however, to keep her from talking in public. She was street. Loveable, but street.

———— ◆ ————

Marla watched the first days of the BNP Paribas Open on television. She grew restless and decided to drive down to Palm Springs. She was hoping to get there early to buy a ticket for the day. She loved driving into the sunrise in the wee hours of the morning, although difficult, it was spiritually uplifting. She remembered Sebastian and his players. It seemed that the top seeds liked playing against Sebastian's team because while they were often destined to lose, they would give anybody a tough match. And, frequently surprising only the uninformed, one of those Spaniards would come out and rise all the way to the top ten.

Indian Wells in the Coachella Valley desert seemed an unlikely place for a world class tennis event but over the years the fans have made it a smashing success, the crown jewel of tennis in the famous Palm Springs resort destination.

At the tennis complex she found out that they would start late because of the overtime of international soccer television scheduling. The scalpers were not ready to drop ticket prices but she hoped they would as they would get closer to the start time. In the meantime, she wanted to check into the local shopping possibilities. She had not been in Palms Springs for over a year and a lot of changes can happen that would interest her.

It was still early in the day. She drove over to the El Paseo Shopping District known as the Rodeo Drive of the Desert. El Paseo boasts a wide spectrum of stores from Sak's Fifth Avenue to world-class shops, clothing boutiques, art galleries, jewelers, restaurants all lined along a beautifully maintained picture-postcard floral and statue-filled mile.

Sak's Fifth had only been open for a short while when she pulled up in their parking lot. Out of the corner of her eye she thought she recognized best-selling author Sid Sheraton coming out of Sak's. She had seen him on talk shows pushing his books but Marla wasn't entirely sure it was he. She could not explain exactly what impulse compelled her when she went over to him.

"Hi, Mr. Sheraton. Are you? Excuse me, but I'd like to ask a question." She talked fast but was instantly cut off by body guards. She now knew for sure that he was the real thing.

The shoppers around the parking lot were blasé. Too many famous people lived in their midst for decades and none of them required any special attention. Discouraged, Marla gave up, turned and headed for the store entrance when one of the two body guards came after her.

"Miss, Mr. Sheraton would like to talk with you."

She followed him to the Chrysler 300 stretch limousine and got into the back where the great author was sitting. The tall grey haired man, wearing orthopedic shoes, dressed casual expensive, still looked intimidating. His long legs extended to the middle of the interior where the normal bar area had been customized to give room to book shelves and magazine racks and an oversized TV screen.

"Welcome to my mobile living room suite," he said, gesturing around toward the driver and passenger seats which were assigned to the body guards and the two additional folding swivel seats that could face the front or turn and relax in the *living room suite*.

"I am Sid Sheraton. And if I recall correctly, you work in a bikini when it's too hot." He smiled as she turned beet red. "You have a question, you said?" His lips seemed to hold in a perpetual smile and the way his eyes settled on her she was sure he was listening closely.

"Yes." She was trying to catch her breath. "Did you know my mother, Kathi Hayes?"

He looked like he was trying to recollect the name, anything.

"I'm afraid the name doesn't ring a bell. Perhaps if I saw her face?"

"She's dead now but she had some memorabilia." Marla could hardly push the words out of her throat.

"Well, here is a postal drawer," he said reaching into the side pocket of the car, pulling out a business card and handing it to her. "Send it to me. The memorabilia. Maybe it will ring a bell."

"Now, if you don't mind, I have to get going."

Marla got out of the car, reached in to shake his hand.

"I'll be looking forward to your weather reports. Maybe it'll get hot again." He liked his own humor and laughed a rich laughter.

"Oh, by the way, there's a tennis tournament in town. Do you like tennis?" he asked.

"Are you kidding? I love tennis, even more than…"

"Well, let's not go that far. Here, have a ticket. My wife only goes to the finals so I only go to the finals."

He drove off. She stood there with a post office box number and a tournament ticket.

Marla couldn't believe what had just happened to her. She gave out a scream and this time people stopped to see what that was about. She drove back to Indian Wells. The Tennis Garden was filling up. She had a bite to eat. Her favorite tennis park snack, the big pretzel with Gulden's yellow mustard and seltzer. She walked around, watched some of the warm-up matches, then went to her seat.

Minutes later, one of the ushers handed her a note. The director of the broadcasting company wanted to know if she, Marla Hayes of KMRTV, would mind being on camera since she was in Sid Sheraton's box. She wrote back "No, thank you. Marla."

But the ESPN camera picked her up anyway and while she didn't appear on the network, she did appear on cable briefly and was seen by Pablo in the players' lounge. He was alone, resting, glancing at the TV screens on the walls all around him when he suddenly recognized Marla. He put on a weird, cover-up cap and sunglasses, and headed out to find her. Marla didn't want to deal with other misunderstandings and left her seat to move elsewhere. She almost ran into Pablo.

She was startled by his voice. "Miss Three Sheets," he said to her curious face.

"Pablo?" she said, unsure until he took off his sunglasses. "Hello," she reached out for a handshake but Pablo kissed her on both cheeks.

"My name is really Marla, you know."

"Si. Sebastian explained it."

"Marla," he said slowly. "Marla," he said again.

"Yes?"

"Where do you sit? I saw you in the box?"

"I made a mistake. I shouldn't have sat in that box."

"OK, OK," he took her by the arm. "You come and sit with us."

With that, Pablo guided Marla to the Spanish players' box at center court. They sat down quickly. A match was starting.

Marla didn't notice until after the first set that Sebastian in a floppy hat was sitting next to her. They looked at each other. She reached her hand for a handshake and once again, was kissed on both cheeks. Back to the match.

Later on, it was time for cocktails at the Marriott lounge.

"It's amazing," Marla said. "To be running into you."

"I was going to call you," he said. "Right after the tour. We're staying here for a few days, then off to Miami."

"Is everyone playing in Miami?"

"No, only Pablo and David. David is really hot. He came from 156 to 28 in the rankings this past few months."

"Wow. He'll surprise everyone in Miami." Marla was enthusiastic.

"That's the idea but it depends on the draw. Right now we'll go one step at the time."

"And one point at the time," she laughed.

"How long are you staying in Palm Springs?" he asked.

"I'm going back tonight." She stopped suddenly. "You know, I owe you an apology."

"Why is that, Marla?"

She took a deep breath. It was difficult. "This is hard. I should've stayed in touch with you, Sebastian. You were the best thing, the best man, who ever happened to me, in my life." She stopped to think. "Yes, in my entire life. And I ran away from you and I was sorry at one point."

"Are you still sorry?" His face lit up. "Can we do anything about it?"

"Why do you care? Why are you so nice to me?"

"That's a two-part question. Let's just go slower," he smiled.

"OK, OK, you're right."

"Do you have to go back tonight? We can get you a room right here. Then we can talk. About everything."

His calmness brought back good memories.

"You know, why not? I could stay the night."

"Be my guest, please."

"I'm always your guest. This time, I have a good credit card plus an expense account."

"Why would you think like that. You're with me." He reached for the in-house phone in the back of their booth and reserved a room for Marla.

"Yes, Ms. Marla Hayes," he said on the phone.

"Yes, from TV," he said nodding.

"How do you know?" she asked when he hung up.

"I know everything."

"I'm serious," she grinned. "How do you know? "

"It's the gossip magazines. You and your ex-husband and another beautiful woman."

"Yeah, I fell for it all. People don't change. When will I learn?"

"Let's take a swim and have a little dinner, hm?" He waited for her to finish the cocktail.

Marla was completely comfortable with him.

"Like old times, Sebastian. I follow you anywhere like a puppy dog." She laughed. "You may be the only friend I have. Definitely the only one I can trust."

They went into the hotel's *Colonnade* shop loaded with designer labels. He bought a bathing suit for her and a change of clothing for the next morning. He put his key card down and the entire transaction took seconds. One of his players called. He wanted to know whether or not he would join them for dinner. He told them he was with his friend, Marla Hayes.

In the pool, she splashed and played like a child.

"What were you doing in Sid Sheraton's box?"

"I made a mistake."

"It didn't look like it. You sat down exactly where your ticket took you."

"It was still a mistake."

"All right, we'll get back to that when you're ready."

She became serious for the first time. "Are you watching me? Why?"

"Not exactly watching you but keeping abreast of your life. I'll be honest, Marla. For some inexplicable reason, you got under my skin when you were in Spain. Time flew when we were together. I have tried to analyze what it was. The attraction? Besides the exterior," he spoke slowly, "Your moral values impressed me. Your curiosity, your grasp of everything that was important to me came so naturally."

Sebastian leaned back in the chaise lounge, looked at the people around them. "There's no one else here right now. Just you and I. We're alone."

Marla soaked in all that he had said. "I had no idea. Why didn't you say anything?"

"I had no idea for the longest time. Until I saw myself comparing every other woman to you. They didn't have your anything. Your magic."

"You'll make me cry."

"See, that's it. Exactly. I want to make you laugh. Not cry. But I have to wait."

"For what?"

"Until you see your way to me clearly. Until there is no one else cluttering your life. No Warren, no bosses, no Michael, no Jonathan, no Reed."

How do you know?

"I know. I have to know."

"You're spying? That's terrible."

"Marla, slow down. You told me about running away from it all. Then I saw Warren in the gossip papers. There are stories I can read."

"I'm pretty much going after the career, Sebastian. After Warren I thought I had a good thing with the writer, Michael. As you say you've read about me. He got taken by another woman."

"But at work? What about work?"

"I love what I'm doing. I have so much to learn. Every day is new. In advertising there was Jonathan who taught me, then turned on me. And Carol. Well, you don't want to know about her." She made a gesture with her hand, indicating that Carol was not a nice person for him to know.

"And your boss?"

"Evelyn is the best. I'm so lucky."

"I read an interview with Reed Rhoades, he was glowing about you."

"Well, I glow right back about him. He is a beautiful person. Unselfish, professional."

"And did you take special fancy…"

Marla rose, pulled on her wrap. "Sebastian, don't go there. Especially not now after what you've said."

Sebastian followed her. "A mistake, Marla. I was joshing. I know you're sensitive about intimate things. I apologize."

"You and your special fancy.… Do you think you're talking to some child? Do you expect a report of some kind? Really…" She got up. "I'll be out of here first thing in the morning. Thank you for everything," Marla said.

Sebastian looked after her. She wore the designer labels as if she were born into them. There was something dignified about her that was positively appealing. When she disappeared inside the hotel, he dialed his sister.

"Nuella, I've just put both feet in my mouth with the woman of my future," he said.

"Hello, Sebastião. It is dawn here. Early, early dawn. Way before my time," she whispered.

"I had to tell you. You're the only one I can tell. I feel terrible. I did the only thing I know makes her angry."

"What?"

"Pried. For the second time, pried into her personal life. I don't know what gets into me. I just want to know everything from her." He took a deep breath. "I'm such a fool."

"Do flowers, Seb. Flowers. Big, Big flowers with a nice note."

"She's not the Big, Big flower type."

"Then do little ones. Do small flowers. Don't come back here without making peace with her."

"And you, Nuella?"

"Someone, a beautiful, beautiful man, happens to be bringing me espresso even as we speak. You're on your own, my dear. I have to go now. Ciao."

She hung up. Sebastian was happy for his sister. And he had to devise a plan. He came a long way to see Marla. She mattered to him and he hated how she would confuse him, set him on the wrong track. With everyone else, he was in absolute control. Not with Marla.

Sebastian said 'good bye' to his team. Told them he would go to Los Angeles instead of Miami. His assistant in *Tolédo* received instructions about his change of plans and needs, while he asked the Marriott Concierge to make reservations for him at the Beverly Hills Hotel, have a driver pick him up at Los Angeles International Airport and reserve a late model convertible to be waiting at the hotel. He wanted to do as much as possible by himself to keep things private.

———— ◆ ————

The new white Thunderbird, Sebastian's rental car, pulled up at KMRTV's gate. Carefully packed in a box to keep it anchored, a flower arrangement sat on the floor of the passenger seat. He asked to see Marla. She was not in, but expected shortly.

Then he asked for Evelyn Baker. The guard turned his back to Sebastian as he talked on the telephone in his booth. After describing Sebastian to Evelyn, he was given a pass. A perky little woman, Evelyn's secretary, Barbie, introduced herself and asked that he follow her to Evelyn's office. Barbie wore a midi-skirt with wedge straps and a very high collar, long sleeve blouse. She was skinny and some part of her seemed to always be in motion.

"This is for Marla," Sebastian said, handing the flowers to Barbie.

"I'll put it in her office." Barbie walked away.

"I'm Evelyn Baker, the manager of KMRTV. How can I help you?"

"My name is Sebastian *de Pombal*. I'm here to see Marla Hayes."

Evelyn sat down on the couch and signaled Sebastian to sit.

"I don't believe you, sir. Whatever business you have with Marla, you can discuss with me. She does not represent the station."

"Even personal business?"

"How personal?"

Sebastian sensed that he came upon some hidden situation. His business nose wanted to probe further.

"Well, Ms. Baker, it has to do with her future."

"Her career? She's very testy about people trying to make decisions for her."

Sebastian poured himself some water. "You're telling me?" he nodded knowingly. "She's very private. I know that much."

"Let's get down to the bare facts, sir. Are you connected to the Pooles, or to Jonathan Kaplan? Because if you are, you'd better talk to our attorneys."

"Neither. I am not connected to those people. I don't know those names."

"Then please forgive me. We're on high alert and very cautious about strangers." Evelyn apologized. "We've had some weird people lurking around here."

"Is there anything I can do?"

Evelyn's look said "but who are you?"

"I am a business man. I have many businesses. *De Pombal*? Maybe you've heard of us. Although, I have no experience in the communications industry. My family has some holdings in this country."

There was knocking on the door and Marla entered.

"Barbie tracked me down. Sorry, Evelyn, for the interruption."

Sebastian got up. "Perhaps we can continue this conversation in the foreseeable future, Ms. Baker?"

He reached out to shake her hand and Evelyn smiled at him. "Why?"

Marla jumped in. "Because Señor *de Pombal* has an uncanny knack for interfering."

"That's not all bad," Evelyn said. Sebastian smiled at Evelyn.

"Shall we go?" Marla said.

Marla remained formal as she directed him to her office. Her face was tight, serious until Reed appeared, walking toward them in the hallway. She smiled.

"Reed, this is Sebastian *de Pombal* from Spain. Sebastian, this is Reed Rhoades."

She watched the two gorgeous men shake hands. "I'm a fan, Mr. Rhoades," Sebastian said.

"In Spain? You know me in Spain?"

"No, I actually have read some of the local papers. I follow Marla's career."

Marla turned red. "Please, Sebastian."

"I'd better leave you alone. Good meeting you, Sebastian," Reed said and moved passed them.

Inside her office she saw the flowers on the sofa table that served as a side desk under the window sill. Her face softened at the sight of a spray of tiny red roses amid lushly smiling gerbera daisies.

She stood still then touched them, inhaled their scent and looked at him. "My favorite flowers." Her gaze always took him off balance.

"I remembered," he said.

"Yes, in Portugal. Cascais. That seems like another century."

"Just a few months. Marla, I'm not too big to apologize. But, I keep making a fool of myself in front of you. I would like to get something going and I am stumped. You have a most unusual affect on me."

"Sebastian, you're the best thing that happened to me. I told you that before. But people don't change. We are who we are. We all have a past. We all know a lot of people. We care about people in different ways. Do not ask."

"Marla Hayes. May I take you to dinner tonight?"

Marla was touched by his formal approach. "Yes, please."

"When?"

"We can go right now. I have no deadlines. "

"Would you suggest a restaurant?"

Her face lit up. "Have you ever been to Malibu? To San Simeon? The Hearst Castle?"

"No. I have not spent any time on the west coast. All my business is on the east coast. "

"Well, then, it is my turn to show you my country, Sebastian. The place that I call home." She was sparkling. She put a daisy in her hair, put her arm through his and they headed for his car. He handed her the key.

"I think you should drive." Marla loved the idea.

"Topless?"

"By all means," he said.

The hard top of the brand new car rose up and receded into its casing. She drove west on Melrose Avenue, then onto Santa Monica Boulevard toward the Pacific Ocean, her hair blowing in the wind.

"You must tell me about the Pooles and Jonathan Kaplan, the people Evelyn was talking about. Isn't that the Jonathan you worked for?" he asked once out on the road.

"I don't know much about them except that Jonathan hates me since I left him and he introduced me to this rhyme-making rich girl, Missy Poole, who claimed to be my boss and own this station. Evelyn assured me that there is a Board of Directors and no Missy Poole."

"And that was enough for you?"

"Sure. Evelyn told me early on that this was a small independent station owned by a family for three generations and run by the Board."

"Owned by a family?" he asked.

Marla drove on in silence. After a few minutes, she yelled out, "Oh, my God! Jonathan is in cahoots with the family Poole,… because I left him…. And that is Missy…. Oh, my God! Let there be light! And the light came on!"

They were going north on the Pacific Coast Highway.

"We'll stop at the Beau Rivage. They have a lovely wine bar," she said

Malibu's Old-World romantic charmer was exactly what suited Sebastian. The Mediterranean cuisine had the familiar touches of home. She held the petite loaf of bread up to him. He broke it and took half. Sitting by the large plate glass windows facing the Ocean, they witnessed an incredible sunset.

Sebastian cradled her hand in his. He wanted to give her the world. He wanted to hold her the way he held up the tennis club on the flier. "This is one of those rare perfect moments in life, Marla. Do you agree?"

"Moments like the one at Porto Santa Maria in Portugal, except maybe better" she said dreamily.

"You said before that I am the only man you can trust. It's an honor. I'll always be worthy of your trust."

Marla smiled. "I know that. I believe that."

She let him hold her hand as the heat of the sunset forged the two souls.

Back at the Beverly Hills Hotel, behind the closed doors of the bungalow, they stood, their eyes locked. Trembling, she moved into his arms. Their lips touched slowly. Almond in velvet. Exactly as she remembered the taste and feel of Sebastian's soft, warm lips. Moisture broke through her skin making every inch of her an erogenous zone. She clung to his body. He unbuttoned his shirt and guided her hands to a slow circular motion on his chest. More and more his body responded. His face was burning with desire. They probed. She felt his muscles tighten under her touch and let him pull her torso against his. They tested each touch, tested each taste of the lips, tested each quick lick of the tongue. They shed their clothes as their heat became the glue tying them together and their lips and tongues would not separate. Their bodies became one. They held their breath. Trembled. Exploded. Shrieked. Then breathed again, as one. Later, much later, their bodies drew apart.

Sebastian studied Marla's face, a mixture of bewilderment, amazement and wonder. He gently held her.

"It's not what you see, it's what you feel," he said. "I AM what you feel."

CHAPTER TWENTY-FIVE

Carol looked at the sign on a storefront, *Clean, Eat and Party!* Ornate white wrought iron on the windows matched that on the outside of the main entry door. Inside, she found herself in a pristine white-on-white space that once may have been a hamburger and hot dog stand in Santa Monica. It was not large but the high ceilings and cool single color made it appear spacious. Sitting behind a white desk, was Xiùměi, wearing a suit and tie. She got up to welcome her and showed her around, pointed out the little kitchen, the supplies, the equipment, the dainty bathroom and everything she needed to operate the business.

"I decorated. Allan painted," she said with pride.

"What's with the suit and tie?" Carol asked.

"Oh, that's for ladies who come in to hire me," Xiùměi said. Then she unsnapped the tie which turned out to be no more than an insert, revealing her breasts with nothing else under the jacket. "That's for gentlemen who come in to hire me. Smart?"

"Clever," Carol said.

Xiùměi proceeded to show her the rest, pointed out a corner with shelving for supplies and equipment, and some folding chairs for what she called training meetings with employees.

She pointed out a room next door that would become available for rent shortly. She would make that into the full kitchen. Xiùměi proudly showed off the Occupational License and the Labor Commissioner's license for her and her agency. She was clearly proud of the License for first employee, Měi Wong.

"I will thank you, Carol, for your money," she said.

"But no one will ever know, correct?" Carol asked.

"Accountant only knows Investor Number 1, and does not ask name. You got fictitious name published?"

"Yes. Out-of-state bank account, also."

Now Carol was comfortable. She had a business where she was a silent partner and profit participant. This way, if anything would go wrong in her life, she would never have to worry about money. Clearly, with Xiùměi , her secret was safe.

"Do you to keep a copy of the book that…" Xiùměi was searching for a word.

"The structure, right? You mean the business structure," Carol said.

"Right. That. Hard word for me," Xiùměi smiled shyly.

"No, I don't want to have any around the house. This is private between you and me. Besides, you have already shown me your master plan, the cost of licenses, the space, equipment, training videos for the staff. What is important is that you have everyone bonded. That is very, very important."

"I will keep secret. You are client, not partner. Yes?" Xiùměi was sugar and spice.

"Xiùměi, I know you're a hard worker and I trust you one-hundred percent."

"If you want contract, I will sign one for you."

"Not necessary. I know you're a good person and I am helping you start your American life," Carol said.

She pulled out a sheet of notepaper from a manila envelope. "Here is a list. I have five names to start you off. Tell them you were recommended by Buzz Kraus and me. Give them your price list and attach an availability calendar." She pulled out a monthly calendar and placed some checkmarks on it, indicating that those dates were still open.

"You want to give the impression that you're busy."

"Yes. Understand."

"Everybody must be bonded before they go to work in these homes. Done?"

"Yes, Carol. All done. We start make money now."

Carol ceremoniously presented an 8"x10" dark metal box. Opened it.

"Here are four envelopes and four deposit slips to start with. Please just have the accountant mail Investor Number 1 checks to my account."

"Carol. Very smart." Xiùměi gushed. She took the box, put it in one of the desk drawers. "Secret," she said, bowing to Carol. Carol bowed back then caught herself and felt silly.

"Now, listen. Buzz has a friend, Michael Gaston. He has a big house and a live-in maid. But he needs the monthly service of a team. For the hard cleaning. Can your people do hard cleaning?" Carol asked.

"Yes. My people, the agency can do hard cleaning."

"There will be a belated wedding reception at his mansion. The caterer needs additional maids."

"I will come, in person and bring one more," said Xiùměi. "Who is caterer?"

"Same as the ones who did my reception."

"Soon, Carol, we will do catering too. I am sure." Xiùměi was bursting with self-confidence.

"I'll tell Buzz to get instructions for you." Then Carol had a second thought, "If Buzz comes by, you keep your tie on, hear?"

Xiùměi grinned. "You my partner. Buzz your man." She reached out and they shook hands.

When Carol left, Xiùměi pulled out the desk drawer and pressed the Stop button. She looked up and mixed among the cleaning supplies was a hidden camera eye. She had plans.

CHAPTER TWENTY-SIX

Linda was coming unglued as the reception neared. She was bigger than she would liked to have been.

"Honey, we've hired the best wedding planner in town. Just call Barbara Squire if you have any concerns. I don't have the answers, she does," Michael said.

"You're always working. You go away, go to the office and work. You come home, eat and go to the computer and work." Linda was whining on and on. "You never stay with me. Am I that ugly?"

"You're not ugly, Linda. You are beautiful. Pregnancy becomes you. You glow, you shine."

"Oh, you talk like a writer," she said.

"Because…?" He held the question mark for her to finish and smiled.

"Because you ARE a writer. See, I know." She started to smile. "The best writer in the whole world." She hooked into her five-year old *persona*.

"Well, then, is it working?"

"Yeah. Yes. It IS working." Linda smiled and started to melt.

"I'll come home early, we'll have Barbara on a conference call and go through the whole thing step-by-step. Saturday will be the most perfect day of our lives. I promise," Michael said as he started down the stairs.

He was barely out of the house when Linda went into her bathroom sanctuary, locked the door out of habit and carefully unwrapped her secret stash of fine quality cocaine. After a couple of quick lines she reclined on the custom-made bath *récamier*. She was at peace. Life was going her way. Finally her father's training was paying off. Although by now she knew that her Father had used her in a self-serving way that could have damaged her, she loved him too much to put any blame on him. Besides, she believed that there was no damage done, she was as normal as she should be and he had been right about preparing her for her future.

She walked downstairs, into Michael's study. She turned on his computer and was happy to see that all the episodes he was writing for the series were saved as desktop icons. She could open any one of them and see the story and the characters that came and went.

When Michael returned that night, she had mellowed out. They had a nice dinner, easy conversation although Michael thought some of Linda's phrases were strangely familiar to him. He wondered why the words rang a bell until realization hit him.

"Are you reading my drafts?"

"What if I am?" she was flippant.

"Linda, my computer is off limits, don't you know? I didn't think I'd have to tell you that."

"Nothing is off limits in this house. It's my house."

"Your bathroom is off limits," he said.

"That's just good manners. That's all it is. Women stuff."

"Well, my work is off limits or I'll have to put a password on the computer."

"You put a password on anything and you know what'll happen to your cock," she said with a sinister grin.

"What?"

"Nothing. That's what. Nothing will ever happen to your cock." She started laughing and, as happened more often, Michael gave up.

------- ◆ -------

By the time Saturday rolled around, Linda had calmed down. Michael asked Judy to spend some time with her which she agreed to do without pay— she had already taken a lot of money and gifts from Linda.

Xiùměi and her staff of four arrived early. Although not asked, they were eager to help the caterer set up and arrange things. Xiùměi checked out the decorations, the table settings, the physical layout designed by Barbara Squire. She saw how the dance floor was laid on top of the clay tennis court, and watched everything the caterer did. Unnoticed by anyone, she went upstairs. She caught a glimpse of the bride on the patio, taking quick tokes of marijuana. Xiùměi smiled to herself. This was new and interesting.

Little-by-little, Xiùměi had grasped the reasons behind the seating arrangements, the keyboard player's location and the carpeted walkway for the bride. Her assistant, a regular working machine, Měi Wong, took care of the labor. She was smart, a hard worker and very grateful to Xiùměi for having elevated her out of her earlier life. The guests began to arrive and soon everyone was in place. The wedding took shape. Who would give away the bride?

When the introductory notes of the Eagles' *Hotel California* started, some of the beautiful people grimaced in surprise or disapproval. How can that be the wedding march? But they soon got into the irrelevance of the music. Then Linda appeared on the arm of Buzz Kraus. She had no relations, and Buzz was a friend of everyone. Linda was a beautiful bride in a gown designed to minimize her condition. Her spirit shone through a rich smile as she attempted to make the small steps down the aisle to the beat of the music, heading toward Michael. She felt victorious. The entire industry, Michael's peers, could now officially acknowledge that she had gone beyond what she considered the stigma of a civil ceremony.

The party was a smash. Linda and Michael chatted with everyone, ate at the dais and danced until her water broke. It came on suddenly and her legs gave out. She slid down into a sitting position against a wall. The ambulance arrived in no time. Michael asked Buzz and Carol to stay with the party, take over the hosting.

Buzz and Carol made sure that a good time was had by all. They held court as the next couple whose marriage was announced. Their planned nuptials on a yacht in Newport Beach Harbor off Balboa Island had everyone interested.

"The invitations are in the mail for the lucky 100," said Buzz to Bernie and his wife, Helen.

Carol went over to Xiùměi, busy in the background. "How are you doing?"

Xiùměi's smile was almost cocky: "I see everything, I learn everything."

"Buzz agreed to use *Clean, Eat and Party!* for our wedding but only if you come in with a reasonable estimate. That's the only way he will pay."

"You can make him do anything, Carol," she answered.

"Don't overestimate my power, Xiùměi."

Carol turned to go mingle and do the hostessing chores. She never noticed in the midst of all the activity Buzz brazenly approaching Xiùměi and talking with her at length in the kitchen.

"You said once we should have lunch, Xiùměi, remember?"

"I do. AA meeting. Sucky-you, sucky-me." She looked at him. "You did not call. Now you engaged man. I am busy for lunch," Xiùměi said.

"I have to take a lesson from an Asian expert how to make a woman happy," he continued, while appearing nonchalant to the onlooker.

"Lesson is money."

"How much?" he asked.

"I tell you tomorrow. 11:00 in morning."

"Where?" he asked.

"Bel Aire Sands Hotel, Building B, Room13A."

Buzz came out of the kitchen just as Carol carried a small plate of caviar and toast points toward him.

"Here, Honey, nutrition for the affluent. Protein. High, high protein." Her flirtatious laugh made Buzz forget Xiùměi. There was something magnetic about Carol that drew him in.

"I'm glad you like Xiùměi," Carol said. "I think her catering and cleaning company will be right for doing our wedding."

"Sure. Let's get an estimate from her," he said.

"I'm on it."

She smiled and surprised him with a kiss in front of everyone, even Xiùměi.

———◆———

Bernie and Buzz arrived early at the production meeting in Michael's bungalow. They were, as always, well prepared. The pros, the old-timers whose experience was invaluable to a new producer like Michael, settled at the round conference table and waited for the rest of the production team.

Bernie was paging through a script. "Whose tootsie is getting this bit part?"

"I don't have a tootsie right now," Buzz said. "You, Bernie?"

"No. Besides, mine comes last, anyway. I'm just the director," he joked then turned to Michael. "But Linda said she wanted it. Said it could be a small running part in the show. That it may get bigger."

"She said that? When?"

"You didn't know? She said she read it in your computer."

Michael was at a loss. "This is embarrassing, guys. I'm really sorry."

"Don't sweat it. If it makes her happy, it will make you happy," Buzz laughed at his own innuendo.

Bernie's face lit up. "This way, she won't be bothering you for guest starring roles."

"She wants to keep her hand in acting," Michael said with sadness in his voice.

"She did say that in case anything happened, she wanted to keep her *résumé* current," Bernie added. But he could feel Michael's pain.

"OK. OK. Onward." Michael had to break out of this box.

"Brian and Santiago. Let's see."

The three of them studied photos and *résumés* provided by the casting director.

"This guy is gay like the character. He's supposed to be a real good actor." Bernie picked up one of the photos. "I haven't seen his work, though."

"Don't we have footage?" Buzz asked. "We never hire without footage. What's this, the amateur hour?"

"Either way, I don't want gay actors because they are gay," Michael said. "I want actors who can ACT gay, whether or not they are, who have the nuances. I don't care what they are, OK?"

"OK, OK," Bernie said.

"I don't mean to come down on you, Bernie, or Buzz," Michael said. "I just want us to have the same focus, the same vision. Speak the same language. That's the only way we can get the right thing on screen." He got up, walked around, poured himself some water. Bernie and Buzz waited. But there was nothing more.

"That's all, I guess," Michael said and sat back at his desk.

The other production people arrived and they switched from casting to the details of mounting not only the first episode but the structure of the series. Not much later Buzz looked at his watch and got up. "Sorry, guys. Hope you don't mind but I have to go."

"You got a date, or something?" Bernie joked.

"Now that you mention it."

Buzz was at the door. "Back at three," he said. Michael and Bernie nodded as the door closed. The others continued with their tasks.

"Let's check out the set, people," Michael said.

"You suppose he is boinking someone?" Bernie asked.

"Keep your mind on the job."

"Isn't he engaged to be married? What kind of a game is this?" Bernie's mind was not on the job.

"Maybe that's the way to go," Michael said. "Separate the wife from the lover, hm?" They looked at each other.

"I heard that in Europe it's common practice," Michael said.

Bernie and Michael headed for the door.

"Let's get some lunch, I'm starved. Then we can check out the sets when Buzz gets back."

———— ◆ ————

Buzz was having a different kind of lunch at the Bel Aire Sands hotel. At first he thought three hundred dollars might be too much for a one-hour quickie but ten minutes into the act, he was not at all sorry. Xiùměi was ready for him. He never saw her body only the short batik tunic with peek-a-boo slits teasing his senses. Xiùměi knew that when he was spread out on the bed and she was massaging his body the right way with the right oils and right pleasure tools, and he was inhaling the aromatic incense of the whorehouses of her native land, he would be putty in her hands.

"Oh, sucky-you, sucky-me?" she purred. She smiled at him once in a while. Opened up a silk bag filled with fruit-extract douches, offering him to choose one.

"Mandarin orange?" she held it up. "Nice selection."

She started to prepare her own body in front of him, letting him watch her ritual, rubbing the scent on her thighs, spanking her thighs, arousing hope with slowly crossing and uncrossing her knees. Each time she uncrossed, the spread between became wider, more and more inviting, ready for insertion. He was hard as rock, but she took his face in her hands, put it between her thighs.

"Sucky-me. Sucky-you."

He really wanted intercourse and tried to pull his face out of her strong hold. He felt she could crunch his jaw the way she held him.

"No inside, Mister." Her eyes became narrower, her face frightened with an old memory.

"No inside. Never inside temple of joy. My temple." Xiùměi's look was forbidding.

He accepted her firm word at which point he felt his face released from her grip. He was in *lala land*, floating on clouds. She took control and gave him slow pleasures, all he wanted. She asked questions. He didn't even know he was talking. Xiùměi learned that he had no sex with Carol. Coming from the traditions of an old fashioned country she understood proper courtship. She praised Buzz for his commitment to Carol and strength to hold back. When Buzz told her that Carol's son had moved out, she didn't let on about being pleasantly surprised. She wanted information about Carol and it suddenly fell into her lap. She now knew that Carol, as a mother, had become weak which made her more vulnerable in general, an easy prey.

At the right time, she brought up the issue of catering Buzz and Carol's wedding and charging the same as Barbara Squire, a woman with more than 15 years of experience.

When he was getting dressed, she laughingly told him, "It is Japanese women famous for art of sex."

"Don't be so hard on me. Asian includes Chinese, Japanese, Xiùměi." He laughed, checked his watch. "Well, my dear. I have to go." She bowed. He bowed. Her eyes downcast, not meeting Buzz's, she said "I will go check-out desk. Pay for room."

"You have enough money?" He took the bait, gave her some more bills. As he left, she pressed the off button of the hidden camera and smiled with satisfaction.

On her way home, she picked up a bottle of champagne and flirted with the Asian owner of the liquor store.

Allan was happy to see her walk in with alcohol.

"Guess we're not going to AA tonight?" he asked with a hopeful grin.

"I'm not. You can."

"I'm not. I want a drink."

"You know you can't have any," she said as she opened the freezer, took out two chilled glasses and poured. He watched. There was no more discussion. They drank and he went berserk. He started to turn the small apartment upside down in search of more alcohol, marijuana, crack, anything.

When the bottle of champagne was finished, Xiùměi saw him take a gun out of the bottom of his dresser drawer and put it in his pocket. He drove off.

Xiùměi got on the phone, called Allan's father.

"Hello, Papa Burke. Xiùměi speaking. Big problem with Allan."

"Xiùměi, what's the matter now?" Victor Burke asked.

"He went out. Drinking" she said. "You must stop him. I am now businesswoman. I need good reputation."

"Where did he go?" he asked.

"Out. Only out with the car," she said innocently.

She heard Victor talk with his wife away from the phone, then he came back on. "Xiùměi, I am sorry you have to go through this. We will try to help. We are leaving now. See you as soon as possible."

"Thank you, Papa Burke," she said and hung up the phone grinning with satisfaction.

CHAPTER TWENTY-SEVEN

Sunday morning at the tennis club. The weekend's added festivities started with mimosas, spritzers, sangrias and included a varied spread of assorted berries, dips and chips, and other goodies served on the main terrace. Marla, Buzz, Evelyn and Reed had just finished playing. Carol watched them from a table, a small bowl of berries in front of her. They came off the court and joined her while cooling off.

"Well, lovely people," Evelyn said. "I can't linger. I have to get to the station. Today's a work day for me." She headed for the locker rooms. Marla followed.

"What's going on?" Marla asked.

"It seems that a couple of people who have been on our Board of Directors for the past ten years are planning to give up their seats. You're not familiar with these elements of management, Marla. Neither is Reed." She poured a cup of coffee from a carafe off to the side on a self-service bar and continued walking.

"I have promised the Pooles, you know, the founding owner family, to provide them with replacement names. The replacements have to be of the same mind as the rest of the Board. Otherwise, if they get ideas about joining the big guys, selling to the networks, they can infect the entire Board and we will never be the same again. Who knows," she laughed. "We may not even stay on the air."

"Is this immediate?" Marla asked.

"Mergers and acquisitions only end at the Board room. They can start anywhere, though."

"I can't believe that little worm would do this to us," Marla said.

"What little worm do what?" Evelyn asked.

"Jonathan introduced me to Missy Poole, the rhyming heiress. What have I done, Evelyn?"

Marla was concerned and most of all, angry with herself.

"It is supposed to be the 'woman scorned' not the man. I really pissed him off, didn't I? Enough to go after the whole station." Marla was beside herself. "How can I fix it?"

"It'll be fixed by diplomacy, Marla. Have faith," Evelyn said.

"He reminds me of Donnie Brown. An attorney I dated before Warren. An unforgiving man. Looking for revenge."

"People who are that cold, get old fast," Evelyn said and disappeared in the shower.

"You know, Marla, we have a good Board of Directors with a long history of service. They're loyal people. We can count on them. That's all we need."

When she came out of the shower, Marla was sitting there, nursing her drink.

"They say you're a programming genius. You could go anywhere with your track record."

"I like where I am, Marla. I have freedom, decisions are mine, problem solving is mine, victories are mine, and failures are mine."

"Is this a good time to run by you some ideas, more like concepts, for interviews I'd like to do?"

"Sure, shoot." Evelyn was getting dressed, drying her hair, packing her gear.

"I am thinking of an immigrant who worked in the produce market downtown and through sheer diligence, working 20-hour days and giving attentive service, he became a millionaire. He never finished high school. His daughter is graduating from medical school. There is his honorary degree and *chair* named for him. A Hungarian."

"Sounds possible. Need notes. What else?"

"I'm thinking of a street guy who became an office supply millionaire by cheating on his customers and the government caught up with him and he is in a white collar jail now. His family cannot really leave their house for fear of getting attacked."

"Sounds possible. Need notes."

"Evelyn," Marla spoke.

"You have more?"

"Not an actual person in mind but if I stumble upon some curious situations, can I do, I mean try to do investigative stuff? You know, like the big guys? 60 minutes?"

Evelyn laughed. "We're independent. We can do whatever works. But remember,…"

"Need notes," Marla and Evelyn said simultaneously.

"Yes, we can do whatever works but we have to be just as careful as the big guys. Now, I'd better go."

"I'm getting some more berries. See you later," Marla said. "Will you still be there at 4?"

"Maybe. Bye."

Evelyn left and Marla returned to the food spread. To her surprise, Carol and Buzz were still there.

"We are going out to the yacht, Marla. It's time I took a close look," Carol said. "Buzz, darling, let's get going, OK?"

Buzz got up. "Just be a minute," he said, leaving for the shower.

"Well, we hired Xiùměi's people to do the wedding." Carol announced with some kind of complacency. "I got Buzz to give the young immigrant a chance."

"That's very generous of you," Marla said. "Do you think she can handle it? It's only a start-up business. Does any one of them have any experience?"

"I trust her. She had a good presentation."

"I hope you're saving money," Marla said.

"I don't care. What if I'm not."

"Excuse me," Marla said. "I just thought to do something this big on a 110 foot yacht, requires know-how. The kind of quick thinking that comes with years of experience."

"Do you know anything about wedding planning, Marla." Carol's ugly side surfaced to save her from more answers.

"Did you do your own wedding? No. Warren's mother did. So, you shouldn't try to tell me what to do." Carol got up.

"When you're mean, you are the queen," Marla said. She picked up her racket and walked over to the information board, looking for a game, looking to hit, to run, to sweat.

———◆———

Driving on the I 405, Buzz and Carol were on their way to Newport Beach.

"I'm so glad you're over forty," Carol said. They were relaxed with each other.

"Forty-two," came the answer. "I'm so glad I don't have to lie about my age anymore."

She gave him a loving squeeze.

"The best thing is that I finally understand that a relationship starts with friendship," Buzz said.

They both smiled, nodding, thinking of their own experiences.

Buzz opened up. "I love this business. The creativity reverberates through everything, every aspect. The heat of creativity seeps into every element. Show-business is a hard business, Carol. The work is hard, the stakes are high, the players are beautiful, time is of the essence and a lot of quick fixes do not hold."

"That's poetic. Really, really nice."

He was pleased with himself. "You bring out the best in me," he said.

"Because I'm comfortable with you." Carol laughed. Their private thoughts melded together.

"I think we can make it," Buzz said.

"I think we should try," Carol answered.

"I think I can hardly wait to sleep with you. I mean to sleep, through the night," Buzz said.

"I think we have a good life ahead of us," Carol said.

"My kids are about Sammy's age. What do you say we try to get him back," Buzz said. "Make a family."

"Let's go."

"Now? You'd rather go there than to the yacht?"

"Yes, Buzz. The kid comes first. The yacht can wait." Carol had tears in her eyes. "Look at me, I'm becoming a regular mom." She dug in her purse for the telephone book. "Here. Here's Sally's number," she said.

"A woman of action. Just what the doctor ordered." Buzz laughed and pulled off the road.

"You're pulling off?"

"I don't know where we're going," he said.

"Oh." Carol got on the phone. "Sally, this is Carol Livingston soon to be Kraus. We are coming over. Buzz and I. I want you to pack Sammy's things and I want him to be ready. Thank you." She hung up. She was shaking. Buzz gave her a kiss and started the car.

It was a good half hour before they arrived at Sally's apartment, or over the garage loft she laughingly called her apartment, in Redondo Beach. The Sunday afternoon parking was difficult. Carol had to change into sandals to make the walk from the distant parking spot.

After they found their way up to the garage apartment, indeed, right on the beach, they were surprised. Inside, the place was spotless. Inviting, pleasant.

When Sammy came out of the bedroom, he was clean, neat, shaven, bright eyed.

"Ma, what are you doing here?"

"We came to take you home," Buzz said. "We're getting married and our families will be one."

Sammy brought out a tray of soft drinks with glasses. "Cool."

"What do you mean, cool?" Carol asked, anticipating an argument.

"Nothing. It sounds good," Sammy said.

"Where's Sally?"

"Getting ready for work. She'll be right out," Sammy said and glanced toward the bedroom.

"Are you packed?" Carol asked.

"He'll be ready," Sally said, appearing in a small cocktail waitress dress. "I got a new job, Buzz. It's really good money but the late Saturday nights might screw up the Sunday morning tennis," Sally continued. She sat down, poured herself a soft drink.

"You were right, Carol. Being responsible for another human being is not easy. I did my best." She looked at Sammy.

"Do you know he is working after school?"

"Working? Carol asked.

"Restaurant. Sally told me if I work in a food place I'll always have food. So, I am a waiter at McKenzie's and in the summer, when the manager goes on vacation, I'll be the manager." Sammy spoke with so much pride, Carol and Buzz were floored.

Sally's smile was rich, almost parental. "It was nice to have Sammy here. To have a family, someone to go home to. I know you're probably angry…"

Carol touched Sally's hand. "I was upset. I'm not now." Her grin assured Sally of no hard feelings.

"He can go home with you on one condition," Sally said.

"Condition? He's my son," Carol said.

Buzz remained calm. "What condition?"

"I want to be the Maid of Honor at the wedding. Did you select one yet?"

Buzz and Carol looked at each other, smiled, nodded. He put his arm around her and in an official tone he said, "Sally, would you do us the honor of being the Maid of Honor at our wedding?"

Sally jumped with joy, hugged Carol, and screamed. "Thank you! Thank you!"

Sammy went into the bedroom and returned with his duffle bag. They looked at each other, Carol took Sammy's hand and the three of them headed down the stairs.

Sally's eyes were moist as she waved after them, "Bye!"

———— ◆ ————

It was time for the Sunday afternoon news and weather. The weather girl, Marla, was reading weather. She was so at ease on the job that the worst predictions sounded reasonable coming from her. She dressed for the camera in casual elegance and designers started to send her clothes that she could keep, requesting only on-air credit. It was granted. Everyone was happy. There were no committees making decisions, only Evelyn.

As Marla finished the first report, she had time to kill and went by Evelyn's office. She knocked.

"Enter."

"Let there be light," came Marla and suddenly stopped talking. Evelyn was on the telephone.

"Jonathan, I'm going on the speaker phone now, someone has come in who should hear this conversation," Evelyn said.

"Who came in?"

"Marla."

"Hello, Jonathan," Marla said. "I'm sorry you feel this angry with me."

"This is not anger. This is business. I was hired to represent the interests of the Poole family regarding overseeing the advertising that is being bought by the station. It has to be reviewed. It has to be evaluated. I spoke with the lawyers. We are within our rights in bringing the station to the next level. As a member of the founding family, Missy Poole can exercise hierarchy."

"You're not making sense. Evelyn has been handling the advertising for years. Years before I came here. It has nothing to do with me or my leaving you."

"Evelyn, please get off the speaker phone. I called to talk with you," Jonathan said.

"But you're on a speaker phone, I can tell. Are you alone?"

There was a long silence. "No, Missy Poole is here. She is the boss."

"Not really. I tell you what, Jonathan, Ms. Poole, let me prepare the documentation you need. I will prove that the advertisers fit right in with the posture of this station. This independent station. This money-making independent station."

"When?" Jonathan asked.

"A week?"

"You have three days," he said and hung up.

Marla stood there, dumbfounded. "I'm so sorry. I'm so sorry," she said repeatedly."

"Marla, we can beat Missy Poole. I have chewed up and spat out bigger opponents in my day," Evelyn said. "A drink?" She walked over to the wet bar, then changing her mind, chose the wine rack.

"I still have a report to finalize," Marla said.

"I've seen you live dangerously before." Evelyn smiled and poured two glasses of wine. Marla settled in the guest chair. "I'm trying not to think this is all my doing, Evelyn."

"I know. But either way, it's an issue that has to be solved.

"A pretty big issue, isn't it?"

"Looks that way now, but things like this don't scare me. Something has to be done. Whatever it is, it will be done."

"You're a strong woman. Do you need me? Is there anything I can do?" Marla said.

"No, nothing, Marla." Evelyn put down the half full wine glass, went to her desk, picked up some papers and seemed to have forgotten about Marla.

"I'll be going out-of-town for a few days," Marla said. "But call me on my cell if you want me back sooner. You can count on me, any time."

Evelyn looked up. "Go have fun, Marla."

Marla walked back to the newsroom and waited for her weather girl turn.

CHAPTER TWENTY-EIGHT

The Thunderbird practically flew on the Pacific Coast Highway with Marla behind the wheel. They had spent a couple of days laughing, sightseeing, stopping at quaint Bed & Breakfast lodgings on their way north. Now, it was time to get back to Los Angeles, to reality, but first, she felt the urge to do something really special on their last day.

"The *pièce de résistance*! I just thought of the best place for us!" she said. "Let me make a call." She pulled off the road and got out of the car.

"It's a surprise. Just wait," she said, turning her back to Sebastian.

He watched as she talked with her hands, nodded, smiled and even laughed out loud, before hanging up. Her face radiated as if she had just made a major scientific discovery that would save the world. He waited patiently to find out what this wonderful thing could be.

Marla's mysterious smile never left her face until she rolled into the driveway of the *Madonna Inn,* the jewel of a hotel in the hills overlooking San Luis Obispo. She got out of the car, took Sebastian by the hand and walked toward the main entrance. They were expected by the staff and informed that the *Austrian Suite* was available for the one night. Marla had heard about the magical suites of the *Inn,* but had never been there before. As if opening a precious gift package, she and Sebastian almost tiptoed into the impressive accommodations. The bellman explained that Alex Madonna, the hotel's founder, hailed from Switzerland and this was his favorite home-away-from-home whenever he stayed there.

Marla and Sebastian did not hear a word he was saying. They were drawn to one of the two balconies with its incredible view. They stood there, holding each other, unaware of the wine and snacks being delivered, unaware of the chambermaid coming in and hanging their clothes, and unaware of the outside world. For this moment, this rare, exquisite moment, there was no outside world for them.

Their lips found each other and their bodies called each other. Hours passed in the wonderland of lovemaking. Emotions burst through with each movement. Every pore of their skin attached to that of the other. They were one.

Much later, they strolled around the grounds.

"How can this be real?" Marla asked.

"My sentiments exactly," Sebastian said. "You mean us, or the hotel?"

"Not funny," she laughed. "I mean us, you dear man. I mean us."

"We are the luckiest people in the world."

"You are my reward," she said. "I must have done something to deserve you."

He squeezed her tighter to himself.

"I'd like to keep you in my world," he said.

"Somehow, part of me wants to plunge into the unknown."

"Not all of you?"

"Maybe down the road," she said. "My mother said that *If your love and your career don't mesh, something has to give or give-up or give-in.*"

"She was wise," he commented.

They woke up early next morning, inhaled the air once more before driving out, heading south, heading out of the dream, back to reality.

"The next time you come, we'll go to Catalina, and San Francisco, Calistoga, and San Diego. Just so much I want to show you," Marla said enthusiastically.

"There's time."

"Maybe you can come here on business and stay longer. That'd be wonderful," Marla said and pulled into the Beau Rivage parking lot. "Well, this is where it all started, Sebastian."

He opened the car door for her. "This is where it all came together, Marla. I'm happy to say."

The maitre d' recognized them from their earlier visit. He even seated them at the same table where they admired the sunset. Sebastian told him how much they appreciated the outstanding cuisine. Marla chose the chef's unique Cappellaci Napoletana, a folded sheet of pasta filled with spinach and the Ahi Tuna Cajun Style accompanied by a lime sauce. Sebastian shared the Prosciutto and Papaya appetizer with Marla and went for the Rack of Lamb Cypriot, stuffed with a puree of mushrooms, onions, Feta cheese and served with a fresh mint sauce. Neither of them asked for dessert, only coffee. They grew silent as the sun dropped off the horizon and candle lights brightened their faces. It was that time.

Marla drove him back to his hotel where her own car was waiting.

"This was the best week of my life and tomorrow is work day, Saturday."

"I'll be on the airplane when you do the *Must See TV* portion of your life."

They let the bellman unload the car and went back to the bungalow. Suddenly, neither of them knew what to say.

"All right. Let's take my bag and I'm on my way. Make it simple."

He kissed her. "Yes, make it simple."

She got in her car. "I'll call you," he said.

"I hope so."

The drive home to the Beverly Glen seemed like only minutes. Her mind was filled with Sebastian. Wondering what was happening? This was not fun fucking. This was overwhelmingly beautiful. All the luxury that came with him was of no real interest to Marla. Long distance romance was the last thing she would seriously consider. Call it a *fling*, she told herself.

As she got ready for bed, the telephone rang.

"You know, Marla, I've never been good at long distance romance either. But we should make a plan to beat the odds. Oh, hello, this is Sebastian, last week's lover."

"I thought it was Marco," she said. "I thought I just spent a week with Marco and now you tell me you're not Marco."

"You want Marco, I'll be Marco."

There was a long beat of silence.

"I'd like to see your plan, Sebastian. I'm really interested in your *beat the odds plan*."

"That's all I wanted to hear, Marla. Thank you. Sleep well."

"Will you be back for Carol's wedding?"

"I'm working on it."

"That's all I wanted to hear, Sebastian. Sleep well."

She hung up the telephone and went to sleep with a smile on her face. Her last thoughts were of her mother. What was she thinking now as she was looking down from Heaven. Was she happy for her? Could she foresee the outcome of this romance from up there somewhere?

———— ◆ ————

Sunday morning at the tennis club. The usual crowd gathered. Marla's partner was Reed.

"Where's Sally?" Marla asked.

"She works late Saturday nights. She'll try to get here next weekend."

"She works?"

"It's quite a turnaround for her," Buzz said. He looked at his partner.

"Lucky for us, Joyce was available. Joyce, meet Marla and Reed."

"I recognize both of you," Joyce gushed. "It's an honor."

Marla shook her hand. "We're just people," she said and started to hit the warm-up balls. And the match began.

Carol watched. Out of nowhere, Rhonda Smither appeared. She sat down next to Carol and started waving to Marla and Reed.

"Hello! Marla!"

"Hi, Rhonda." Marla turned to Reed. "What is she doing here?"

"Scooping *Must See TV Marla TV*?"

They were hitting hard but missing. Both of them lost their tennis concentration and eventually the match. They attempted to shake hands with their opponents graciously but didn't mean it. Winning was important except now they had to deal with something else. They looked at each other, looked over to Rhonda. Carol already had her star struck antenna up, drooling at the anticipated upcoming excitement. This was too good.

Marla and Reed helped themselves to mimosas and a fruit snack in order to put off going to the table where Rhonda now settled.

"Don't leave me, Reed. Please. She scares me," Marla said.

"Hello, Rhonda. What a surprise," Marla said and sat down across from her, making Reed take the middle seat.

"I'll be back in a jiffy, Carol," Buzz said, leaving for the shower.

"I know you don't like me, Marla. That comes with the territory," Rhonda said. "Nobody likes me."

"I like you," Carol said quickly.

"No, Carol, she's talking about us, not real people. Real people love her," Marla said.

"They do? They love me?"

"Why do you think you have a job, Rhonda?"

"You're right, real people."

"Must see TV. Must see gossip."

"I'm good, right?" Rhonda patted herself on the shoulder. "I got your attention. What about the next interview? Who will it be? What about the next weather report? Are you wearing any clothes? Who designed them? There's so much to know." Rhonda took a deep breath. Looked at Marla. Looked at Reed.

"You're not talking. You're ignoring me." She gulped down her drink. "People think I have answers. How can I have answers if you're not talking. Help me out here. Colleagues."

"Oh, this is too good." Carol was beside herself. Buzz returned,

"Let's go."

"No. I want to hear what happens," Carol said.

"Nothing happens, Carol. Rhonda will leave and you'll see on the air tonight that she will say something nice about me, hoping that I break down and give her a scoop. Yes? Am I right, Rhonda."

Rhonda took a sip of the melted ice mist in her drink. Got up. "Yes, Marla." Then she looked at Carol. "She's right. I have my work cut out." Rhonda walked out leaving Marla almost feeling sorry for her. But she changed her mind and dramatically returned to her seat. She opened her sport tote, pulled out a newspaper page and with the mystery that surrounds a magician, placed it in the middle of the table.

"And this, what about this, Marla?"

"What?"

The newspaper proof contained a list of the 'sexiest men in Hollywood.'

Warren's photo was among the top ten.

"Next issue. The proof!" Rhonda said, searching the faces for reactions.

"Whoa!" Reed said.

"I did it. I did this." Rhonda was swelling with pride. "And besides, I could increase your audience if there were anything going on between you two!"

She was unstoppable, full of her own creative gossip of inventing unchallengeable tidbits. She pointed at Marla and Reed. "What about you two?"

"We're very small potatoes in the large scheme of things, Rhonda." Reed gave her his *knowledgeable host* look.

"You're right." Rhonda left.

"I almost feel sorry for her," Marla said.

"She got to you, didn't she? Very clever woman, Rhonda Smither."

Marla started for the locker room.

"Do you want to grab a bite?" Reed asked.

"How come? Where are the kids?"

"It's not my weekend," he said.

"Actually, I could discuss an interview I am thinking of doing."

"Need notes," he said, then added "why do you need an agenda to have lunch with me?"

"You're a guy. Very, very, very handsome guy."

"Thank you, thank you, thank you." He laughed. "Am I your type?"

"No. Not really."

"It's not a date, OK? You're being too sensitive. What's going on?"

"I may be in love. I just spent the most wonderful week of my life with the most wonderful man on earth."

"Then you need a girl friend. Tell me all about it over lunch."

CHAPTER TWENTY-NINE

The entry to *Clean, Eat and Party!* was locked. Buzz could not get in. He was fuming. He dialed his cell phone. Xiùměi answered, apologized. She should have told him that the door was always locked. Only she and one assistant, Měi Wong, had a key. She told Buzz that without a staff there, being a storefront office that opened onto the street, it was safer to keep the door locked.

As Xiùměi talked with Buzz on the telephone, she appeared inside the door and let him in. They both hung up. She smiled and bowed. He bowed.

"Mr. Buzz, I am happy to see you," she said.

"I'm here on business."

"Which business, please?"

Buzz thought for a moment that she was being a wise guy but then he decided she couldn't be that clever. He pulled out the neatly folded estimate from his briefcase.

"This is way too high," he said.

"But you can write-off," she answered.

"I cannot justify it, Xiùměi. We know what the other companies would charge. Please be reasonable. Carol wants to use you."

"Accountant said, silent partner said, I can charge any amount." She walked around the back of her white desk.

"That's bad advice. You were given bad advice."

"You think? Mr. Buzz? Please sit."

Xiùměi switched on the TV monitor. She moved behind him and proceeded to gently massage his back. He watched the video. He saw himself getting her sex treatment. He shivered. He was speechless. When it was over, he got up, signed the contract on her desk and left.

———◆———

The seven islands of Newport Beach Harbor lie cradled inside the Balboa Peninsula. Surrounded by fantastic multi-million dollar homes, their small yachts anchored behind them. A grand yacht named *THIS IS NO DREAM [It is real]*, was where Carol and Buzz's wedding was about to take place. Anchored just far enough out from the residential mansions, the wedding yacht was accessed by a pontoon party boat that delivered as many as 12 guests at a time. It also ferried additional supplies as needed to fuel the extravagant celebration. Carol's designs and Xiùměi's execution of the decorating resulted in bright colors rendered low key by soft, easy-on-the-eyes accents. Before long, some sixty people were milling around, enjoying drinks and snacks on deck and in the spacious salon. The public areas of the yacht's beautiful interior were admired by everyone. Xiùměi's uniformed staff members were visible and helpful. Měi Wong, as always, reliably took charge and guided Xiùměi's team to perform non-stop.

The music changed, the small wedding procession started. The bride wore purple and looked magnificent. She walked down the aisle on Sammy's arm. Ironically to some, the Maid of Honor was none other than Sally. Her lilac dress, just a little too tight, matched Sammy's lilac shirt and blended into the scheme of rich colors, making her look as if part of that family.

Marla knew very few people at the wedding and stayed in the background on the bride's side. The guests on the groom's side were unknown to her except for Michael and Linda and his secretary, Judy. Bernie and his wife, Helen, Buzz's teenage kids, Marshall MacIntire the lead actor from the new show arrived stag, and others were strangers to Marla although most of them recognized her, the TV weather girl. She had a lot of gracious smiling to do.

On Carol's side she knew only the Kaplan staff. No one was angry with Carol about how she left the company. This was her dream, being important, fashionable and a homemaker.

After the ceremony, the dancing and partying went into high gear. Linda looked better than ever, her weight just right, her high just right.

"Let's not get too involved, here, OK? I really have to get back and get some work done," Michael said.

"No. I don't want to go." Linda would not cooperate.

"Honey, little Mike's at home, we belong with our baby."

"The nanny is fine. OK? She'd call if there was something wrong."

"Are you up to something, Linda? Because this morning you were happy to just make a brief appearance here. What has changed?" He quizzed.

"What do you think?"

"Are you looking to make a deal? I think you're up to your tricks and want to barter. What is it?" Michael said.

"A yacht. This is simply too, too cute, sweetie. I want one. Let's get one."

Michael stopped in his tracks. "A what?"

"A yacht." She walked around him and let her hand slip inside his pants. They were leaning against the railing. Linda was doing her job. Michael crumbled.

"Maybe a smaller one. We'll look into it."

"60 foot?" she asked.

"How about 40 or 50? Let's start smaller. Pretend it's a training yacht. We'll learn."

She kissed him on the lips. "See what you get? In front of all these people yet!"

"It's OK, honey, we're married."

"Back in a sec," she said and disappeared below.

Michael was left alone, wondering how come, once again, she turned everything around, made him feel like the bad guy who owed her something. She had it down pat.

He started after her. Which way? In the master stateroom he ran into Marshall just pulling his pants up. Marshall waved to Michael, who was looking for the master head when he heard Xiùmĕi's voice from the opposite direction.

"Mr. Gaston, Sir. You like small snack? Big snack? I bring." She chatted away, too fast for her, almost garbled.

"Maybe you come with me to table?" She guided him out of the master suite, to the salon. Linda could hear them in the master head. As the sounds became more distant, she came out.

On her way over to Michael, Linda stopped by Xiùmĕi.

"How did you happen to be here? Did you know I was in the head?" Linda asked.

Xiùmĕi looked around, lifted her uniform jacket and Linda got a glimpse of a small video camera.

"I know many things," Xiùmĕi said.

"Well, I don't care."

"I'm friend." Xiùmĕi bowed. "I can be better friend."

Linda became more interested in Michael sitting at a table with Marla. She took a drink off a tray and sat down between them. Michael looked at Marla with embarrassment.

"I turn my back and see what happens. I can't believe this."

"Linda, honey, try to be civil."

"It's all right, Michael. Life's too short." Marla got up but was stopped by Penelope and her handsome escort, a man in his 70's. They sat down.

"Marla, I want you to meet my beau, Nicholas."

They shook hands.

"Is that what happened at the Shubert Theater party?" Marla teased.

"We're actually old friends, since our youth," Nicholas said.

"Things work out the way they are supposed to," Penelope added. She was comfortable and in her element.

"Meet Michael Gaston and his wife," Marla said.

"My pleasure," Michael said as he rose to shake hands. "My wife, Linda." Linda nodded briefly toward them and looked in the other direction.

"How nice," Penelope said. "Are you the writer friend of Marla's? I recognize your voice. I'm the receptionist at The Kaplan agency.

Michael's face lit up. "It's a pleasure to meet you."

Linda made no secret of being unhappy at the intrusion.

"If you have time some day, Michael," Penelope said, "I'd like to tell you some funny stories about my neighbors. Reckless housewives in their forties, once gorgeous but still trying to be powerfully sexy, can't accept the aging process. Trying to push their men around with their sexuality. Could be funny. You know, pathetic funny."

"I doubt that the world is ready for over 40 women running around in T-shirts without bras," Michael said pleasantly.

"That's a nice touch. I see you're already creating," Penelope said.

"Old women using sex as a weapon? It'd never fly," Linda said and purposely looked at Penelope.

"It's unique. You think about it, Michael. Call me."

Linda took control and Michael didn't fight.

"He likes to write about historical times," Linda said as if she knew it all.

"Whatever you say, then." Penelope stared at Michael. "I can call Gary Aletter or another writer to do the housewives idea."

"Good luck, like that's going to happen," Linda said with a *gag-me-with-a-spoon* look. Michael, however, was listening.

"Women's sexuality should not be used to emasculate their men. They lose everything. Their virility first of all," Penelope said.

"I think women over forty should know their own beauty without needing constant reinforcement," Marla said.

"Look at Penelope," Nicholas said. "Did not miss a beat."

Michael observed the warmth between Penelope and Nicholas. Linda was drinking. She seemed unattached to him.

"You know, maybe you have something here, Penelope," Michael said.

"Just call me. I'll give you up-close details."

"Michael has his own ideas. He doesn't need yours," came Linda with an attitude.

"Excuse me," Marla said.

She headed for the pilothouse to get an overview of the harbor, and maybe the surprise arrival of Sebastian. Carol's softest whisper traveled down from the pilothouse.

"Xiùměi, this is my last warning. I just checked again. Your accountant is not depositing my share. Or is it you?"

"No, Carol. I will tell accountant." Xiùměi also spoke low but the deep tones traveled.

"I'm coming over to see your records. You have to show me. You've had a lot of business because of me. Don't make me lose patience."

"I want you be happy, Carol. Nice looking son. Young. I hear he not live with you." Marla sensed a nasty undertone in Xiùměi's voice.

"You hear wrong."

Carol came down the stairs and saw Marla quickly walking in the other direction. She could not get away. Carol caught up with her.

"I saw you with Michael. Linda must be going mad."

"I hope so, Carol," Marla said, smirking. "Great party."

"I'd better find Buzz. My husband."

Marla smiled. "Congratulations. You got what you wanted."

"It wasn't easy but it was worth it."

"And Jerry?"

"He's out of the picture."

"And Xiùměi? Is everything all right?" Marla ventured.

"Yes, yes. Why do you ask?" Carol evaded her eyes.

"Oh, you just seem jittery. Maybe you should calm down before you find Buzz."

Inexplicably, Carol couldn't be sure about trusting Marla, the TV person. "Yes, I should." Almost involuntarily she glanced up where Xiùměi was. Marla's eyes followed.

"Is she giving you a bad time about anything?" Marla asked.

"No, no. Not at all. She's doing a good job here, don't you think? I'm pleased with her. Are you surprised?"

"Why does it matter?"

Xiùměi walked down the steps from the pilothouse, carrying a bag of trash.

"Excuse me," she said and walked by them. "I went up to see if little boat comes with more drinks."

"Fine, Xiùměi. Just go ahead," Carol said, fear flashing through her eyes, then her face hardened. Turning to Marla, she continued, "What about you? Why were you going to the pilothouse? Looking for your invisible Spaniard?"

"You don't know when to stop, do you?"

Marla let her go find Buzz. He was in his element, hosting their guests, joking, thanking them for being with him at his happy time. When Carol came over to him, he kissed her with love and care. Carol had a tear in her eyes.

The ferry, bringing more supplies, also brought more guests, Jonathan and Missy. Their late entrance was planned. Missy Poole liked drama and, as Marla already sensed, liked confrontation. They greeted Buzz and Carol with loud apologies. Missy was delighted to meet both of them and hoped to see them again.

Xiùměi saw that she was off the hook when Marla's attention changed direction. Jonathan and Missy took a drink off a tray and with ominous looks in their eyes, moved in on Marla.

"How lovely to run into you again," Missy said.

"I really don't want to ruin my day," Marla said and turned away.

"This is a social event, Missy, let's leave it alone," Jonathan said.

"You're not exactly the macho man I expected. Leaving it alone when she's insulting me, soon to be the boss."

"Right, Missy." Jonathan turned to Marla.

"This is not over, Marla. You're in for a real awakening when you find the station gone and yourself without a job, without a future."

"Is that your goal, Jonathan? Will that make you happy?"

Marla walked away and went back to the pilothouse to look out again—see whether or not Sebastian was making it.

No Sebastian. She was resigned. Marla headed back to Penelope and Nicholas. Why would Missy follow? How could she make her go away? Missy almost ran head-on into Nicholas. He gave her a stern look. Missy appeared more surprised than concerned.

"I thought you moved to Switzerland," Nicholas said. "Does my sister know where you are?"

"I'll move when I'm good and ready," Missy Poole said defiantly.

"I'll be talking with your mother tonight, young lady."

"But I'll tell her first that you are with the woman nobody wanted in the family."

"Your mother and Penelope were like sisters. I should have listened to her. I would've had a happier life."

Nicholas took Penelope by the hand and guided her to the ferry ladder. "Penelope, things turned out the way they were supposed to turn out."

"Time is our friend, Nicholas," Penelope said, holding on to his hand tightly.

CHAPTER THIRTY

Michael's television series reached the top of the ratings. A hit show. The critics considered it smart writing, an entertaining way of introducing the audience to early American history. Marshall MacIntire, the actor who played the wagon train leader, went from unknown to TV stardom and promptly divorced his wife who had stood by him during his hungry years. It was the way of show business. His co-star, who played his love interest in the series, had already signed to do a Playboy spread and did interview after interview where she expressed her desire to be seen as other than a wagon train maiden, covered up in vintage garb, wearing no make-up. She wanted to show it all and she wanted to be a *film actor*.

Michael had seen and heard all this before. He decided to kill her off at the beginning of the new season, get the high ratings for such an episode and find a new leading woman for the show. Maybe there are some humble actresses out there. Nice work if you can get it but too much of an oxymoron.

Michael stayed away from his cast's personal lives. He stayed away from everyone except his production team and his friends, Bernie and Buzz. That was his family. He attended essential meetings with the high brass but he preferred e-mails and long written instructions to personal sit-downs.

The end of season wrap party promised to be the usual. Lots of drinking, eating, congratulating one-another and lots of flaunting of phony camaraderie that would disappear with the show's hiatus or demise. Generally no husbands, wives, family members were present only the cast and crew. Linda, having secured herself a small running role on the show, was among the first to show up. Michael still worked in his office when the party started on the soundstage where the series shot. The soundstage contained the permanent interior sets of the show and the celebrants were milling around, settled in the kitchen set, or the bedroom set, or one-sided wagons that served as the homes of some of the characters.

Linda almost immediately sought out Marshall. He was still wearing his western garb with pants a little tighter than they wore them in the real west.

"You started something at the wedding, Big Guy," she said.

"You started it."

"All right, if that's the way you want it." Linda kept drinking then opened her Judith Leiber purse, flashing a condom at him.

"Shouldn't we finish what we started?" she said with her sexiest glance from the corner of her eye.

"I brought a date," he said.

"I'm not proposing marriage," she said.

Linda walked away, looking for easier prey. A well-built young grip caught her eyes. She slithered toward him.

"I'm Linda," she introduced herself.

The young man's face lit up. He was a tall, open-faced country boy.

"Are you an actress?" he asked.

"Don't you recognize me? I'm insulted."

"I don't mean to insult you."

"I'm in the show. I was in the episode just two weeks ago. Where were you? Weren't you working that day?" She was annoyed. The young grip still smiled.

"Oh, you're a day-player? That's why. Maybe that's why I don't remember you."

She was angry.

"That's all right. I don't have anything against day-players."

"I'm no day-player. It's just that in the last episode I only worked one day. Don't you look at people? Don't you know the scripts? What do you do?" Her temper rose.

"I'm a grip, ma'am. I know the equipment. Where it goes. When it goes. What it does." He stopped smiling and waited. Linda stared at him. She was at a loss for words.

"Ma'am," she repeated with disgust. "Ma'am." After a long beat she turned and walked away. She went to the stage phone to dial the office.

"Judy."

"Hi," came Judy's voice. "Michael is tied up, Linda. He'll be a while."

"And you? I need company," Linda said.

"Can't leave just yet, but soon."

Linda hung up.

"You really need company, Mrs. Gaston?" she heard the raspy voice of the lead actor.

She didn't turn around, she caught the scent of his cologne. "Yes, Marshall. I really do." She started for the exit door. Outside, she stopped to look back. Marshall and his date were following. Linda walked over to the next soundstage only a few feet away. There was no one in there, only sparse lighting that marked the various exit doors were visible. Linda entered the bathroom. Marshall and his date followed. When Linda saw both of them enter, her eyes lit up.

"Only the best." The *crack* came out of her purse. Three of them crowded into the handicapped toilet, sat on the floor and let go. Being in the moment called for touching each other. Intoxicated, well-endowed Marshall was actively touching himself. His girl friend's breasts burst out of the narrow uplift bra under a silk tank top. Linda grew excited. Competing with the girl friend, she took off her top to entice Marshall. But it was the girl friend whose lips closed in on Linda's nipple and Linda automatically reached for the other woman's crotch, all to Marshall's entertainment and delight. Linda was loose, floating in a nice place.

CRASH! The door was kicked down.

One of the "extras" on the show came in with two uniformed police officers.

"I'm afraid, you're under arrest," the extra said, showing his badge.

"I'm the producer's wife," Linda said, trying to stand upright, collect herself and look into his eyes.

"I'm afraid I know that, Mrs. Gaston."

"But you're a fellow actor. How can you do something like this?"

"Acting is make-believe. I'm a real life cop, ma'am."

As he said that, several uniformed policemen and women entered.

Linda made a break for it and ran into Michael's arms. The uniformed officers handcuffed Linda and the other two. Before they took them outside, Michael unlatched the sliding stage gate and pushed it open. "Drive right in," he said to the cop. "I don't want my wife walking outside with handcuffs."

Judy, who came in with Michael, was stunned, trying to grasp what had happened. She watched the police van drive in, the three stoned people get seated inside and off they went. The party on the soundstage next door never missed a beat. No one but Judy knew of Michael's real pain over both, his wife and his show.

The undercover extra turned to Michael. "I saw her looking for trouble, Michael. I'm trained, you know."

"Did anyone know you were a cop?" Michael asked.

"Besides you? No one."

"You did?" Judy asked.

"Yes." Michael didn't explain. "Go in, apologize for me, tell them I wasn't feeling well, or something, OK?" he said to Judy. "I'm going over to the precinct."

"You want me to drive you?" the undercover extra asked.

"Just take me to my car. I'll follow you."

----—◆—----

And a night of hell came down on Michael Gaston. The Van Nuys police station always had paparazzi on its doorsteps. It was the station closest to the studios and restaurant row on Ventura Boulevard. By the time Michael entered, Linda had been booked, Marshall's agent was tearing down the house and Marshall's girl friend, who was not spoken for, was taken to the holding tank. It was a moneymaking night for the paparazzi. The flashlights never stopped.

Michael, treated with due respect, did manage to get Linda released in his custody. In the car, he called the nanny and advised her that on account of an emergency, they would be out all night. She'd have to pull double duty. There would be a bonus for her. At the rate the nanny was paid, she happily obliged.

The white Rolls Royce rolled silently through the gates of *Mountside Malibu.* A white, two-story building making an *L* shape around the pool and facing the Pacific Ocean similar to a secluded motel. The middle-aged woman who came to greet them wore a terry sweat-suit and looked like someone just getting ready for a workout in the gym.

"Hello. I'm Mrs. Rosa Taylor, the director," she said, reaching out to shake hands with Michael.

Michael held Linda in his arm until Mrs. Taylor took over. She hit the bell on the admission desk and a uniformed attendant appeared.

"Charles, this is Mrs. Linda Gaston. Is her suite ready?" Mrs. Taylor asked.

"Oh, sweetie, what a great idea," Linda said to Michael. "We should go away more often."

Charles brought a wheelchair, a white wheelchair for Linda.

"Sweetie, look, a white wheelchair! How wonderful! Let's go for a ride." Linda sat down and Mrs. Taylor gently administered a sedative. Linda peacefully went to sleep. Charles rolled her out of the lobby.

"I'm sorry I had to wake you but there was no sense for me to take her home and then try to bring her here."

"Mr. Gaston, you know we are the highest rated drug treatment center in Southern California. Tomorrow, when she wakes up, we'll explain to her what has to be done."

"I'll be back in the morning," Michael said.

"No, you should probably sleep in our guest quarters. It's almost sunrise," said Mrs. Taylor and walked him to a simple, functional, bedroom.

"Is your child well attended?" she asked.

"Yes, he is. Good night." Michael went inside and collapsed from exhaustion.

———◆———

Early next morning Michael called the nanny. Little Mike was fine. He called Judy and was assured that she was prepared to fend off all calls for a day or two, including that of Marshall's agent. The only good thing in his life was that it was shooting hiatus and the writing pressure was not immediate.

After a quick shower he met with Mrs. Taylor. Together they watched Linda in a therapy room. One way mirror allowed observation of the patient who would normally be left alone for brief periods. Linda helped herself to coffee and Danish, checked herself in the mirror, lifted her breast and viewed herself sideways. Finally, of all the available reading materials she chose the gossip magazine, *US*.

Linda didn't appreciate being brought in without her prior knowledge but once she was sober, she agreed that she should stay and detox. Maybe a few days is all she would need. She didn't think she had a serious problem that would require weeks and weeks of therapy. In fact, at some moments, she was glad that she had help to kick the ugly habit of drugs. Her attitude was positive. Mrs. Taylor and her staff were almost as optimistic about Linda's improvement as she was.

As he came out of the therapy room Michael walked through the plush lobby. He never noticed the night before how the interior was reminiscent of a fine hotel and once behind the *pearly gates,* indeed swinging doors with designs of pearls and glass of all colors, you were in the medical facility.

In the spacious lobby, enhanced by an espresso bar, was Marla, having a cappuccino. Michael did a double take.

"Marla? I can't believe this. What a sight for sore yes," he said and gave Marla a bear hug. She held him for a moment. Human assurance. You're never alone.

"Hello, Michael. Judy called," she said.

"I never know what to expect from her. I think she's really on my side."

"I'm sure she is."

"You know, there is a chance that Linda may come out or just see us accidentally. That wouldn't help her rehab."

"I'll buy lunch. Meet you at the Hideaway Café, remember, by the Country Inn on the cliff?''

She jumped into her car and drove off. Michael followed.

Atop a hillside at the edge of a bluff overlooking Zuma Beach, this small country-style cottage with a spacious view patio and warming fire pits was a favorite of the upscale Malibu crowd and a welcome discovery by the Inn's guests. The midweek lunch business was slow, soothing and romantic. Exactly what Michael and Marla needed.

"I wish I could help, Michael."

"Things sure have changed, haven't they," Michael said.

"Yes, you were my man, I was your woman—for five minutes," she tried to joke but nobody laughed.

Michael nodded. "Everything I wanted two years ago,"

"Is gone," Marla finished the thought.

"But not the kid. I'm crazy about little Mike." He pulled out his wallet with the baby pictures.

"He looks like you, Michael. The spitting image," she said.

"Sure he does. Why wouldn't he?"

"There were stories. At first, I was worried for you. I felt sorry for me. Then, later on, I thought if she could just scoop you up out of the air, like a low flying tennis ball that's about to bounce at your foot and become unreturnable, she is masterful. Hats off to her."

"Well put. And yes, that's a good metaphor," Michael said, digging into the famous grilled fish, his main course.

He was deep in thought. Marla watched as his face turned to laughter.

"I saw you on the beach. Bikini and all." He took a drink, smiled. "Warren and the model and all."

He chuckled.

"Would you rub it in, please." Marla smirked. They broke out laughing.

"All my journalistic and meteorological prowess is overpowered by the one hot day on the beach," she feigned insult.

"The bikini," he added.

"The bikini," she agreed.

"And while we're at it, what journalistic and meteorological prowess might you possess?" he asked laughing.

"The bikini."

Their laughter illuminated the already sunny restaurant. Anyone watching them would think they were lovers. The laughter slowed down. The laughter became smiles. When the laughter diminished their burning gaze took center stage. Silence followed. Angst weighted him down like a centuries-old anchor. She could see his pain but could not touch it.

"We could've been good together." He gazed off to nowhere.

"In another life, Michael."

"I did love you, you know."

"You never knew me," she said. "You never knew me, we never connected in a real way. Our bodies never knew each other."

"Linda and I, we know."

"Right. Linda and you know each other. That's what counts. And in a way, I am happy for you. Your baby."

"Yes." He sat silently then got up and walked her to her car. "Well, thank you for the smiles," he said after a long beat. Marla gave him a reassuring bear hug and before driving off she said, "Go, spend time with you baby."

Back at her condo, Marla took the normal bubble bath that would relax her. She read the paper and could not stop wondering why Judy would have called her of all people. Next morning, Marla called the office. Judy answered.

"Why did you think I could help him, Judy?" she asked. "His life is full."

"You did. You already did, by showing up. He called me last night."

Marla was taken aback. "It's strange, Judy. I wish I could help him but I'm in a different place now."

"Those were exactly the words Michael used when he called me. But he was happy about seeing you. So, maybe I did do some good."

"He couldn't possibly have a better person in his corner, Judy. I believe this."

"Then there's no chance that you'd come back into his life?" Judy asked.

"I'll always be a friend. Not a floor mat to be stepped on again.

CHAPTER THIRTY-ONE

Linda was on her best behavior at the *Mountside* and returned home in only ten days. Mrs. Taylor tested her time and time again as to the *mantra* and face-to-head-to-neck exercises that would help resist her urges. Whom to call and where to go if she felt she was falling and Michael was not enough to hold her up.

Linda was an absolute angel when Michael came to pick her up. She was dressed beautifully, her face rested and bright. Michael had not seen her look this good in a long time. He was thrilled.

On their way home she wanted to lunch at Neptune's Net. Had a craving for lobster.

"Craving as in pregnant?" Michael asked.

"No, silly. Not yet," she laughed a lighthearted laughter.

"It wouldn't be a problem." Michael was happy.

"Do you want to make a baby now?"

"Tonight?" he asked.

"This afternoon. In daylight," she said.

He pulled off to park in the Neptune's Net lot and kissed her with great love. Michael was happy. He had a life ahead after all. His day was getting better and better. Starting with Linda's release, her promising kiss, then the best lobster in the world served by the Neptune's Net just off the Pacific Coast Highway before the county line. The succulent, juicy food was a sexual turn-on for both of them. They never stopped touching each other during the drive all the way home and to the bedroom. The nanny heard them come in but had no reason to bother them. She knew that when Linda was happy the entire household was happy.

———— ♦ ————

Unbeknownst to Marla, Sebastian arrived in Los Angeles earlier than she had expected, checked into the Beverly Hills Hotel and went directly to the station for a meeting with Evelyn.

Sebastian knew how to wear Armani, casual or otherwise, but he was also a fan of his countrymen, Spanish designers such as Antonio Miro or the up and coming Purificación García. Sebastian was a looker, always set apart from other men, but his best quality was his ability to listen and hear. He knew he was blessed by a unique family life and felt that continuing the task of making the family fortune grow was his natural calling. He was smart, educated and curious, motivated by positive ideas.

Evelyn treated him to a special lunch created by her in-house chef. There were thinly crisped lobster bites with a sour orange and mustard sauce; Asian shrimp potstickers with plum dipping sauce; shaved Okeechobee hearts of palm salad with avocado, tomato and Panela cheese; seared sea scallops, tiny green beans and fruit sherbet to top it off.

"This is a fabulous lunch, Evelyn. My compliments to the chef," he said.

"You can thank him yourself later on. Chef Patrick will step in before he leaves for the day."

"Do you eat this well all the time?" he asked.

"I have to admit I wanted to impress you, so we did something unusual for your palate." Evelyn was proud of herself. "This is not an every day visit. Your idea interests me. Actually, it intrigues me."

"That was the intent," he said. He opened his briefcase, pulled out a portfolio of photos of Emanuella's Models of the Continent.

"You see, my sister, Emanuella, thinks that California girls are most beautiful. She had been talking about enriching her stable with the long-legged variety sporty looking ones."

Evelyn was nodding along, wondering where this was going.

"You may be wondering where I am going with this, Evelyn," he smiled softly. "I'll cut to the chase. The bottom line is that Emanuella would never buy into a network, or into a cable company and have no control, but she wants her hands in television. You've explained to me that this is an independent station with its own brand of programming, your brand."

He walked around, poured himself some coffee, sat down, looked at her and then, as the *toreador*, moved in for the kill. "We want to buy the station. Emanuella wants a forum in California. Your Board of Directors is being threatened by imbalance that could be taken advantage of, possible unfriendly takeover."

Evelyn was speechless.

"What *sayeth* you, ma'am?"

This time she walked around, she poured herself more coffee and looked at him quizzically.

"I say, it is food for thought. Definitely food for thought." She took a long sip. "It is, obviously a possibility which never occurred to me. I would like to get into the nitty-gritty," she said.

Sebastian nodded thoughtfully, then took a thick velo-bound book from his deep briefcase. He walked around the table, placed it in front of her and opened it.

"Look at the table of contents, Evelyn. I believe I've covered every aspect. Besides the financial offer, I have outlined the percentage of time Emanuella would like to control and the type of shows she would like to do. She is only interested in promoting the beauty of modeling, having contests for girls, lectures on how to dress, eat, move, and so on, which is what girls' schools used to do for all girls a few decades ago."

Evelyn's thinking cap kept getting larger. "Not too bad. We could attract a bigger and younger audience. But we don't intend to depict or promote promiscuity in any form."

"You are the final word in programming. In fact, Emanuella would rely on your guidance since there may be different rules on the Continent. Emanuella also attached a plan to show that she would be responsible for a certain amount of revenue and if she is not fulfilling that end, she would walk."

"She would?" Evelyn was amazed.

"We are fair business people. We do not take without giving. That's how we were raised."

The telephone intercom buzzed. Evelyn pressed the speaker button.

"We're on the speaker, Barbie."

"Just wanted you to know that Marla is in her office," Evelyn's assistant said.

"Thank you."

"Is there a way out for me? I don't want her to see me," Sebastian said.

"You don't?" Evelyn was surprised.

"I suppose I should give you an explanation since you're her friend. I'm not arriving officially until Monday, after the weekend. But she loves the locations north of Los Angeles so much, that I think I will be buying a home there. I have appointments to see some in Santa Maria and Santa Barbara areas."

"May I remind you that she doesn't like her life planned by anyone other than herself," Evelyn said

"Believe me, I have that carved in stone on my mantle," he laughed. "That's actually the reason for my buying a place. I don't want her to feel pressured by the distance."

"Pressured?"

"Yes, with the ways of global business, I can operate anywhere. But her face, her weather, her interviews, are all here. In Los Angeles, for Los Angeles."

"I'm touched. I hope she'll like your surprise."

"By the way, the acquisition is between us. After you have read the entire prospectus, we will decide how to present it."

Evelyn buzzed her assistant. "Barbie, would you occupy Marla for about 15 minutes while we get Señor *de Pombal* out of here?"

"On my way," Barbie answered.

Sebastian and Evelyn shook hands and headed out of the conference room.

"I'll be eager to hear your thoughts, Evelyn."

"I'll be just as eager to collect them," she said, laughing.

CHAPTER THIRTY-TWO

Marla and Becky walked back to the advertising agency after lunch. Becky was the head writer now but she reported to Marla that she was not happy. Jonathan has changed since Marla left and his taking up with the Poole woman was not good for them at all.

"I thought the Poole family had hired him to review the advertising at KMRTV and propose a plan of his own," Marla said.

"No. He went after them to get their business and Missy intercepted and took over with him. I don't think she speaks for the family. I think the family has nothing to do with Jonathan. I think she's just leading him on."

"Really? How do you know that?" Marla asked.

"I don't know it for a fact, Marla. I just caught some tidbits of information along the way that make me think that."

"Well, I'll tell Evelyn to check it out."

"Don't mention my name."

"I wouldn't. Don't worry."

Becky headed into their office building, Marla walked toward the parking lot. She saw a red Ferrari pull up in front. Jonathan was being dropped off by Missy. Marla turned away and continued to her car. She heard the typical wolf whistle but did not stop. She was opening her car door when Jonathan caught up with her.

"You ignore me now? Is that it?"

"I don't respond to wolf whistles. I'm too dignified, remember?"

"But you knew it was me."

"Jonathan, I am not going to reduce myself to your games. Your evil games. I don't know what happened to you and I don't want to know. I used to have great respect for you."

She got into her car. He blocked her from closing the door.

"Let me go," she demanded.

"I need you."

"Let me go, I said." She started the engine.

"I'm not evil."

"If you can do what you're doing with the Poole woman, you are evil. Let me go."

"I'm not evil."

"I have a hazard siren and I will use it."

He held the door for a beat, then stepped back. Marla was glad her car went from zero to fifty in sixty seconds. She was out of there.

———◆———

Marla headed to her next appointment in Santa Monica. She drove the few blocks to *Clean, Eat and Party!* and parked in the parking building off the street. She walked by a small wine shop and a bakery where she inhaled the fresh smell of baked bread and pastry. She looked longingly at the pastry window display. Some days she could eat anything in sight. It was tough to pass it up, but she managed to keep walking.

"Welcome to my place," Xiùměi said as she opened the front door to let Marla in. She gestured around. "Very little now. Will be bigger soon."

Xiùměi opened a side door which was part of a wall unit and lead to the kitchen that was adjacent to the bakery next door. She was proud of the continuous space. "State of art very soon."

"You have to have dreams to know where you want to go," Marla said.

She saw the open shelving of supplies, dishes and equipment. The delivery boxes ready to go.

"Měi Wong will come at noon. Will deliver. She lives in house on corner. Takes care of place."

"You don't deliver?"

"Only friends. To friends. I deliver to friends only," she carefully corrected herself by putting the sentence in order.

"I want to throw a surprise birthday party for my boss. I would like to see your price list and catalog," Marla said, sitting down.

"You, weather girl. I recognize. Mistress of executives," she said while producing her well-designed catalog.

"Little funny, yes? Something your good friend Carol said," she laughed, then waited for Marla to join in. She did not.

"You're less naïve than I thought. 'Mistress of executives' is not a nice thing to say, especially if you want to do business with me. Do you?"

Xiùměi bowed, her eyes cast down. "I am in shame, Miss Marla," she said.

"I'm sorry," said Marla. "That's the correct apology."

"I am sorry," Xiùměi repeated.

Marla smiled. "OK. No more of that. Let me see what you have."

"How many people?" Xiùměi asked.

"Somewhere between forty and sixty. I want to invite everyone at the station. I'll need prices."

"We select menu, yes?"

"Yes. But menu depends on the budget. We select prices first. I have an idea," Marla said. "Let me have the list of your menu with the per serving prices. I will take it with me and work up some combinations. Then I'll call you back with the details," said Marla. "Can we do that?"

"Yes. We can do that." Xiùměi pulled out the relevant pages from the catalog to make copies for Marla.

"Miss Marla, I am happy. I have citizenship celebration."

"Well, congratulations," Marla said. "When is that?"

"July 4th. Big party at China Garden in China Town. I will ask many clients to come," she said, her eyes filled with sincere excitement. "You like date? July 4?" She was proud of herself. "Birthday of America, birthday of Xiùměi."

"Very good idea," Marla said. "Maybe the station will let me bring my cameraman and do an interview? Would that be all right?"

"Very much all right. Good for business. Nice Chinese girl, American citizen, private business. Very much all right," she said enthusiastically.

Xiùměi handed Marla the pages and Marla headed for the door.

"I'll call you after the weekend, in a day or two. Thank you," Marla said and waved *good bye* to the bowing Xiùměi.

———◆———

Xiùměi sat back and ran the video of Marla's visit. There was nothing wrong about it. Nothing she could use.

Loud banging startled her, made her jump up and rush for the front door. She did not stop the video tape. In front of her business entrance was Linda, dressed in teenage grunge look that absolutely did not become her. Xiùměi quickly let her in.

"Miss Linda?"

"Yeah, yeah, Xiùměi. I have to talk to you," Linda said.

"About? Another party maybe?"

Linda saw the Marla conversation tape running and stopped to watch it. She paced up and down, her eyes searched around suspiciously.

"Interesting. The bitch will give a party for the other bitch. They do fit together, don't they." She was talking more to herself than to Xiùměi.

"And she wants to interview you. How can you be as interesting as my husband? What is she thinking? Dumb broad."

She continued pacing then abruptly stopped.

"I want my tape."

"What tape?" Xiùměi asked innocently.

"From the wedding. Carol and Buzz's wedding. I'm sure you remember." Linda was on edge and impatient.

"Maybe we talk. Talk about tape. Would you like some tea?" Xiùměi asked. "How much is it worth?"

"It's not worth anything. My husband saw me with Marshall."

"Then why do you come here?"

"I want it. That's all."

"How much?"

"You know, I can blackmail you right back. I can expose you. You're invited into fine homes to do a job, you get a lot of money and then you spy? That's criminal. I can stop that nice big citizenship celebration with one phone call." Linda pointed toward the video and stared into Xiùměi's eyes. "Think."

Xiùměi busied herself with the tea kettle and placed the setting on the coffee table in front of the guest couch. She poured for Linda.

"Cream? Lemon? Asian?"

"Asian," Linda said and sat down.

"Why do you keep me waiting?"

"You in hurry?" Xiùměi was slowly gaining back her footing. "I have nice little stash. You wish to see?" she asked Linda.

Linda squinted at her from the corner of an eye.

"Stash? Stash of what?"

"Stash of things. Assorted stash." Xiùměi said. "Little this. Little that."

Linda got up. "Are you taping this?"

"Yes."

Linda could not make up her mind.

"Turn off your camera."

"Fine." Xiùměi walked toward her desk and made Linda believe that she was stopping the tape. Linda was tempted by the dope. Temptation versus her security? What to do?

"I can't do business with you, Xiùměi," she said. "You are not worthy of my trust."

"I am only one worthy. You have secret. I have secret. We trust. I am only one."

Xiùměi got up and brought a huge gift basket of foods to the coffee table. She ceremoniously opened a *faux* cheese ball. It was a container for cocaine. That caught Linda's interest. Xiùměi unscrewed a decorative pear and disclosed that it, too, was a hiding place for drugs. Crack. Linda's eyes were glued to the process. She reached for some chocolate squares. Looked at Xiùměi. Xiùměi nodded "No." Linda reached for a box that had "mints" written on it. She opened it and there was a neat row of *roaches* and a snazzy *roach clip*.

Xiùměi picked up the basket and moved it out of Linda's reach.

"What are you doing?" Linda was disturbed. "Do not tease me."

Xiùměi smiled and poured Linda some more tea.

"You like the tea?" she asked. "Damiana. You want to remember the name. Sometimes it is all that you need for excitement, for feeling very, very sexy."

"Is that what I'm drinking?" A twinkle appeared in her eyes. "I like, Xiùměi. I like."

Linda was childlike in her delight of discovering a new aphrodisiac.

"I want some. I want some of everything."

"You have money?"

"I have money." She started to put bills on the desk. Xiùměi was surprised to see the amount of cash Linda carried on her.

"Here. Is that enough?" Linda looked at Xiùměi.

"Yes." Xiùměi made a little *care package* reminiscent of an ice cream container and put it into several double bags as one would an ice cream container. She pulled out the monthly calendar.

"About cleaning mansion?"

"Cleaning what?" Linda asked.

"Mr. Michael mansion."

"My house?"

"Yes. Monthly big cleaning. Very big." Xiùměi put an "X" in a calendar box.

"I can do final Monday."

"Final Monday of what?"

"Final Monday every month. I send contract to house."

Xiùměi finished the packaging and sent Linda on her way.

Linda stopped at the first market, purchased a few more containers of ice cream and put them all together on the floor of the back seat.

———— ◆ ————

Xiùměi went home and found Allan sitting on the worn out couch in his shorts and undershirt, staring at the TV. She took some leftovers out of the refrigerator and set it on the dinner table.

"Did you work?" she asked.

"Yes."

"Many hours?" She looked at him with eyes of scrutiny.

"Five hours."

"When get paid?"

"When I finish the house I will get paid," he answered.

"Five hours? Very slow painting."

"It's very hard work, Xiùměi."

"You buy groceries?"

"You make more money, Xiùměi. You buy groceries."

"Don't order me. You are not boss of me." She was annoyed and angry. She walked over to the TV and turned it off. "No."

She stood facing him, looking down on his slouched figure.

"No. I not buy groceries. I put my money in my bank. I will buy house." She turned her back on him and went to the kitchen. He followed.

"That's a good idea, to buy a house. Owning property is smart."

"I buy my house," she said.

"We're married. It's community property. We both own it."

"Not if you don't stop addiction."

"Not what?"

"Not your house. My house. Not married."

"You're going to divorce me? I laugh at that," he said, gleaming.

"You laugh. OK," her voice rose, her face turned red with anger. "You want married, you want house, you stop addiction. No drink, no drugs. Stop!" She stood erect, locking eyes with him.

"You don't understand," he yelled. "You're not U.S. citizen. You can't do a lot of things!"

"I give you laugh back!" she screamed. "I U.S. citizen July 4, birthday of U.S. of A."

"Before you go off buying houses, remember that I brought you over to America, good old U.S. of A. You owe me!"

"Owe you? I laugh back!" she replied. "I pay. I give you money for airplane ticket. I give you money tomorrow! No, wait, I give you check now!"

He grabbed for her but she got away. She ran to the drawer where Allan's gun was kept. She took it. Pointed it at him. She went to the bedroom, all along pointing the gun at Allan. He was scared, unsure whether or not she would pull the trigger. She was still flushed, losing self-control.

"You sleep on couch. You stop drink, drugs, you sleep in bed."

She slammed the bedroom door closed.

———— ◆ ————

Michael called it a day and went home early to see his loved ones. He casually dropped off his briefcase, walked up the stairs and opened the bedroom door. Through the sliding glass balcony doors he saw Linda, still dressed in teenage grunge, dancing around the balcony over the pool, carrying the baby, making him giggle by tossing him in the air, singing along with a rock group, squeezing him tight, and tossing him in the air again. Without startling her, Michael watched closely and jumped in to catch the baby during one of the tosses.

Linda started laughing. "Good catch!" she shouted.

"I trusted you, Linda. I believed you." He had tears in his eyes. He wanted to hug Linda but she danced away. "Stop it, sweetie. Settle down." He sat on the bed, little Mike in his lap, indicating for Linda a place next to him. She slowed down dancing but still wouldn't settle down. Michael was afraid to let go of the baby and giving Linda a chance to pick him up again.

"I married you because I love you."

"It was just sex," Linda said.

"It was love," Michael said. "I still love you. I'll see you through this."

Linda settled down. Michael put the baby in his crib in their bedroom and held Linda. The baby didn't want to be put down. He started to cry.

"Damn him," Linda screamed.

"It's our baby, Linda."

"I hate him, I hate him!" she screamed. Little Mike cried louder.

"Don't get angry with him," Michael said and picked him up. "Look at that face. How can you hate that face?"

Linda looked at the baby, smiled and kissed the teary little face.

"How about if we take a ride? Just the three of us. The family."

Michael took little Mike in one arm, put a jacket over Linda's shoulders and they walked down the stairs to the garage. In the car, he secured the baby, asked Linda to put on her seat belt and started the engine. He pressed a speed number on the telephone keypad and heard Mrs. Taylor's voice through his ear phone.

"It's OK Mr. Gaston. We are here."

He didn't say anything. He knew that Mrs. Taylor's Caller ID was enough of an advance notice of them being on their way. Michael felt himself aging by the minute.

The white Rolls Royce rolled silently through the gates of *Mountside Malibu.* Mrs. Taylor greeted Linda as if she were a long lost best friend.

"We're so happy to see you, Linda," she said, taking her by the arm. "You'll never guess what we did. We repainted your room. It is now shrimp color. Easy on your eyes."

"Easy on my eyes," Linda said in an obviously regressed stage.

"We'll have a good time together. You know what else?" Mrs. Taylor looked at her with a warm smile. "Your old friend, Amy, the one you liked so much when you visited before, remember?"

"I remember Amy," Linda said, walking slowly with Mrs. Taylor, forgetting about Michael and little Mike.

"Well, Amy has your special cocktail ready. Then, when you wake up, you will go for a swim."

"Goody, goody," were the last words Michael heard as Mrs. Taylor and Linda disappeared down the corridor and the *pearly gates* closed.

Baby Mike had gone to sleep in Michael's arm. Michael's feet were lead. He could not move. He stood in the lobby until an attendant directed him to the guest room where he had stayed before. They rolled a crib in for Baby Mike.

Michael couldn't sleep. The silence was deafening.

CHAPTER THIRTY-THREE

Working on the weekends made Marla more tired than if she had been in front of the camera all week long. Just the same, Sundays went fast. She could hardly wait to get home and relax but the brain was buzzing, going into overtime again. There were some "Need notes" she wanted to do for Evelyn and Reed on Xiùměi. It was a hunch thing. She had to prove that some of the available information and her first-hand observations were contradictory. Who was this woman? Was she a nice immigrant trying to do well? Was she trouble? If so, what kind of trouble? What were she and Carol talking about on the yacht? Could she or should she call Carol and ask?

She poured a glass of wine, turned on the computer and got the best news, an e-mail from Sebastian. He was coming to town.

She couldn't deny that her heart went *pitter-patter* and beat that extra beat. She looked up at the sky and said, "Thank you, Mother."

Since it was impossible for her to relax, she started her list of questions regarding Xiùměi. She was not sure that she could sell the idea of interviewing this immigrant to Evelyn and Reed, but it was really under her skin. Nevertheless, her thoughts were interrupted time-and-again by thoughts of Sebastian. What will he say? What will she say? It seemed so long ago that they spent that incredible week together. It seemed that she had not come to terms with her feelings about him. It seemed that she was not ready. But, he was coming. Ready or not. That was that.

Monday morning found Marla at the tennis club, fitting herself into a doubles game that was about to start. By the time she was in the third set, she saw Buzz come out on the courts. She looked toward the terrace, and as expected, Carol sat by herself with a cup of coffee. Poised to watch.

The service counter on the terrace always had coffee, tea, lemonade, water and fruit available for the members. Marla finished the match, shook hands and headed over to Carol. Buzz had already started a match with Sally as his mixed partner. Carol was cool as a cucumber.

"Good to see you," Marla said. "I think." She snuck in a little chuckle. "I never know for sure which one of you I am talking to."

"This is the good me. The happy camper me" Carol said.

"All right then, I can deal with that."

"How does it feel to be famous? Even a little bit. Just L.A. famous?"

Marla picked up an apple from the service counter, took a huge bite of the crunchy, juicy fruit and sat down at Carol's table.

"I tell you, it is very strange. You never know when it'll hit you but you can never be in a bad mood about it. Carol, it's like a perpetual fishbowl. Being just L.A. famous. I don't want the BIG famous. No way."

They laughed. Buzz played at his best. Watching him was a pleasure.

"I took your lead about a caterer, Carol. You know, you're the homemaker maven so if you think Xiùměi is a happening, why shouldn't I. I'm hiring her for Evelyn's birthday gathering. We all have to start somewhere." Marla broke up laughing. "Don't we?"

Carol caught the idea and started laughing. "Who would've thunk, as they say," Carol said and tried to keep her laughter low.

After a while Marla returned to her original topic. "Somehow, I have some inexplicable misgivings regarding Xiùměi. Some confusing thoughts."

Carol's instant response was freaky, "What do you know?"

"Know? I know nothing. What's there to know?"

Marla couldn't believe that her own reactive mind caught Carol's body language that gave away too much immediately.

"I want to know everything. I'm thinking about covering her citizenship celebration. That would give her business a push. Is she worth it?"

"You know, Marla, you have interviewed a top television producer, larger than life. Then you have interviewed a top con, loveable and cuddly, but larger than life, who screwed a lot of ordinary middle class people out of money. I thought that was high quality interview with a Marla touch. I am beginning to understand what people like to watch about you. You come right into their living room and they sit down with you. You don't sit down with them. You make it so easy."

"Wow! Thank you. That's a real compliment."

"What can you gain by featuring someone like Xiùměi? It's like a round peg in a square hole. No fit."

"My handle would be that we have too many immigrants who're doing nothing just living off us. Here is one, etc., etc."

Carol was faking nonchalance. Her face grew tighter, her eyes shrunk squintier. "Far be it from me to advise you."

"Why stop now?" Marla said this in good spirit.

"I don't know anything about television."

"You're the audience. You know a lot."

"Well, no. I don't think you should do her. You said you have misgivings.

Listen to your inner voice." Carol poured herself some more coffee. Marla watched her every move.

"Profound."

"You're mocking me, aren't you?" Carol was on guard.

"I want to test myself as a journalist."

"A journalist? Since when? If you're trying to make me laugh, you're on the right track."

"Are you milking the money cow on both ends?" Marla asked. Then put her hands on her mouth. "I'm not sure why this came out of my mouth."

"I'm not sure that it makes any sense. You can burn a candle on both ends but you can't milk a cow on both ends." Carol stayed calm. "Money cow? Is that a journalistic device?"

"Guess I'm losing it. Thanks for pointing it out to me."

"I'm your friend."

"Yes, I remember. Not my mother. But I'm curious how come Xiùměi is so busy so fast?"

Carol got up. "Why don't you ask her if you're so curious. I have to run some errands."

"OK, see you." Marla started for the lockers.

"I think you're looking for a story where there isn't one, aren't you?" Carol said. "Jonathan makes a better subject than Xiùměi, especially if he falls on his face. Which I'd hope."

"Do you see that coming?" Marla asked, sensing that Carol kept herself inside the loop.

"You're doing it again, Lady. I'm not your *deep throat*. Bye." Carol left. Marla felt her instincts confirmed. Carol knew something. Carol wanted to change the subject from Xiùměi. Why? Marla realized this was bigger than what she had experienced as a television journalist. She went to the station.

"Evelyn, can you spare a minute?" Marla asked, walking through Evelyn's open door.

"Yes."

Marla rushed up to Evelyn's desk and spurted out an unbelievable concept.

"Evelyn, this Xiùměi is not what she seems to be, there are little signs of her being connected to all the people who hire her. I tell you, there is a string, a tie of some kind that gives her the upper hand. She's too successful too fast. She acts subservient but is very smug at the same time. I don't know what and I don't know how to find it." Marla practically collapsed in the guest chair after saying all this in one breath.

"We have investigators on retainer, Marla."

"Oh, is that how you do it?"

"Yes. That's how we find facts before we report on them. It's called responsible journalism."

"Wow!" Marla laughed. "Thank you. So I have to be a responsible journalist? "

"Yes, my dear. It's not all glamour. The glamour is up front. The substance is behind it."

"Can you find an investigator who speaks Chinese?" Marla said.

"Good thought. I'll check into it," Evelyn said. "We have the best private eye company on retainer, so they should be able to help us."

"Oh, well then, I can relax. Xiùměi will cater your surprise birthday party and the investigators can get on her tail."

"That's one way. By the way, thank you for my surprise birthday party. When is it?" Evelyn laughed.

"On your birthday, Evelyn. Friday. Don't leave town. Can't start without you."

They laughed. "You are such a breath of fresh air."

"But I don't know what I'm doing," Marla said.

"Listen to your hunches but don't act upon them before telling me. That's the only rule you have to follow. Do not act upon them before telling me."

"I will not act upon them before telling you." Marla crossed her heart.

————— ◆ —————

Back in her office, Marla e-mailed invitations to all employees about the party the following Friday. Then she called Xiùměi, faxed over the delivery order. Marla was very happy to find out that Xiùměi would bring the food over in person and there would be one or two of her helpers along. The investigator could get a good fix on her, maybe go undercover and get a job with Xiùměi?

Marla told Xiùměi to bring all utensils and settings but that Marla would take care of the decoration. She would handle that. Marla could hear Xiùměi moving around as they talked.

Xiùměi said on the telephone, "Excuse me, moment. Someone at door."

Marla heard her going to the door to let someone in. "Hello," said a female voice to Xiùměi. It sounded vaguely familiar, or was it just Marla's imagination? Then Xiùměi got back to her.

"OK, Miss. I will prepare for next Friday," Xiùměi said.

"Call me if you have any questions, please," said Marla and hung up.

She stopped by Evelyn's office. Barbie was at her desk and Evelyn's door was closed.

"Barbie," Marla said. "I'm out of here. I'm getting my hair done, manicure, pedicure, facial, the works."

"A date?"

"I think so," Marla smiled.

"Tonight?"

"No. Not tonight. But soon." Marla grinned.

"How soon?" Barbie asked, as if doubting Marla.

"As soon as Sebastian gets here."

"You have to admit this is funny," Barbie said.

"What?"

"No date date."

Marla could not be more secure in having a date.

"Believe me, it's a real date."

"Marla, there's something wrong with this picture. Do you hear yourself? A real date but you don't know when."

"Not exactly. Approximately. But, just to make sure, I'll be ready!" She added a girlish wave of her hand, kicked up her heel and danced out.

The telephone rang. "Evelyn Baker's office," Barbie said.

"Hello. I'm fine, thank you. Just a moment, please." She buzzed Evelyn. "It's *Sebastian de Pombal*."

After a lengthy conversation with Sebastian, Evelyn rang Barbie, asked her to call a special Board of Directors meeting for as soon as Saturday since she could not miss her own birthday party. Was it forty or fifty? Hard to remember. Time flies.

CHAPTER THIRTY-FOUR

"What? No pizza?" asked the handsome Chinese-American man handing a bouquet of flowers to Evelyn. "This can't be a real party without pizza. But if it is, happy birthday, Evelyn Baker."

"Thank you, Chang," Evelyn said. "Let me introduce you to Marla Hayes, our…"

"No need. I wouldn't miss the weekend weather for anything," he said, shaking hands with Marla. As if on cue, Sebastian appeared in the doorway of the decorated conference room, with a wrapped gift for Evelyn. Marla instantly lit up and moved toward him. They kissed on the cheeks and Sebastian handed the gift to Evelyn.

"Somebody did a beautiful job decorating," he said, looking around.

"Somebody did a beautiful job cooking," Evelyn said. "Let me introduce Ms. Wang Xiùměi, our caterer."

Xiùměi bowed and Sebastian shook her hands while Chang bowed as well."

"Mr. Jiǎng Chang, our good friend is always welcome at our parties, with or without pizza."

Xiùměi looked questioning, "Pizza? Is good at party? Birthday party?"

"I was joking," Chang said. "This looks like great food. Would you care to tell me what everything is?"

"Come with pleasure, I show everything," Xiùměi said. Chang and the others held back their laughter at the humor of the faulty English.

"I come," he said to her and followed her from dish to dish, from area to area as she had grouped up exotic foods with simple settings and simple foods with exquisite settings. The way she walked, with so much pride, was noticed by everyone. Although it was Evelyn's party, Xiùměi felt special as well.

"She did a fine job here," Sebastian said to Marla. "I would like to remember her name, maybe get her card."

"Sure, thing," Marla said. "I'll tell you about her later."

"Much later?" he smiled seductively. "I have other things in my mind for us first."

Evelyn was surrounded by her staff and executives. A small band made up of employees playing various instruments, started to mess around and make some kind of music. Some of it was even recognizable and that which wasn't they called *jamming*.

Barbie lead a conga line, Rhonda tried to sing and Reed became the chief bartender. Evelyn and Marla saw Chang and Xiùměi chat, Xiùměi blush as he whispered something to her before he left.

"I can't believe you got a Chinese investigator," Marla said to Evelyn.

"Yes, I remembered Chang from using him before. He was born in L.A. but his parents never learned English. So this job is really right on the nose for him," Evelyn said.

"Looks like Xiùměi trusts him," Marla said.

"Yes. It does," Evelyn replied.

Sebastian stepped over to them.

"I'm happy I came to your party, Evelyn. Everyone's having a good time. Are you?"

"Oh, yes, Sebastian. This was a good idea. Thanks, Marla. I haven't had a birthday party in ages."

After everyone has cleared out, Xiùměi's staff cleaned up. By the time Evelyn, Barbie, Marla and Sebastian were ready to leave, the entire building was back to normal, back to business.

Sebastian followed Marla to her home and parked in her garage. She was quiet, he was quiet when they rode up the elevator and entered the condominium. Dimmed accent lights gave it a soft hue. Marla reached for the light switch. Sebastian stopped her.

"One moment, please. Let my senses capture this first impression," he said. He took her by the hand and she slowly walked him through the living room, the guest room, the den, the open dining area without stopping at the master bedroom.

"It's jasmine or gardenias?" Sebastian asked, inhaling the fresh cut flower scent.

"Gardenias," she said.

He pulled her to him and they kissed.

"I never forget 'firsts' and this is a 'first'." He kissed her again.

"A 'first' in your home," he laughed, wanting to ease her tension. She was clearly nervous and started to light candles around the dining room, that was once the *table for twenty networking center*. It seemed like another century.

"There, now," she mumbled. She opened the wine closet.

Sebastian glanced at the wine selection. "Malbec?"

"Yes, sure. Please." She could not relax. She switched on the dining room light so he could easily find the wine glasses. Marla was still working on coring the apples and pears when he came to the kitchen, put down the wine and with her back to him, put his arms around her. She could feel his nostrils against her neck, his breathing like a ribbon of velvet slithering on her skin.

"I want us to feel comfortable and free together," he said. "Anywhere. Our emotions have to be the same anywhere. It's who we are that matters, not where we are."

She turned to face him. "I know." She took a deep breath as if trying to get rid of the ghost of Warren.

"In Palm Springs you said 'until you see your way to me clearly, until there is no one else cluttering your life' we cannot be. You were right."

She slowly dropped her clothes to the floor. "And here I am. Uncluttered."

She reached for his hand and walked him to the bedroom. When he pulled her to him it was just like the first time. She trembled under his touch. She could not get enough of the feel of his skin against hers, the scent of his light cologne, the way her body fit perfectly into his muscular arms around her and the taste of his lips. She carried that taste with her ever since the first time. Unforgettable. Another night of magic locked out the rest of the world from their lives.

The early morning light found them in the shower, playfully starting the day. It was Saturday. She would go to the station sometime in the afternoon. Before that, she would run a couple of errands and definitely try to get in some tennis.

"Are you sure you don't want to come with me to the club and hit a few?"

"Actually," he said, careful to appear truthful, "Nuella asked me to check into something for her here in Los Angeles. Some business. I made an appointment."

"All right, then. I'll miss you," Marla said.

Sebastian looked at his watch. "How would you like to have dinner with me tonight?"

"Oh, I thought you'd never ask," she said.

They held hands in the elevator and shared one more passionate kiss before getting into their cars and driving off in different directions.

———◆———

The Board of Directors was settled around the conference room table by nine o'clock Saturday morning. Coffee, muffins and fruit were served. Barbie proved herself over and over again as a most professional assistant. Once a court reporter, she would frequently apply her dictation-taking skill at Evelyn's meetings.

Chairman of the Board, Nicholas Poole, ran through the formalities. They waived prior business, previous minutes and moved to accept the one-issue agenda of the special meeting, that of the Offer of the *Family de Pombal*.

Evelyn introduced Sebastian who pointed out the highlights of his acquisition proposal. He then gave them some time alone.

Unexpectedly, Missy Poole arrived with Jonathan and immediately started to speak.

"Gentlemen, Ladies, I am the sole heir here. Why was I not invited?" Missy was beside herself.

Evelyn turned to her. "You seem to have forgotten that first, you did not ask to speak; second, you are not on the agenda; and third, you have no voting power, Ms. Poole. Maybe some other time."

"No voting power? How about the two seats? I want a seat."

"At the moment the gentlemen filling those two seats are present. They have not yet retired. But since you've taken upon yourself, to come to this special meeting may I introduce a witness to your current status. Penelope Kaplan Marx Just.

Penelope entered the room and stood next to the Chairman of the Board, Nicholas Poole. Missy stared at her with disgust and looked at Jonathan.

"Your receptionist?"

Jonathan was taken aback. "My mother."

Missy was about to faint. Penelope smiled her victory smile.

"Ladies, Gentlemen of the Board. Many years ago Evelyn Baker's mother mentored me and made sure that I did not stray from the straight and narrow path." A sexy smirk passed through her face. "Which I had a tendency to do." She took a sip of water.

"I was engaged to Nicholas Poole. We were in love, but the family didn't like a Jewish girl, so I married Morris Kaplan, an entrepreneur, the father of Jonathan. Mr. Kaplan died too young."

"I then had the rare opportunity to guide Evelyn to her independent thinking and watch her take KMRTV to previously unknown heights. There never was any kind of action or interference by any member of the Poole family."

"Although I married Howard Just, I stayed in touch with my dear friend, Missy Poole's mother, and Nicholas' sister, Annabelle. Jonathan Kaplan, my son, is a quick study, but Missy got ahead of him. I knew he had to learn a lesson when he and Missy started to plot against the interests of the Poole holdings, including KMRTV.

"So, in the end, if things remain under the control of Evelyn Baker, Missy Poole will, one day, inherit a fine operation." She turned to Missy.

"But Missy, you have to stop misrepresenting the family and provoking lawsuits against the family by your unauthorized dealings and self-serving methods."

Missy was shrinking in her seat. Evelyn rose.

"Thank you Penelope." She then turned to Missy. "Ms. Poole, your family was advised, pursuant to the Rules and your uncle Nicholas, Chairman of the Board, is present. It was not required that you be advised but a mere courtesy. You have nothing to do with these proceedings."

"I want to stay," she whined.

"If there is no objection by anyone here, you may stay," Evelyn said. She then looked around. "Any objections?"

"Let it go on record that the members of the Board allowed Missy Poole to stay and hear the proceedings."

"There is certainly no place here for an advertising man," Evelyn said.

"I don't want to be here, thank you," Jonathan said and scrambled out the door as quickly as he could.

The meeting continued. Sebastian's proposal was accepted unanimously, pending full review and final answer within one week.

Jonathan hurried down the hallway to the parking lot. Outside, he took a deep breath. A breath of relief. His mother saved his skin once again. As he reached his car he saw Marla drive in. He decided to wait for her. She got out of her car.

"What now, Jonathan?" she said annoyed.

"Apology?"

"Yeah, right." Marla walked past him toward the building entrance.

"I am very serious, Marla. I taught you to do research and I neglected to do my own research. Missy lied. She's actually a little soft in the head."

"You don't say. Who would've thought?" Marla's look was filled with pity.

"Jonathan, you fell for the money. I can't believe it."

"Does that mean you accept?"

"What?"

"My apology," Jonathan said.

Marla reached out her hand to shake his. "Yes. Apology accepted. But the rhyming. Wasn't that a hint to beware, that something is off kilter with her?"

"Are you never going to let me forget that? She's soft in the head."

Marla gave him a hug.

"But you're incredible," he continued. "Like I said, 'leaps and bounds,' You're reaching amazing heights."

"Thank you, Jonathan. Yes, you did predict something like that. Now I have to go to work."

Marla went inside directly to the sound studio where the news was broadcast, bypassing the administration building and the conference room.

CHAPTER THIRTY-FIVE

Xiùměi carefully straightened out her office, prepared the tea set-up ready in the kitchen, dusted the coffee table, the couch, the shelves. When finished, she took a last look around and smiled with satisfaction. Her little kingdom, soon to be empire. She proceeded to look out to the street through the window, through the white floral design tulle curtain. Past the wrought iron bars she saw Chang getting out of his car.

She was nervous when she opened the front door to let him into her shop. He brought some flowers. She was visibly touched. Her demeanor shy and modest.

"Tea ready," she said with eyes cast down.

"I like whiskey in mine," he said.

"If you wish." She went to the kitchen and returned with a small bottle of Kentucky whiskey. He poured, she declined.

The telephone rang. Xiùměi checked the Caller ID, her grimace expressed annoyance.

"So sorry," she said to Chang and picked up the handset. "Clean, Eat and Party!"

"Hello Xiùměi, this is Marla Hayes."

"Hello. Is this important?" Xiùměi said. "I in big hurry this moment."

"I'll be quick," Marla said. "I'd like to come by with a cameraman to photograph you in your shop and talk a few minutes. Can I do that?"

"Yes."

"Can I do that before your citizenship party?"

"Yes." Said Xiùměi impatiently, aware of Chang's eyes on her.

"When?"

"I call you at TV office."

"You have my card?" Marla asked.

"Yes." Xiùměi hung up.

Chang sat on the guest couch, watching her every move.

"You're the first beautiful Chinese woman I ever saw in this country," he said flirtatiously. "Is it true what they say about the genuine article?"

"What you mean?"

"Come here, Xiùměi. Sit down."

She did not move. Could not. Her feet seemed to be glued to the ground. He got up and moved so close to her that she could feel his masculine membrane brushing by her crotch, taking on rhythm.

"That is private," she could barely whisper.

"Yes," he said without stopping.

"I have husband."

"Is he here?"

"No."

"Is he coming here?"

"No," Xiùměi said. She couldn't resist him. She involuntarily cupped him through his pants with both her hands. As she was rubbing him, she felt herself get moist between her legs. This was new for her. She quivered while his face almost burst with sexual ecstasy. He kissed her with passion inside her mouth at the same time he reached his crescendo. She lingered a moment, then she pulled away, walked to the kitchen.

Chang took a deep breath, switched modes and hurriedly started to photograph the space with a panoramic camera. He wanted the full picture. He also dropped a small microphone into the planter box behind the couch. The tiny remote camera got squeezed in among the floral window decorations. It was perfectly camouflaged. By the time she returned with a tasteful arrangement of bite-size snacks, his job was done.

Chang tasted the food, had some more tea and watched how this big, unattractive Chinese woman came alive in front of his eyes. He liked his powerful affect on her.

"My apologies, beautiful Xiùměi. Today I have to hurry. Will you see me again at another place? Not your place of business?" he asked.

"I like that very much," she said almost blushing.

"I will be sure to call you." At the door, he kissed her with roughness previously unknown to her, then left. For the first time in her life she felt sex, she felt the tingle of every inch of her body, she felt the moisture of anticipation beneath her pubic hair. She held her breath as she grasped the new possibilities of what wonders might await her.

CHAPTER THIRTY-SIX

Sebastian drove Marla north on the Pacific Coast Highway past Carpinteria to the town of Montecito at the lower foothills of the Santa Ynez Mountain range. He turned onto a narrow, paved mountain road and did not stop before reaching the very top.

"My surprise for you," he said. The front gate opened electronically and he pulled up in front of the rambling Spanish Colonial Revival style house. He opened the car door, took her by her hand, lead her up to the entrance and with a grandiose gesture read out loud the freshly painted words over the entry. "Casa de *Pombal* y Pacifica."

He started to enter the code numbers to the front door in the security pad when it popped open from inside by none other than Carlotta. Supermodel Carlotta Rainee. Marla was annoyed and surprised.

"Not you again. Do you need all my men? Can't you get your own?" she said without any charm.

"Oh, a touch of ire," Sebastian said. "It's good to see a new side."

Marla was embarrassed

Carlotta kissed Sebastian on both cheeks than leaned to kiss her. Marla stepped back. Carlotta playfully ignored that. Before more was said, Emanuella appeared.

"Sebastião, my dear," she said and kissed him. It was her turn to kiss Marla on both cheeks. "Marla, my dear," she went on. "You please meet Carlotta Rainee, my dear, dear client. She came with me. She is my guest on business."

"I'm here for the team, not Warren Traynor" Carlotta explained.

Amused, Sebastian looked at his watch. "Right, almost time for the boys to get here."

Marla looked at the three of them in bewilderment. "What team?"

"The tennis team," Sebastian said.

"Wonderful," Marla said.

"You say 'wonderful'" Carlotta said. "Now, you want my men?" She watched Marla at a loss for words. "I made a joke," Carlotta said. "I tell you now that Warren is filming movie in Montana? Wyoming? Some faraway place. He is with movie star girl friend."

"And you wait?" Marla asked.

Carlotta's laughter had a sharp edge to it. "No, I don't wait. I was done with him."

"Well, darling," Sebastian said to Marla. "Let's have a nice glass of Port, and Stilton. Let's sit on the balcony, behold the ocean. The Pacific Ocean."

A uniformed Spanish maid started to set up for al fresco dining. Marla calmed down.

"Luiza is my surprise for you, brother. She was available, so I brought her until you make different arrangements," Emanuella said with great pride.

"Marla, I hope you don't mind," she added, as if talking to the true mistress of the house. "Luiza has been in our family for a few years. She knows everything we like."

"I've no idea what's going on," Marla said, looking to Sebastian for answers. He grinned.

"It's all right. You will. This is marvelous, Nuella. Thank you. Marla, let me show you around while Luiza gets things ready." He walked her through the house. Maybe five bedrooms that Marla could remember. Maybe more. Exquisite baths, garden windows, lap pool, lanai gym. His face radiated pride when he showed her the state-of-the-art wine cellar.

"And see, Marla, I am discovering California wines!" He pointed to a couple of cases that needed sorting. "Franciscan Oakville Estate. This is very good. We shall try it."

He took out a couple of bottles and carried them with him.

"What do you think?"

"You're the connoisseur, Sebastian. I drink what you give me," she said.

They continued their walk through the barely furnished house.

"Those are my favorite pieces," he said, gesturing around.

They saw Emanuella appearing, disappearing, reappearing with measuring tape and notepad, making a list.

"She'll furnish this beautifully," Sebastian said. Then caught himself. He was trying to avoid cornering her into any commitments. "I'm sorry, Marla. I meant that my sister will give you her ideas. You can make all the decisions."

"What about you?"

"I'm easy. I do what I'm told."

"Well, then," Marla said. "I'll give you my ideas, too, but *Casa de Pombal y Pacifica* has to be furnished to suit you."

"Your ideas will suit me." His self-assurance put Marla in a secure place. "In fact, we can get your mother's art and memorable treasures out of storage and display them here. There's room."

Marla didn't have to answer. Her face, her eyes, expressed her gratitude.

"Well, what do you think?" he asked.

"It's beautiful. Positively gorgeous."

"It is mine. You can stay here or at your condo. I can stay here instead of a hotel when I come to visit or to work."

"I might sell my condo," she volunteered. "Too much Warren there. I'll get a smaller place. You know, something in town…" She was on the verge of saying 'for us,' but stopped herself.

"Well, we will work it out, I am sure. Are you sure?" he added.

"I am sure. No doubt in my mind." Marla was happy.

Not much later the tennis team arrived. They dropped their luggage inside the entrance. There were only four of them. Pablo had fallen in love and wanted to skip this trip. The boys were staying at the house until the Countrywide Classic started at UCLA. Then they would move into Westwood. Carlotta put her arm around a couple of the guys.

"I'm going with you, boys," she said. "You will win for me! Lots of money!" She said the word *monnney* with several *n*-s and winked.

She then turned around with grandeur befitting the Queen of England. "After the tennis, I will meet a few film producers and I will become great movie star!"

Everyone adored her. She was an unassuming, undemanding, charming beauty.

"We go down to the village, bring supper." Amidst *Ciao*-s and a lot of waving, she and the players left.

That evening, over cocktails, Sebastian and Emanuella announced to Marla that they became major stockholders of KMRTV. They would have the details ironed out within one week. Marla was elated.

"You saved Evelyn. It's incredible." She was so excited she couldn't stop kissing them and laughing. She looked up at the sky. "Thank you," she whispered.

"It seemed like the right thing to do," Sebastian said with his usual understatement. "It is not public knowledge until everything is signed and there is an official announcement, but you should know."

"I didn't expect you to make ties to Los Angeles," Marla said, deeply moved.

"It's simple. I wanted to be near you."

Emanuella excused herself.

"I knew I had to prove it. Now we're on our way, aren't we?" He drew her into his arms. They understood the possibility of happiness opening up to them. Relaxing, they savored the moment.

The silence was interrupted by the noisy return of Carlotta and the players. They were loaded down with food from the supermarket. The cooking began. Each of them wanted to make a dish, something that was special to him or her. The laughter, joking, cooking and eating lasted into the wee hours.

CHAPTER THIRTY-SEVEN

Carol and Buzz pulled into the circular driveway of Michael's house. A new nanny let them in. She was older than the first one, chunky, moved a little slowly, but her calmness seemed to affect everyone around her.

"My name is Lena," she said with an unusually warm voice. "Mr. Michael and the baby are in his study."

She led them to the wide-open double doors where Michael was working and little Mike was playing in his playpen next to the big desk.

"Thank you, Lena," Carol said. "I'll get some coffee for us. I know where it is." Carol headed to the spotless, roomy kitchen where everything was put away, a large fruit bowl on the tiled cooking island made a colorful accent for the otherwise ivory and beige kitchen. The aroma of rich fresh coffee called to her. Lena pulled back and let Carol pour coffee for the three of them and carry it to the study.

Michael's study was quite unlike his old fashioned, almost dark office. His desk faced the sliding glass doors leading to the balcony and looking toward the tennis court. The space was airy, green plants and exotic cut flowers in a vase breathed life into the work-oriented décor. Couch, easy chairs, loungers and, of course, toys, reflected the life of a working writer.

"I see you have a new nanny," Carol said.

"Yes, the young one was afraid of Linda, so she became her playmate. Don't even start me on that," Michael said.

Buzz played with little Mike while they talked.

"I don't know how to help you, Michael. The whole thing is bizarre," Carol added. "She can be such a delight and then…"

"And then she's a monster. Never a dull moment." Michael smiled lovingly as he spoke about Linda.

"I have not raised my voice to her, I have not punished her. I have been encouraging recovery, describing the wonderful possibilities ahead of us. I believe still that we can make something of our lives if she sobers up. Really sobers up."

"Remember when years ago your biggest problem was how boring your marriage was?" Buzz's mind was traveling time.

"Yes, Buzz. I remember it too well. I don't miss it, though." Michael was very firm. "I have really thought about that and no, I would not go back to that life. This one can be fixed."

"Does she love you?" Carol asked.

Michael took his time answering. "I think she is getting closer and closer to it. I know now that she didn't at first."

The doorbell rang. The nanny came to announce that the cleaning crew has arrived so there will be some noise.

"What cleaning crew?" Carol asked.

"You know, the Chinese woman, what's her name," Michael said.

"Xiùměi?"

"Yes. She convinced Linda. I didn't even know they knew each other," Michael said.

Carol went to the foyer and saw Xiùměi at the door, about to leave.

"Xiùměi," Carol called to her.

"Oh, yes, hello," Xiùměi said.

"I would like to talk with you."

"I have to go now. Delivery."

"When will you be in your shop?"

"In office?"

"In your office, yes."

"Afternoon. Little time. I will come back here pick up workers four o'clock."

"Then I'll see you at two o'clock, OK?" Carol turned around and went back to Michael and Buzz.

"I'm going out to *Mountside* this afternoon," Michael said. "They'll tell me what and how the additional therapy will be done. I think this time it'll take." His face reflected his strong belief in the success of the treatment.

"If you need anything, if you want us to take little Mike when the nanny is off, if you want to talk or not talk, please call," Carol said.

"We mean it, Michael," Buzz added. "Anything, any time."

"I do have to get this series back on track. None of the episodes are finalized. The hiatus will be over in two weeks," Michael was shaking his head in disbelief and walked them to the door. "I'm glad I can count on you two."

They hugged, patted each other on the back reassuringly and left.

———— ◆ ————

Evelyn and Marla were reviewing the pictures taken by Chang. Reed popped in and stayed for the discussion of the new plan. The enlargements showed hidden cameras in two places. Chang assumed there could be more. "Why would she want cameras?"

"Who would be her target?" Marla asked.

"What is she after if not a successful business?" Reed questioned.

"I have an appointment with her at six tonight," Marla said. "She said she would be busy all day and would be easiest to talk with after work hours."

"Are you taking the cameraman?" Reed asked.

"Yes, I thought we could get the little things done and then build up to the citizenship party."

"Pretty flashy!" Reed joked.

"I hope so. That's the idea." Marla laughed wholeheartedly.

"I'd better go. Now that you come in with your occasional segments you've raised the bar. I really have to stay on my toes to be in the same league."

"I know you're kidding, Reed, but it sounds good. Thanks."

Reed left and Chang headed out too. "I have to make a date with her and see whether I was on camera. Pretty racy stuff," he said.

"No bragging, please," Evelyn said and waved *good bye* to him. "See you later."

"Evelyn," Marla said. "Sebastian is The Prince, isn't he?" Her face glowed with joy.

"I never knew men like he existed," Evelyn said. "To think that all this happened because Jonathan wanted to control you."

"Well, he sure got his comeuppance."

"It's too bad. I feel sorry for him," Evelyn said.

"Yeah, me too." Marla nodded.

The Missy Poole thing was really dumb. That's when I lost respect for him," Evelyn said. "In a way, I wanted him to get the account. Who knows, if he had come to me directly, maybe he would've. But to take the offensive, that was not like the man who had trained you."

Marla turned around, headed out.

"You know something?"

"What?" Evelyn asked.

"I'm crazy about Sebastian. That's what."

CHAPTER THIRTY-EIGHT

Carol arrived at Xiùměi's office. Xiùměi was her sweet, calm self. Prepared tea and cookies for her guest.

"You always welcome here, Carol."

"I have to ask you not to talk with Marla, not to do the interview."

"I like interview. Good for business," Xiùměi said.

"You could jeopardize my name by saying anything."

"Your name not anywhere. My business." Xiùměi smiled.

Now Carol was stunned. "Your business? What do you mean, your business? I gave you the money. I gave you the contacts. Without me you would still be cleaning at the Hilton," she spoke out loud.

"Can you prove?" Xiùměi asked.

"You show me the accounting books and I will show you my deposit. Your start-up capital."

Xiùměi walked around to Carol's back. Switched on the TV. Buzz, naked, having sex.

Carol turned away. "You cannot blackmail me. I am smarter than you. What other tapes did you make?" Carol asked.

"You not smarter than Xiùměi. My business. Not your business." She turned her nose up and posed in a superior stance.

"I don't pay you money," she added.

"Xiùměi, I gave you my life savings. I did everything I promised. Now, you have to show me the tapes, the blackmail money you receive. I want my money," Carol said growing crazed.

"Don't order me. You are not boss of me." Xiùměi was turning redder and redder, losing control.

"I set you up. You owe me money."

"There is no money," Xiùměi said, changing to fighting stance.

"Your name not on papers, not in bank. No money. No. No. No."

Carol slapped her. Xiùměi slapped her back. They fought. Carol's fury scared Xiùměi. She was kneeling on top of Xiùměi.

"Stop," Xiùměi said.

Carol let down her guard just long enough for Xiùměi to roll out of under her, reach for Allan's gun and shoot. Carol fell. Xiùměi ran out of the office, paper-towel in hand, avoiding fingerprints, she locked the front door. She jumped into her van and sped away. She had a plan.

------◆------

Marla and her cameraman knocked on the door of *Clean, Eat and Party!* There was no answer. Marla was annoyed. She called Xiùměi's office number inside but all she got was the answering machine. She didn't know what to do. She told the cameraman that they will wait a few minutes. But before she even finished her sentence, Xiùměi arrived. She was in a great rush.

"I sorry, Miss Marla," she said. "I pick up my workers. I drive home my workers. Much traffic."

She unlocked the front door and the three of them walked in. On the floor was Carol, dead. A bullet through her head. Xiùměi fainted.

------◆------

At the police station Xiùměi was the picture of innocence. Her fainting underscored her lack of knowledge of who would have done that. She was believable in every way. She told them Carol was a client but what was she doing there? How did she get in? Who was with her? Xiùměi was more concerned with the crime on her premises than the death itself. Her business was everything to her. Xiùměi was helpful and eager in offering information. Her husband had nothing to do with her business. He didn't know her clients. But what was his gun doing there? Did he break in? Did he see Carol come in? Did he think she was an intruder?

The interrogators believed every word she said. Xiùměi was released.

------◆------

That night, Marla and Sebastian went to see Buzz. Buzz was a mess. Sammy was a mess. Marla hugged and kissed both of them on their cheeks.

"This is *Sebastian de Pombal.* Carol never believed he existed and called him a figment of my imagination," Marla said. "My invisible Spaniard."

The men shook hands and Buzz let Sebastian put his arm around him.

"I don't know what to say," Sebastian said. "I can't say that everything will be all right. It's not. I can't say things happen for the best. Some don't. But I can say that Marla and I are here for you to help you both heal."

"Carol was the best. She turned my life around."

"You turned hers around, I saw it with me own eyes," Marla said."

"Xiùměi is evil. She blackmailed me into hiring her for the wedding. She is now on a retainer at Michael's house. I wonder who else had she videotaped?" Buzz asked.

"We have to go."

"Go where, Marla?" Sebastian asked.

"There."

"It has a police tape around it."

Sammy jumped up immediately. "Yeah, we have to bring her down."

He walked over to Buzz and stared at him until Buzz understood Sammy's need for revenge. Right or wrong, he and Sammy had bonded.

"We have to bring her down," Buzz said, looking at the three of them. "What about the police tape?"

"The kitchen had a separate entrance. I remember the house where her assistant, Měi Wong lives. I saw her go in," Marla said.

Měi Wong was at home. They scared her into letting them use the spare key to the back door and made her stay as their lookout. The door was at the other end of the kitchen. It did not appear connected to Xiùměi's business. It could be a door or a three-dimensional painting, trompe l'oeil.

Once inside, Marla got on the computer. She figured out fast the system Xiùměi used and while she didn't know exactly what she was looking for, she stumbled upon evidence of alterations to the accounting files. They were copies of each other, named to identify the recipient. There was one for "X," which was the master, one for "I," which was the IRS, a blown-up version named "CP," for Client Presentation. Very interesting but not murder.

All this time Sebastian and Buzz searched through everything the police had already checked. They went over it again and again. Sammy was no real help. He was too distraught being at the scene of the crime. Buzz fell back on the guest couch in desperation and defeat. His feet accidentally kicked the bottom of it. A thin drawer popped open. It was filled with videotapes. There was Buzz, Linda, Carol, Marla, Chang. Apparently everyone who came in was photographed.

"What a sneaky, ugly soul this woman has," Marla said.

Měi Wong knocked on the outside of the kitchen door. "Someone coming," she said and ran.

Sebastian turned off the light. They watched as a tiny laser flash illuminated the hands of someone who knew about the connection between the once separate premises. It was none other than Chang cracking the back door. Chang and Evelyn quietly snuck in. Chang panned the entire reception area with a small laser light and saw the four. Měi Wong was gone.

For a long beat they just stared at each other in the low lighting.

"Didn't I ask you not to act upon your hunches without first telling me?"

Evelyn said.

"Yes, you did," Marla said.

"Why are you here?" Sebastian asked. "Didn't you see the police tape?

"Carol was killed here. Did you know?" Marla asked. Buzz was leaning on Sammy.

"Oh, my God!" Evelyn said. "We didn't know."

"Chang's hidden microphone was not transmitting and we wanted to find out what was wrong," Evelyn said.

Chang went over to the planter where he had hidden it. It was there all right, but it was soaked. "Oh, shit. These flowers are real."

He took some tissues off the desk and wrapped the wet mike with them.

"I was too busy with the wrong thing," he said to Evelyn.

Her reply was a cold gaze that could have killed.

Chang reached for the hidden camera in the window and almost immediately found it.

"Here it is! The pictures! Evelyn, I can dry the mike. We'll have the whole story.

"We'd better. It could be homicide now," Evelyn said.

"Let's get out of here." Chang sounded official.

"I'm not done," Marla said.

"If you came through the police crime scene tape and made it, you can be sure we are staked out."

Just as Chang said this, the lights were switched on by the police. They had watched the activity inside and waited to make their move.

"This is not a pretty picture. So many fine, upstanding citizens caught with their hands in the cookie jar," said the detective. "Let see, what do we have here?"

And they were taken to the station with their evidence. And there were lawyers called and the entire event was going to be made public. No way to stop that.

"One minute, Captain," said Marla. "There may be a way of getting a full confession. May I talk with you in private, off the record?"

They went into one of the interrogation rooms and Marla told him, without a lawyer present, what her original plan was. Her hunch about the strange connection between Carol and Xiùměi. Her curiosity about the fast growing success of Xiùměi's business. Marla informed the police Captain of Chang's investigation, the wet mike that will dry, the surveillance video, the blackmail videos. She finally announced that she was planning to report Xiùměi to the police as soon as there was real evidence, more than her hunch.

"So, can we work together?" she asked.

The police Captain was fascinated by all this falling in his lap. This will be good publicity for the Department and for himself.

"I have to go by the book, Ms. Hayes." He started to smile. "Let me see what we can do."

"That's great!" she yelled out, then caught herself. "I mean, thank you. I really appreciate it."

She got up and headed for the door. He got up and opened the door for her. She took a deep breath. A free woman.

CHAPTER THIRTY-NINE

Xiùměi was in her element. Dressed in an American flag skirt and Chinese silk blouse, she was celebrating becoming a citizen and that morning having taken the Oath of Allegiance in a group ceremony in front of City Hall. Her private, by invitation only party, had closed the Chinese Garden restaurant where she had one of her first jobs as a new immigrant. She decorated it herself with Americana motifs and even arranged some of the Chinese dishes in a patriotic design.

Měi Wong made sure that everything went the way Xiùměi had planned it. Měi Wong had owed Xiùměi her wealth, her new future and was beholden to Xiùměi. The entire staff of *Clean, Eat and Party!* was in attendance both to serve and celebrate. Xiùměi's other friends from the AA and some uniformed housecleaning staffers from the beachfront Hilton were there. And a few clients.

Xiùměi took a bottle of Remy Martin and headed to the back room. The door was unlocked. Allan was inside watching an old TV set and snorting cocaine. His feet propped up on a broken down coffee table in front of a couch covered with torn fabric. His face lit up on seeing her with the booze.

"Just what the doctor ordered," Allan said, reaching for the bottle. She handed it to him.

"You don't go to AA with me so I don't go," he moaned.

"Oh, take control. Be a man!"

"I brought you to this country."

"Yes."

"You did good. You make me proud."

"You don't make me proud. Understand? You make me mad. You make me hurt." Xiùměi looked at the broken down drunk with disgust.

"You bring me here. You lie. You have nothing. You are nobody. You want to be nobody." Her face took on a proud look.

"I want to be somebody."

She turned and headed for the exit. He tried to get up but could not. His eyes rolled inside-out. His brain was scrambled.

"I will take care of myself now. I will give you divorce and moncy for your drink. Papa Burke will see I have big future."

———◆———

Marla arrived with her cameraman. They thought it would be more dramatic to have the camera rolling as they went in search of Xiùměi.

Outside, Buzz and Sammy pulled up but did not get out of the car. Buzz looked at his watch then at Sammy. They could hear the music of the party from the restaurant and saw an unmarked police van arrive. They crouched low to be unseen from the entrance to the restaurant and watched as undercover policemen and one woman headed inside.

The officers entered and looked around. They spotted Xiùměi as she came out of the back room, smiling at her happy guests. They stepped up to her. One of the officers showed her his badge.

"Xiùměi Burke?" he asked.

"Yes."

"You're under arrest for the murder of Carol Livingston."

The music stopped. There was silence. The female officer placed handcuffs on Xiùměi's hands behind her back.

Victor and his wife arrived in time to see Xiùměi being guided out of the restaurant. They looked closely into every face, looking for Allan. Not seeing him, they headed through the kitchen to the back store rooms, opening every door on their way. And he opened the door to the small smoky, smelly room where Allan was collapsed on the dirty couch. Victor reached for his cell phone, dialed. "911!?" he shouted. His wife went over to Allan to check his vital signs. He was alive. She wiped his face clean, put his head in her lap and waited for her husband to get help.

Outside, as Xiùměi walked to the police car, she looked around the dark street, her gaze pierced into each car within sight. She saw Buzz. Their eyes locked. Buzz gave her an "up yours" finger. She turned away, bent down to enter the police van.

Buzz leaned back, tried to breath. Sammy, sitting next to him, let out a scream, the guttural cry of a wounded animal. Buzz put his arm around him. He reached for his wallet, opened it. Carol's picture came alive, smiled at him as his tears freely rolled down his face. He hugged Sammy. They stayed that way for a long time, comforting each other.

CHAPTER FORTY

Montecito on a sunny, dry, perfect California day. Wearing tennis gear, Marla and Sebastian were heading out of the house to the beautifully maintained tennis court. Holding hands, they walked in silence. When they reached the equipment closet courtside, they got their rackets, balls, towels, drinks.

"You know, I think my mother is happy for me. Up there, somewhere." She looked up to the sky. "Maybe. Maybe I did grow up the way she had raised me."

"You're not angry with her."

"I hope she's not angry with me."

"You would know."

"Yes, I would," she said in a firm voice. "She wouldn't have rewarded me with your love."

His eyes were moist. She gave him a big hug and playfully ran out on the court. "Enough tears!"

They started to hit the balls back and forth, gently, warming up. Marla's cell phone rang.

"Oops, I forgot to turn it off. So, sorry." She went over to the table and answered.

"Hello."

"Marla Hayes? It's Sid Sheraton."

Marla's knees gave out.

"Hello, are you there?"

"Yes. I had to sit down," she said.

When Sebastian saw the excitement on her face, he came over and sat next to her. She pressed the *speaker* key on her phone.

"That's good. My point is that I read in the trade papers about KMRTV eluding an unfriendly takeover."

"You're not too busy for that?" Marla asked.

"True, I keep turning out bestseller after bestseller, but in between, they let me read the paper. A little reality." He laughed at his own humor. Marla smiled.

"I should have treated your mother differently. Know now."

"Thank you for saying that."

"We can talk about it if you like." His voice was calming.

"I will think about it. I am not sure," she said.

"Would it help me redeem myself in your eyes if I did an interview with you?"

Marla's hands gave out, she lost her grip on the telephone and Sebastian caught it as it was falling to the ground.

"Mr. Sheraton, hello. This is Sebastião Emanuel *de Pombal* y Martín."

"Ah, Señor *de Pombal*, I hope we will meet one day. I've read about you, as well."

"You have?"

"I have. I read a great deal." Again, he was laughing his soft, deep laughter. "Is Marla all right?"

"She is collecting herself."

"Here I am. I am so embarrassed, Mr. Sheraton."

"That's normal. I have that affect on several people. By the way, I do remember your mother. She was a sweet part of my life. Maybe we can talk about it before or after the interview." He was quiet for a beat. "When should I call you at the station?"

"Usually Thursdays and Fridays."

"Until then," he said and hung up.

She stood there looking at Sebastian. Speechless. Sebastian held her.

"It's pretty amazing, Marla. Sid Sheraton is pretty amazing."

"Isn't he?" She was still dumbfounded.

"Can you imagine me interviewing him, the great author?"

"It'll break the ratings meter," he said. "Or whatever it's called."

She took a deep breath, picked up her racket and walked out to the court.

"If you win the next set," he said jovially, "I'll let you stay here free of charge."

"And if I don't?"

"I'll let you stay here free of charge."

"Then I'll win," she said with a playful giggle.

THE END